Sniper!
A Natalie McMasters Mystery

Sniper!
A Natalie McMasters Mystery

Thomas A. Burns, Jr.

Published by Tekrighter LLC 2020

Cover designed by Thomas A. Burns, Jr.
Cover images used under license from Shutterstock

Thomas A. Burns, Jr.

Printed in the United States of America

First Printing: October 2020

ISBN-13 978-1-7331140-6-6
ISBN-10: 1-7331140-6-8

Dedication

To the Monday night beta readers – Craig, Skip, Paul, Ilia and Sam

Table of Contents

"I have a very strict gun-control policy: If there's a gun around, I want to be in control of it."

CLINT EASTWOOD

Chapter 1.

The psychologist William James wrote, "The progress from brute to man is characterized by nothing so much as by the decrease in frequency of proper occasions for fear. In civilized life, in particular, it has at last become possible for large numbers of people to pass from the cradle to the grave without ever having had a pang of genuine fear."

My name is Natalie McMasters. I'm twenty-one, short and blonde (OK, it's bleached), a pre-law student at State and a private detective trainee at my Uncle Amos's 3M Detective Agency. And I am not one of those lucky people who have never had a pang of genuine fear in their lives.

I'm back on State campus after nearly a year, with three semesters left before I can apply to law school. My first class this morning was Psychology, and the prof read James' quote to convince us that what he termed "a state of mild existential dread" is the best frame of mind to have if you want to lead a fulfilling life. He claimed that in these times, most people live in a state of perpetual boredom, which has many negative consequences—repeated failure, depression, and the acting out of self-destructive behaviors such as smoking, drinking, drug use, promiscuity and even suicide, all in a vain quest for a more interesting life. OMG, I wish that that was my problem!

It's a fine early fall day in the South; just a hint of chill in the air, but still warm enough for shorts and t-shirts. Sweat tickles my back as it runs down inside my Shinedown tee, where my backpack holding my laptop rests against my spine. I'm crossing a crowded wide brick courtyard on central campus—the New Commons—not only full of people going between classes, but many informational displays and booths also contribute to the chaos, welcoming, enticing and exploiting the returning students. Spicy aromas from a couple of food trucks remind me that lunchtime is approaching, but the long lines induce a mild existential dread that the food may run out before I can get any. That's good, right? Various academic departments have set up tables where students can explore opportunities for a major in their discipline, as well as various political, religious and mundane extracurricular groups seeking followers. In the center of it all, a stage rises six feet above the bricks, rimmed with red, white and blue bunting and American flags snapping in the breeze. Half-a-dozen city police officers occupy different stations on top. The banner hanging above reads *Capital City Police Department Gun Buyback - Take Back our Campus Now!* A lone microphone stands in the center of the stage.

My hand creeps down to my right hip to caress the comforting lump beneath my extra-long shirt—my new Sig Sauer P-365, filled with 11 rounds of 9mm +P jacketed hollow points. Yes, campus is a gun-free zone, and yes, I'm committing a felony by carrying a pistol here. However, I acquired my current case of severe existential dread, otherwise known as PTSD, when I was caught unarmed. Because I'm carrying, I'm way sus of the cops, and give the stage a wide berth as I head to Dr. Rebecca Feiner's office in the Counseling Center on old campus. She's been helping me with issues that have arisen in my not-so-boring life over the last couple of years.

I descend a long concrete staircase to a grassy courtyard the size of a football field, where students lounge on blankets with their backpacks for back rests, listen to music, play frisbee, or just chill. A vague uneasiness arises. I've been on this campus for three years and still don't feel part of it. I've seen too much misery, too much evil, too much death, some of which is my own doing. I want to go back to being just a student, get my law degree and live a normal life. Maybe Rebecca can help me do that. However, I'm not sure she even wants to—I had no trouble making an appointment with her through the counseling office, but I'm pretty sure they didn't ask her permission first. Because I also consider her a friend, I invited her to my recent wedding, but she didn't show. She and me recently attended the same relationship clinic in Georgia; me to resolve family issues, her to deal with a traumatic experience that I was involved in. I learned some disturbing things about her, and I'm not sure that she doesn't think she got her wig snatched. Maybe that's why she left me on read about the wedding.

The Counseling Center is one of several red brick buildings on the courtyard, all children of FDR's WPA. I ascend a long, two-stage staircase and pull open a heavy wooden door, entering a modern office that smells of paper and old building musk. A receptionist tells me to take a seat after giving me a clipboard full of forms. I don't understand, why in this electronic era I have to fill out the same damn forms every time I come here, but there's totally no use bitching about it.

I keep an eye on the doors leading back to the counselors' offices as I transcribe my life history. The doors open and a woman and a man come out. The woman is Jay Howell; she goes to a veterans' support group that my husband Danny runs. She's a twenty-something, a head taller than my 5'1", dressed in camo pants and a tight olive drab t-shirt with a ranger logo and a patch showing a snake coiled around an arrow on the sleeve. Her auburn hair is tight on her head like a skullcap, and she's struggling to swing her heavy black backpack over her shoulders. She sees but doesn't acknowledge me—we're not really friends or anything.

The fortyish dude behind her, Dr. Leland Marks, is not much taller. He's sporting round glasses and a totally awful black-and-white checkered shirt under his white smock. He's got a crew cut and a smooth, boyish face that belies his age. I've met him a few times when coming here to see Rebecca. Marks grabs a strap on Jay's backpack and holds it for her so she can shove an arm through and shrug on the load. She bends a little at the weight—she's probably carrying a laptop like me and some textbooks too.

Jay departs, and Marks turns back toward the offices, then stands to one side waving someone out. It's Rebecca. My breath always catches when I see her—she's absolutely one of the most beautiful women I've ever known. She has on a starched white coat over a dark purple pants suit, and her raven black hair is in a crown braid, accentuating her high cheekbones and dark, almond-shaped eyes. She notices me, but there's no welcoming smile. She just waves for me to follow her. Marks, the perfect gentleman, holds the door for us ladies. I smile at him; he blushes and looks away.

As always, Rebecca's office smells of fresh flowers, bright red and yellow in a cut crystal vase on her glass-and-steel desk. She takes the black leather chair behind it, but does not invite me to sit. I have a bad feeling about this.

"What can I do for you, Natalie," she asks coldly. Natalie, not Nattie.

Standing in front of her like a penitent in front of a priest, I'm at a loss for words. Finally, I answer, "I missed you at the wedding."

"I had other commitments." Obviously. "Sorry I forgot to RSVP. How is your family?" Do you really care, Rebecca?

"They're all Gucci." I reply. "Lupe is still going to NA, and she got her job back. Eduardo is living with us again, and he's in the third grade. Danny is still working with Uncle Amos and Leon Kidd at 3M, and mentoring a veterans support group on campus."

"It sounds like everyone is fine," she says. Oof! From her tone, she could care less. WTF is her prob? I'm pretty sure I know, and I want to just ask, but maybe I'm afraid to hear the answer.

Instead, I say, "I was hoping we could start our sessions again. I'm having some issues..."

"I don't know that I'm the one to help you," she replies. "I've told you previously that I think your troubles are largely of your own making. I don't think you're going to get better unless you change your lifestyle, which you seem reluctant to do."

OK, she's outright lying. She's never said anything like that to me before. But I won't brace her on it. "What do you mean?"

"I mean that you seem to have a propensity for violence. It's no wonder you're a psychological mess."

Wow. "It's not my fault that people keep trying to kill me."

"You know, maybe it is. A violent lifestyle begets violence."

Don't yell, Nattie. "But I don't have a violent lifestyle. I've done everything I can to keep violence away from me and my fam."

"It's your mindset, Natalie. You're paranoid. When you think you're being threatened, your first reaction is to lash out. And when you hit someone, they're going to hit you back."

Now I'm getting way salty. "Paranoid! Was I paranoid when I got raped? Or when my enemies tried to ruin my life last year? Or when that crazy bitch tried to kill me last spring? Was I paranoid when a nutjob murdered fifteen people shooting his way into a hospital to get at me?"

"Maybe if you hadn't been doing what you were doing, those things wouldn't have happened."

"What I was doing was trying to protect myself and my fam," I say.

"That's what we have the police for. It's not your job."

"Not my job? I was raised to believe that we had to take responsibility for our own lives."

"Well, maybe you were raised wrong. Look at where it's gotten you."

At that relationship clinic we both attended a few months ago, I was trying to mold my wife Lupe and my husband Danny into a family, while

4

Rebecca was trying to address an emotional trauma. She fell back into a sick relationship with her old BF, the guy who ran the clinic. He turned out to be wanted by the FBI, and he threatened to come after me because he thought I had a hand in exposing him as a serial killer. Surely, she can't think all that's my fault?

"Is it getting easier for you to kill people?" she asks.

I don't say it, but the answer is maybe. Instead, I opt for, "I haven't killed anyone except in self-defense."

She stares at me, her face frozen. "And you had no part in it, right? You were just minding your own business, and these bad people just tried to kill you for a lark?"

"They were doing bad things, Rebecca. To me, and to people I cared about." A beat. "You were one of those."

She gives a long sigh. "You just can't see it, can you? Every time you commit an act of violence, you rationalize it. It's not your fault, the bad guy deserved it. And every time, it gets just a little easier to do that. Mark my words, Natalie McMasters. One day you're going find you enjoy being judge, jury and executioner. And on that day, you're going to kill someone just because you think they deserve it."

I can't help it. "And then I'll be no better than the guy you were gonna marry," I say.

That last clap back told—I can see the hurt in her eyes. She looks at her watch. "We need to cut this short," she says. "I've volunteered to help at the gun buyback."

That's a cop-out, but I try to lighten the mood with a joke. "Maybe I should go, too. It sounds like a great way to get some money for a new gun."

Now her eyes are totally on fire. "That's not funny! The proliferation of guns and violence in this country is a national disgrace." Her voice rings with the zeal of a true-believer. "It's the duty of every responsible citizen to do something about it. The state legislature is considering an assault weapons ban, and this buyback is State's way of supporting that."

The blood rises to my cheeks—now she's got me full send. "All I've ever gotten in a gun-free zone is fucked! And I seem to remember that I even saved your life once, because I was carrying."

"I wouldn't have even been in that situation if not for you," she claps back, "if you hadn't hurt someone who decided to retaliate. You have a bad attitude, Natalie. You end up bringing trouble down on yourself, your friends and your loved ones. You need to stop it."

"Sorry, not sorry," I tell her. "There are still bad people out there looking for me. One of them is your ex." She looks away; embarrassed or plain pissed, I can't tell. "When seconds count, the cops are minutes away. I'll continue to protect myself, if you don't mind."

She gives me a way sus look. "You're carrying right now, aren't you?" I neither confirm nor deny it, but she knows it from my expression. "Oh my God! In my office! How dare you!" She's so mad she's almost spitting, the indignation clear on her face. She reaches for the phone. "I'm calling campus security!"

WTF? "You wouldn't..."

"Oh no?" She picks up the receiver. After a moment, "Security, this is Dr. Feiner at the Counseling Center. A student in my office, Natalie McMasters, is carrying a loaded gun." A pause. "No, I don't think so, but you'd better send someone right away." She hangs up.

She didn't! If I'm caught with a gun here, it's no more law school—I'm going to prison. She's got to be bluffing, she just wouldn't do that to me! I know! She's trying to get me to give up my gun at the buyback. Fat chance— I just got that Sig last month. We just stare at each other, waiting for someone to give in. Finally, I say, "Look, I'm going now. I'm sorry about what I said, and I'm really sorry that your engagement didn't work out." Not that it could have. "I'll call you next week when you've calmed down." She doesn't reply.

I open the door to the hallway, and a blue-clad campus cop is pointing a gun at me. The heat drains out of me into the floor.

"Keep your hands where I can see them, Miss." he says, "Get back inside. Are you Natalie McMasters?"

I nod. She did it! She really fucking did it! OMG!

The cop is a middle-aged dude with dirty blond hair, a well-coiffed mustache and a Van Dyke beard. His eyes flicker to the lump at my waist. His face hardens. "Are you armed?" I can tell he's nervous from the sweat beading on his brow.

He's going to search me—there's no use lying. "Yes." I back into the office and he follows me, his pistol pointed at my belly.

"Put your hands behind you, turn around and face the desk," he says. "Do anything else and I'll have to shoot you."

Shoot me? Fear curdles into a cold knot in my stomach. Another emotion arises, too. Anger! How fucking could she? This is going to end my college career! I do as he says.

Cold steel encircles my wrists; the handcuffs' rasp grates in my ears as they bite into my flesh. The cop jerks up my shirt, removes the Sig from the holster. He points it at the floor, pops the mag, then racks the slide to eject the chambered round. Rebecca has a look of cold satisfaction on her face.

Sadness wells up in me, and tears begin to flow. I thought she was my friend!

"Natalie McMasters, you're under arrest for carrying a weapon in a gun-free zone. You have the right to remain silent..."

SNIPER!

Chapter 2.

The cop places one hand on my upper arm prior to perp-walking me out of the building. I think fast. "How can I sell my gun at the buyback if I don't bring it on campus?"

His look says *Oh, come on.* "If you were going to turn it in, why were you carrying it loaded?" he asks.

Time to be the dumb blonde most guys think I am. "But that's how I always carry it, officer," I say in a high, apologetic voice. "That's how they taught me to at the class I had to take to get my permit. They said I should always keep it in my holster." It isn't hard to let tears flow—I'm still pretty ripped over what Rebecca did. "I didn't know I was doing anything wrong," I let my voice break a little on the word *wrong*.

The officer seems to have mellowed a little at the sight of my tears. "You know, there is a moratorium today on bringing a gun to campus, because of the buyback. But you shouldn't have been carrying it loaded..."

I let a hint of desperation creep into my voice "But I didn't know!"

Rebecca's totally speechless. She knows goddamn well what I'm doing.

In for a penny... "Because I was attacked before, I thought I needed protection. That's why I got the gun. But I totally haven't been comfortable since it's been in the house. When I heard about the buyback, I decided I really didn't need it anymore."

"You were attacked?" The cop looks shocked. "On campus?"

"No." I don't tell him it was in a strip club.

He looks at Rebecca. "Is this true?" he asks her.

She nods, the anger still evident on her face. She knows I'm telling the truth. But it's killing her.

"That's how many women react after being assaulted," he says in a lecturing tone. "It's understandable, but wrong-headed. You're much more likely to have an attacker take your gun away and use it on you."

Yeah, tell that to the five people I shot and killed before they could kill me, asshole. "I know. I've heard that." My voice just oozes submission.

He unlocks the cuffs. "OK," he says. "You can participate in the buyback." He hands my Sig, the mag and the round to Rebecca. "Will you make sure this gun makes it there, Dr. Feiner?" Hmmph. This cop isn't a complete idiot after all.

Rebecca steps back like he's trying to give her a dog turd. "I can't take this. I don't have a permit..."

"It's OK, today. We have to have a general amnesty on campus for things like that so the buyback can work like it's supposed to."

"Just put it on the desk, then," she says. "Sorry for troubling you."

"You did the right thing," the cop replies. "You can't ever be too careful around somebody who's carrying a loaded gun. *What about you, jerkwad,* I think, staring at his now holstered pistol. *You were the one pointing yours at my belly, threatening to shoot me.* He goes, leaving Rebecca and I alone in the office.

Rebecca's voice drips acid. "I suppose you're really proud of yourself," she says.

I glare back at her. "No. Just relieved." A beat. "What the fuck is wrong with you? You almost got me sent to prison! It's not my fault you decided to marry a nut job."

She grimaces, so I know that jab stung. She retrieves a bright green backpack from a large desk drawer, picks up my gun with two fingers like it's something dirty, and drops it inside. The mag and the bullet follow. "I'll turn this in at the buyback," she says. "And you and I won't be having any more sessions." She shrugs on the pack and heads for the door.

"So, you're a thief now, too?" I say, stopping her in her tracks. "What about my money? That gun cost me almost $600."

"The city is paying $100 per gun," she says. "I'll mail it to you."

Any vestige of the friendship we once had is now gone. "I don't trust you. I'm coming too," I clap back. Just to twist the knife, I follow up with, "I can use the $100 as a down payment on another pistol. I still have my permit."

"You do that. And I'll make sure that the police keep an eye on you to make sure you don't carry it on campus."

We walk back to the New Commons together, but we're miles apart. Rebecca's new persona baffles me. Like many on campus, she's always considered herself totally woke, and she's never been shy about representing her ideology. But she's never fired shots at me because I thought differently than she did. Her sexual assault last year totally shook her, and her recent

10

attempt to deal with it, with help from an old flame who ultimately fucked her over seems to have driven her into fanaticism. I totally want to feel sorry for her, but it ain't her fault that I'm not in jail right now. I don't know if I can ever forgive her for that!

A voice from behind us. "Rebecca, wait up!" It's Dr. Marks, hurrying to catch up. "Are you going to the gun control thing? Senator Sam is going to speak!"

A group of maybe twenty-five people has gathered in front of the stage in the middle of the Commons, and a bunch of suits are now intermingled with the cops. We join the group in front, near center stage. Off to one side is a news truck, and a couple of cameramen have their lenses trained on the proceedings. A forty-something brunette woman in a tight, black-and-white polka-dotted dress taps on the mike. The crowd hushes as the thumps bounce off the concrete buildings, reverberating throughout the Commons. She takes the mike from the stand and holds it to her lips.

"Welcome everyone!" she says, in a bright-and-cheery voice. "I'm Daisy Marks, the dean of your University College." Dr. Leland Marks is staring at her intensely. She's his wife.

"It's wonderful to see such a great turnout for our first ever gun buyback here on State campus." Two dozen people is a great turnout? "It graphically demonstrates the commitment of our august institution to getting dangerous weapons off the street, and to the ideal of an eventual gun-free America!" A ragged cheer goes up from the great turnout. "In a moment, I'm going to turn the mike over to Police Chief Elaine N'Dour, who will explain the mechanics of the buyback, after which you may begin bringing any weapons you want to turn in up on the stage. But before that, I want to introduce some of the dignitaries present today at this historic event." She beckons a fortyish blonde woman in a lavender business suit forward. "First, although she needs no introduction on this campus, I want you to give a warm welcome to our United States Senator, Samantha López, our very own Senator Sam!"

It figures that this broad would show up—she's been beating the gun control drum on the morning shows and late-night TV a way long time. She takes the mike from Dean Marks, waving to the spectators in that annoying way that politicians do. "Thank you, Dean Marks. I won't take a lot of time—

I know that we have super important work to get to here today. I just want to say that I've never been prouder of my *alma mater* than I am right now, for leading the crusade for safer, gun-free America." The great turnout, which has nearly doubled in size since this thing started, goes wild.

"We're at a historic turning point," she goes on. "Our state legislature is poised to enact the first ever assault weapons ban in a southern state. To show support for that endeavor, State University has partnered with the Capitol City police to hold this gun buyback. Every dangerous weapon that we get off the streets today makes each one of us a little bit safer. I look forward to the day when all firearms in the United States are in the hands of competent authorities!" Another ragged cheer goes up from the proles, but a chill goes down my spine.

The senator hands the mike back to Dean Marks. In a much more subdued tone than the one she used when introducing the Senator, she indicates a gentleman in his 50s, wearing a blue suit and bright red tie. "Next, I would like to introduce the Congressman from our district, The Honorable Ralph Bader." Now there's a shock. Bader is a Republican, and a well-known Second Amendment supporter.

Bader gives the Dean a saccharine smile as he takes the mike. "Many of you may be wondering why I have chosen to be present at this event," he begins. No shit, Sherlock. "It's because, first and foremost, I am supporter of liberty!" He ignores the boos and catcalls that arise from the crowd. "If an American citizen wishes to turn his guns over to the police, that is his right. But it is also his right to keep and bear arms, as enshrined in our constitution." He waits for the grumbling to die down, and then continues. "I wanted to make sure that point of view is represented here today. Make no mistake—that wrong-headed assault weapons ban in the legislature is a clear violation of the Second Amendment. Even if it passes, it will never go into effect, because we'll tie it up in court until the cows come home!" A chorus of boos arises from the crowd, which has again doubled in size from a few minutes ago. The congressman hands the mike back to Dean Marks with a flourish.

"Thank you, Congressman," Dean Marks says, totally not meaning it. "One last point. I want to reassure you that this buyback is totally anonymous—if you turn in a gun, you will not be asked for identification of any kind, or even for a handgun permit. You will be paid with a blank city voucher that you can exchange for cash at any bank or check-cashing venue." Wow—now I know what to do when I have a murder weapon to get rid of! Dean Marks hands the mike to a short, fiftysomething, coal black woman in a navy-blue police uniform. "Chief, it's all yours."

"Thank you, Dr. Marks," the police chief says. "Let me add my welcome to yours, and thank everyone who is participating today for making out community safer. The procedure for turning in your gun is a simple one. Line up at the stairs on my right, and come on up on the stage when the officer calls you. Give your gun to the officer at table number one—she will check it to make sure it is unloaded and give you a receipt for it—you can write your name and address on that at a later time. If your gun is loaded, please tell the officer before you give it to her—she will take it from you in a safe manner. Then proceed to table number two and show the receipt to the officer there, who will give you your voucher. Finally, exit the stage promptly via the left-hand stairs. Any questions? Yes, the woman in the gray hoodie."

The questioner is obviously a student, about my height, sporting a nearly white crew cut with a purple stripe down the middle, and wearing a black t-shirt under the unzipped hoodie. She looks vaguely familiar, but I can't place her. "Betsy Kiefer, The State of State. What's going to happen to the guns after you take them?" she asks.

Kiefer? I know that name...

"That's an excellent question, Ms. Kiefer," The chief says. Then her head explodes in a fountain of blood and tissue.

SNIPER!

Chapter 3.

Everyone is frozen in time—an absurd silence grips the Commons. My mind refuses to process what I've just seen, because it's just so fucking wrong. Then a large crimson rose blossoms in the center of Dean Marks' chest, and she collapses in a heap. That's when I finally realize what's happening. But why don't I hear any shots?

Danny taught me that the first thing you do when you come under fire is seek cover. Problem is, I'm standing smack in the middle of an open concrete courtyard a hundred yards wide—a sitting duck! The huge stage right in front of me is about 30'x30', but there's absolutely no cover on top. I'd have to run all the way around to get behind it and be a target the whole way. The sides of the stage are covered with red, white and blue cloth—I have no idea what's underneath it—could be a blank wall, for all I know. But I have to try get under there.

People begin screaming and stumbling among the tables, chairs, and plastic tubs staged to receive handed-in guns on the stage, scurrying in all directions. Dr. Marks dashes up the steps, hurrying toward his wounded wife, but a shower of blood erupts from his shoulder and he goes down. Some of the cops finally get it, draw their weapons and crouch to make themselves smaller targets. Their puny pistols will do no good—the nearest building, where the sniper likely is, is over two hundred feet away. A cop lays on top of the senator, shielding her with his body. Congressman Bader leaps off the back of the stage and vanishes. I grab Rebecca's hand to drag her along with me, but she pulls in the opposite direction. Still holding her hand, I turn to tell her to come on, but now she's falling, a crimson stream spurting from her neck, her shoulder covered in blood. No! I let her go and she crumples to the pavement, and I dash for the front of the stage—I can't do anyone any good if I'm the next one shot. I tear away the patriotic drapery and find a metal skeleton supporting the structure, with plenty of room beneath. It's lousy cover but great concealment, so I dive in, ripping my t-shirt in the process; a protruding bolt opens a long wound on my side. On hands and knees, I crawl toward the center to ensure the gunman can't see me. A tickling develops on my face as I break through a spider web hanging between the struts.

SNIPER!

My scream rips through the air. Flailing at my face, I backtrack toward daylight, heedless of the danger outside. Fucking spiders! I've got to get away from them!

The area in front of the stage is now empty except for prostrate bodies in rapidly widening pools of blood. I tear toward the perimeter of the Commons, away from the shooter.

Once safe inside the Octagon, a classroom building on the New Commons fringe, it takes me a good fifteen or twenty minutes to get myself calmed down. I can't stop shaking, and I'm constantly pawing at my face to remove remnants of spider webs that I'm sure are no longer there. Eventually, a campus cop notices me, probably because the blood on my face and my clothes makes me look like I'm ready for a zombie walk. He's a young guy, prolly a couple years older than me, with blond hair and a skimpy mustache. "Are you shot, Miss?" he asks.

I shake my head.

"Come with me," he says. "The shooter's gone. I'll take you to the paramedics."

I grab my backpack as he takes my hand, leads me outside and back to the stage, where ambulances and news trucks are parked among a throng much larger than the original crowd. A white canopy has been set up for medical personnel, and the cop steers me that way, where a pretty Latino EMT who reminds me of my wife Lupe awaits. She motions me to sit on a gurney. I ask her if she knows anything about Dr. Rebecca Feiner.

"Was she hit?" I nod. "All of the wounded have been transported," she tells me.

"Do you know which hospital?"

"University Hospital. It's the closest." Duh! Of course, it is. I'm really out of it. "Are you hurt?" she asks.

"Not really. I have a scratch on my side. Not from a bullet. The rest of the blood isn't mine."

She pulls on a pair of latex gloves, unwraps a wet wipe and begins cleaning my face. I grab her hand to stop her, but she gives me a petulant look, so I let her take care of me. I reassure her again that I haven't been shot.

"We should still transport you anyway. You look as if a prescription for some tranquilizers wouldn't hurt you."

"Please, no. I'll see a doc if I'm not better by tomorrow." She frowns. "I promise."

"Since you've been exposed to other people's blood, you should get tested for diseases like AIDS and hepatitis in a month or so. They can give you an appointment if you go to the hospital."

"No, please. I just want to go home."

"OK," she sighs, helping me down off the gurney.

As I walk away, a dude in a bright blue windbreaker, wearing a black backpack approaches me. He's holding a microphone, which he shoves in my face. There's a cameraman behind him, recording us. "Miss, can I talk to you?"

Because of several run-ins with them over the years, I'm no fan of the media. "Get the fuck out of my face," I tell him.

He lowers the microphone. "I'm sorry," he says, with an unassuming smile. "We're all a little rattled here. I should have introduced myself. I'm Darren Murphy, WTCD TV." He looks like he could be maybe 40, and his shaggy blond hair peeps from under a white cloth beach hat. He's good-looking if you're into surfer boys, which I ain't. I want to be mad at him for being a pushy journalist, but that grin of his is disarming, maybe deliberately so.

"I don't care who you are." I tell him. "I don't want to talk to the press, I just want to go home."

His denim blue eyes bore into mine. "I understand," he says. "I'm sure this was a traumatic experience for you. A student should feel safe on her campus, especially at an event to get guns off the street."

That hits me wrong. "That's the last place I'd feel safe," I tell him.

"Really? Why is that?"

"Just look at the shitty job the cops did protecting us from this wacko."

"Isn't that just a little unfair, ah... Could I get your name?"

"Natalie."

"Natalie what?"

"McMasters."

He breaks into a broad smile. "I thought I recognized you! You're the one who took down that shooter in Manhattan a few months ago."

Oh God, I really thought I had left that shit behind me! "Look, Mr. Murphy..."

"Call me Darren, Natalie."

"OK, Darren, I totally don't want to talk about that, OK?"

"Sure, Natalie, sure. But don't you think it's unfair to blame the police for this shooting, when that criminal was allowed to get hold of an assault weapon?"

Now he's getting me salty. "It's not guns that's the problem. It's crazy motherfuckers who don't have any respect for other people's lives." Too late, I realize I've just said *motherfucker* on television.

Darren doesn't seem to notice. "But if those crazy people didn't have guns..."

"They're always gonna have guns!" I holler. "You didn't see the asshole who just shot us up standing in line to turn in his gun, did you? The cops will only take guns away from honest people who want to protect themselves. The crazies won't turn theirs in!" I'm so mad now I'm crying.

A woman and another cameraman have noticed us and are approaching. Darren steps up and puts a protective arm around my shoulders, holding the mike in his other hand. "Hey now. I know you're scared..."

"I'm not scared! I'm big mad! That shithead shot my friend!"

Darren's expression flashes between concern and anticipation. "Who is your friend, Natalie? Who did he shoot?"

"Rebecca Feiner. She's my counselor."

"And how is Rebecca? Do you know?"

My tears flow again. "Not good, I think. She was bleeding from her neck."

He hugs me closer, turning me straight on to the camera.

A couple more cameramen now have lenses pointing our way, and a guy with a mike on a pole dangles it over our heads. I see the student reporter who asked the police chief a question, Betsy Kiefer, also in the group.

"Did you see anyone else get shot, Natalie?" A woman reporter asks. Darren tosses a glare her way for poaching his interview, but she doesn't care.

"The police chief," I say. "She was standing right in front of me. And Dean Marks..."

"And after seeing that, you really think we should let anyone who wants to have a gun?" Darren asks.

I wheel out of his grasp and push him away. "You're damn right I do!" I say.

After hearing my answer, Kiefer asks, "Don't you even care about those people who were shot and killed here today?"

"How dare you!" I spit at her. "My friend was shot! But I didn't do it! You have no right to take my gun from me, or tell me where I can carry it, because some nutjob decided to kill a bunch of people!"

Darren's eyebrows go up. "Do you carry a gun, Natalie? Is that why you came here today? To protest the gun buyback?"

Now the alarm bells are blaring- he's putting words into my mouth. "No! I don't care if people want to sell their guns to the city. I just don't want anybody telling me that I'm not allowed to protect myself."

The crowd of people around me has swelled to a dozen or more, and they're barking rapid-fire questions.

"So, you admit you carry a gun," Kiefer accuses. "Do you have one on you right now?"

"How many guns do you own?" Another man asks. "What do you think of the proposed assault weapons ban? Do you own any assault weapons?"

"Do you have any remorse for the man you killed in New York City?" the woman journalist asks.

That does it! "No! Why the fuck should I? He got what he deserved. He killed 15 people!"

Darren tries to put himself in front of me to shield me from the mob, but I shove him away, sling my backpack on my shoulders, and push my way through the crowd. Another guy sticks a mike in my face and I backhand it— it goes clattering across the bricks, and the vultures back off enough so I can get clear and take off across the Commons. They don't pursue me, but they do keep shouting asinine questions in my wake.

Goddamn it! How do I always get myself into this shit?

I pull out my cell and text Danny and Lupe that I'm OK—I don't want them worrying about me when they hear about the shooting.

19

SNIPER!

I want to go home, but my Jeep is parked way out in the fringe lot, a mile or more away. People are saying that the University is canceling classes for the rest of the day in the wake of the tragedy, so I know the buses will be packed. That's fine—I need to walk off my shitty mood anyhow. Any animosity I had for Rebecca is now gone. She was bleeding way bad; I'm way worried. Why not go over to University Hospital and check on her?

Campus is almost deserted as I make my way to the south side. You can totally feel a current of fear crackling through the air like a living thing. I pass under the railroad tracks through a tunnel lit by a row of yellow lights running down the center of the ceiling. The dank concrete tube smells vaguely of urine and bleach—I've seen university maintenance people scrubbing down the floor and sides to fight the odor. The walls are covered in graffiti—the university permits it here, as a way for the students to blow off steam, I suppose. My eye lights on a slogan—squiggly blood-red letters on a black background—*100 people are shot in the US every day! Ban assault weapons now!* Shit, I suppose that many are killed in car wrecks too, but you don't hear them calling to ban automobiles. I don't own any so-called assault weapons, but maybe I'd better score me an AR-15 while I still can.

I make my way to the south edge of campus and cross a four-lane divided highway on a pedestrian bridge. The traffic beneath stands stock still—the cops probably have road blocks to catch the shooter. I descend into the University Hospital parking lot, where an orange and blue bus awaits with doors wide to carry passengers to the main entrance. I hop on so I don't have to dodge the cars and emergency vehicles circulating in the parking lot.

University Hospital is a group of massive, angular, white buildings sprawling over several acres. Half a dozen police cars, both city and campus, are parked at the main doors, and two cops are busy checking visitors' I.D.s. There's a TV truck and several reporters hovering about, but the cops, bless their hearts, are not letting them in. I show the police lady my student ID.

"We're limiting entry to victims' families," the police lady says. That explains why the reporters are being excluded.

I think fast. To my knowledge, Rebecca hasn't got any family. "I'm here to see my aunt. Rebecca Feiner?" The cop checks a clipboard, then she narrows her eyes at me. "How do I know you're her niece?"

"Oh, come on, lady! She's my mom's sister so we don't have the same last name. What kind of proof could I have to convince you?" Her expression tells me she's not buying it. I let my voice break. "I was standing right next to her when she was shot. She was bleeding way bad." I force out a tear or two. "Please?"

She gives in. "I have to check your backpack." She finds nothing suspicious, then runs a wand over me. It beeps, and she raises her eyebrows.

I reach in my pocket and come out with my Swiss Army knife.

"I'll have to confiscate this," she says. "No weapons of any kind are allowed in the hospital."

"Will I get it back? My dad gave it to me."

"No, I'm sorry. We can't return contraband. He'll just have to get you another one.

"He can't, Ma'am. He's dead." I give her a hurt puppy look. I don't have to fake it.

She rolls her eyes. "OK," she says finally. "I shouldn't, but... I'll be on duty here for another couple of hours. If you're done by then, find me and I'll give it back. But if I'm gone..."

"What's your name?" I ask her. "That knife means enough to me that I'll come and find you at the precinct if I can get it back."

She points at her name tag. *Gomez.* "Try to catch me before I'm off duty," she says.

I thank her, and she waves me into the glass and steel lobby, where I join the line at the main desk.

When it's my turn, I give the receptionist Rebecca's name. After a moment's search, he says, "She's in ICU. Can you give me some information about her for our records?"

He needs Rebecca's full name, address and age, which I supply. "You need an ID badge for ICU," he tells me. "See the man over there."

I know the drill from the time that Uncle Amos was here. I have to fill out a form that demands way too much information, then hand it back to the dude along with my ID. He snaps a selfie of me with his PC, then we wait for it to come out of the processor. He removes the backing and takes a badge on a lanyard out of a box on the floor, pastes my picture on it, then scans the barcode into the computer.

"Wear that at all times in the hospital," he says. "ICU is in B wing..."

"I know. I've been up there before." I wish I hadn't.

ICU is on the fifth floor. On arrival, I push a button on the wall next to a pair of locked, plate glass doors. A nurse in pink hospital scrubs at a round counter inside buzzes me in. She's got shoulder-length brown hair with reddish highlights, and she doesn't look a lot older than me. Her name tag says she's April. The counter is surrounded by a circle of glass-walled rooms, in which the patients can be constantly observed. Most of them are occupied, but I don't see Rebecca.

"Oh, she's still downstairs in surgery," Nurse April tells me, after I give her Rebecca's name and she checks her tablet.

"How is she?"

"Critical, or she wouldn't be here," April says. She reads a little more on the screen, then tells me, "Apparently, she's lost a lot of blood. They're giving her transfusions to bring her blood volume up."

"When can I see her?"

"Dunno. It could be hours."

Shit. "What's the prognosis for that kind of thing?"

"Dunno," she says again. "You'll have to talk to the doctor."

More shit. I can hang around here all day, or go home. "Can I get somebody to call me when she can have visitors?"

"Nope, but you can call here and we'll tell you if she's in a bed. I'll give you the direct number, but please don't call us every five minutes."

Fuck! There's no sense in standing around here all day, but I'm finding it hard to leave. The Rebecca I encountered this morning, the one who nearly had me thrown in jail, has vanished from my mind. In her place is the gracious, beautiful lady who helped me find myself when I was so lost last year, held my hand while I was in the throes of PTSD, defended me at the expense of her own career when my enemies tried to ruin my life, and stood by my side when I married my Lupe. She was traumatized by a vicious killer as a result of her friendship with me, and further taken advantage of by her cray-cray ex when she tried to get his help to heal. How can I turn my back on her now, no matter what she's done?

"Please Ms. McMasters," Nurse April says, "go home." She hesitates, then says, "I promise I'll call you when she's up here." She holds out her phone.

I take it and put my number in. "Thanks," I tell her. "I might as well head home before Lupe and Danny start to worry about me."

The elevator stops on every floor on the way down. On 2, the door opens and I see a familiar figure, his arm in a light pink sling. He steps into the elevator and the door closes.

"Dr. Marks! How is your wife?" His face falls and I'm sorry I asked.

"She's gone, Miss," he says softly, hanging his head.

"OMG, I'm so sorry..." Tears well in his cornflower blue eyes behind round spectacles. I can't help it—I step up and give him a hug. The physical contact causes the dam to break, and he's suddenly hanging on to me for dear life, sobbing into my shoulder. The rest of the people in the elevator shrink back against the walls to give us the room.

The elevator shudders slightly and the doors hiss open on the ground floor. We break our embrace and exit so we're not blocking the rest of the passengers. Dr. Marks takes my hand and guides me out of the flow of traffic. "How are you doing, Miss...?" he asks, struggling for my name. "Were you injured in the attack?"

"I'm Natalie. McMasters. It's just a scratch. How about you? I saw you get hit."

"I was lucky. A bullet just creased my shoulder." He hesitates, then, "I saw them putting Dr. Feiner in an ambulance."

"I came to see her, but I couldn't. She's hurt way bad. Critical."

"Oh my God!" Now he's crying again.

I take his hand and lead him to a low bench by a window, help him sit, then hold both his hands in mine while he cries it out. When his sobs subside, I ask, "Have you got someone to call to take you home? You totally shouldn't be driving right now."

He stares at me, a half-smile on his features. He's easily old enough to be my father, but his round face is almost boyish, his skin pale and unblemished. I want to hug him again because I can see he's hurting so badly, but I don't. "I'll be all right," he replies. "I can get an Uber, pick up my car tomorrow. How about you? I know you were seeing Dr. Feiner for counseling."

"That's right." I choke up.

He notices. "What?"

"We had a fight this morning. Before it happened. I said some really ugly shit to her. It was the last thing..." Now I'm crying.

He purses his lips, then reaches to take my hands again. "You know, if you need someone to talk to, I could make room on my schedule. At least until Dr. Feiner is well again."

"But your wife..." His blue eyes are rheumy, and brimming with tears. I feel so bad for him.

"Work is the best antidote to sorrow, Miss McMasters," he says. Seeing my skeptical expression, he goes on, "Maybe we can help each other through this."

"OK." I'm still not sure, but I would like to help ease his sorrow if I can.

"Just set up an appointment through the campus counseling center, like you would with Dr. Feiner," he goes on. He's smiling now. "I'll look forward to chatting with you."

Fuck it! "Okay. I'll set something up tomorrow. Is that too soon?"

He shakes his head. Still holding my hands, he rises, then gives them a little push before letting go. "I'll hold you to that. Be well, Miss McMasters." He smiles that boyish grin of his once more, then rises and heads for the exit.

I wait a few moments then follow him out. I'm not sure if I agreed to his proposal for him, or for me. I tried not to let him see it, but I'm a total hot mess—trembling inside, my stomach upset. I'm continually checking people out, trying to decide if they're going to hurt me, even though I know that the shooter is long gone. And I'm scared to death for Rebecca. If anything should happen to her, I don't want our last words to each other to be in anger. Maybe it will be good for me to talk to Dr. Marks to help get past what happened today.

I find Officer Gomez, and she gives me my knife back. Some cops do have a heart after all.

Chapter 4.

It's pushing three in the afternoon when I turn my Jeep into the driveway of a townhouse complex in the posh north end of town. It's filled with sparkling white sidewalks that wind through green spaces spattered with purple crepe myrtle and white fall-blooming hydrangea between free-standing, two story white buildings with windows all around. I park in my spot, identified by a brass plaque with my name and house number atop a mahogany post. Lupe's tiny Chevy and Danny's battered pickup are in adjacent parking spaces.

I hop out of the car, retrieve my backpack from the passenger seat, and follow the stone path to my front door. As I unlock it and go inside, the aroma of Mexico—corn, chiles and garlic—makes my eyes tear and my mouth water. Lupe sees me through the pass-thru from the kitchen and yelps, "Danny! She's home!", dropping a pan on the counter with a clatter and charging me. Danny, lounging on the sofa with a comic book, tosses it on the floor, springs up and does likewise. A moment later I'm smothered in the crush of bodies. A loud yowling arises from my feet as Buddha, the cat, tries to get into the act, too.

After my husband and wife let me go, I toss my backpack on the sofa, and they guide me to the easy chair as I reassure them that I'm not hurt. I recount the awful events of the day. I can't keep my voice from breaking when I tell them what's happened to Rebecca. "I tried to see her at the hospital, but she was in surgery," I finish.

"She's in good hands," Danny says quickly. "I've seen Marines recover from terrible GSW's when they've been medevacced quick enough."

I think he's just trying to make me feel better, but I reward him with a smile anyway. I go on, "The worst part about it is that Rebecca went way extra on me in her office earlier. She called the cops because she figured I was carrying."

Danny is triggered. "You were carrying on campus! You..."

"Hop off, Danny! You don't get a vote. You ain't got a murderer for a stan!"

That shuts him up. He knows about the letter I got from Rebecca's ex. I continue, hesitantly, "And I guess I'm going to be on the news tonight..."

Now Danny looks like he's heard it all. "What do you mean?" he says.

I tell them how I was ambushed by Darren Murphy.

"Will you ever learn?" says Lupe, shaking her head.

"Hey, I was all tore up about Rebecca. He took advantage."

"It is what they do," Lupe says.

"So, you've lost your sidearm?" Danny says.

"Duh! The rent-a-cop gave it to Rebecca to turn in at the buyback. She never got the chance. I lost track of it when the shooting went down, so it's prolly gone now." I frown. "That Sig cost me $600 plus, and I never even got a voucher for it."

"Maybe you can call the hospital and see if you can get it back," Danny says. "What have you got to lose?"

"Nothing, I guess," I agree. "I can carry my backup in the meantime." It's a little Ruger .357 revolver that I don't shoot much anymore.

Danny gives me a stern look. "Don't you dare carry on campus again! Carrying in a gun-free zone is a felony in this state, permit or no. Because of what Rebecca did, they'll be watching for you. Keep it locked in the console of your Jeep when you're on campus."

"Ok, ok..." He's right. It ain't worth going to jail for.

There's a click as the front door opens, and a small boy carrying a Steven Universe backpack enters the great room. Buddha howls joyfully and trots toward him. As he holds his arms open to receive his leaping cat, I can see that he's got a massive black eye!

Seeing her son, Lupe leaps to her feet. "Aiee! ¿ Has estado luchando de nuevo?" she screeches. She runs to him, snatches him up, minutely examines the damage to his face.

"No fue mi culpa!" Eduardo says, trying to pull away from her. "It was not my fault! The other kids, they say bad things about us!"

"Tell us what happened, little man," Danny says. "What bad things did they say?" He guides mother and son to the sofa, sits them down, then seats himself on Eduardo's other side. I flop down on the beanbag, facing them.

"All us kids in the third grade are new," Eduardo says. "Mr. Woodley ask us to get up, inter..." He can't find the right English word.

I help him. "Introduce?"

"Yeah, that's it. Introduce ourself and tell about our family."

Oh, shit. I think I see where this is going.

"When it's my turn, I tell everybody I have two mommies and a daddy. Mr. Woodley ask if I live with my mommie and daddy sometimes, and my other mommie sometimes, and I say no, we all live together in the same *casa*. Then the teacher ask me if my mommies are les…, lesbi…" Again, he can't find the word. He looks to me for help.

"Lesbians?"

"Yeah, that. I say I no know what that mean, and Mr. Woodley, he say it is two women who love each other." He smiles broadly. "I tell him yes! Mama Lupe and Mama Nattie love each other, and they love Daddy Danny too!"

That's exactly what we told him when we explained the throuple to him.

"So where's the problem?" Danny asks. C'mon dude, are you that clueless, I think.

Eduardo goes on, "Later, when class is over and we're waiting for the bus, this guy Chris, he say that it sounds like my mommies are whoers."

Whoers? Whores!

"I ask him what that is, and he say it is women who fuck anybody."

Eduardo is acquainted with the word *fuck* largely because he lives with me, but he doesn't know what it means, and he's been told not to use it at home or at school. I've been trying way hard not to say it when he can hear me.

"Chris, he starts singing, 'Eduardo's mommie is a whoer!' over and over, and he's laughing, and then all the other kids, they start laughing at me too. I tell Chris to quit, but that just make him sing it louder. Everybody is looking at me real funny, and it make my face feel real hot, so I get big mad. I tell him to stop again, and when he doesn't stop, I hit him."

Excellent! Our kid struck the first blow.

"Chris, he hits me back, and then we're fighting, and all the other kids are yelling and cheering. Then the teachers come and make us stop."

Eduardo reaches into his pocket and pulls out a piece of paper, which he gives to Lupe. She unfolds it and scans it, then hands it to me, looking scared. OMG! Eduardo's been suspended, and Lupe is supposed to bring him to school in the morning and meet with Mr. Woodley, the guidance counselor. Because she was an undocumented immigrant for many years, Lupe has a strong fear of people in authority. Having her green card now totally doesn't make that any better.

"Don't worry, Hon." I tell her. "I'll go with you."

"Maybe I'd better come, too," Danny says. "Our living arrangement is none of the school's goddamn business. That teacher shouldn't have been asking Eddie about his family."

When we enrolled Eduardo in school, we filled out a form to inform the school that they could release Eduardo to any one of the three of us, but we never went into detail about our family structure. I'm totally sure that shit will get way complicated if Danny goes to school with us tomorrow. "Please let me and Lupe deal with it, Danny. It won't help Eduardo if you go off on somebody."

His face says he doesn't like it, but he knows I'm right. "OK," he says. "But don't you go off on anybody, either." He knows me. "Tell them not to single Eddie out like that again, though." I smile. It's amazing how protective of Eduardo Danny's become since joining the fam.

"Go upstairs, change your clothes and clean yourself up," Lupe says to her son. "I will be up to help you after I get dinner in the oven." Eduardo does as he's told. He's a way good kid.

Later, the four of us sit down in the dining nook to Lupe's tortilla pie, guacamole, pico de gallo, and sweet tea. I really prefer beer with her Mexican food, but I've got to go out tonight.

Danny's phone chirps. He looks at the screen. "I have to take this." He goes into the great room for privacy. Returning, he's holding the phone like someone's still on the line. "It's Andy from the vets' group," he tells us. "Since they've canceled all campus events because of the shooting, we can't have our weekly meeting there tonight. Can we meet here this week?"

Danny's been running a support group for some vets enrolled at State, who had emotional issues when they got out of the service. It's been a big help with his own problems.

I look at Lupe. She nods. "Sure," I tell him. "I've got my first Krav Maga class tonight. You won't be in my way."

"And I have NA," Lupe says. "Can I cancel the babysitter?"

Danny nods to Lupe. "Yes. Eddie can play on his Switch in his room." He speaks into the phone. "Tell them to be here at eight." He kills the call and sits down again.

I glance at my phone, lying on the table next to my plate. 6:00. I pull up the app to turn on the TV in the great room.

"Do you have to?" Danny asks.

"C'mon, I'm gonna be on. I wanna see how bad they make me look."

"That's why you should not watch," says Lupe, but of course, I don't listen.

The theme music for the evening news, urgent and full of angst, echoes through the townhouse. The male anchor's voice emerges above it, his tone serious.

"A sniper attack that occurred during a gun buyback on State campus this morning left four people dead, including Capitol City police chief Elaine N'Dour, Dean of the University college Daisy Marks, and two students, Sandy Clemmons of Cameron and Donald Jenkins of Liberty. Several other people were wounded in the attack and taken to University Hospital."

"Hmmph! They didn't even think to mention Rebecca's name. Doesn't she matter?"

"Police say that the shots came from the roof of Overton Hall on the New Commons. The shooter apparently used a silencer, which may have contributed to the death toll, as what was happening was initially not apparent."

The female anchor interrupts. "Tim, isn't a ban on silencers a part of the assault weapons bill currently being debated in the State legislature?"

"That's right, Jill." He pauses to let her comment sink in, then goes on, "Noted gun control advocate U.S. Senator Samantha López was among the group kicking off the campus buyback, and there is speculation that she may have been the actual target."

Cut to a sound bite from Senator Sam. "This disgraceful and cowardly attack only underscores what I've been saying. We cannot allow a vocal minority to dictate public policy on gun control. This kind of terrorism is what you get when that happens."

The female anchor takes up the narrative. "To get the students' perspective on today's events, our own roving reporter Darren Murphy caught up with some of them after the shooting. Interestingly, our first guest, Ms. Natalie McMasters, was present at the mass shooting at Bellevue Hospital in New York City last April, which took 15 lives, and was responsible for taking down the shooter there."

I get up from the table and go into the great room. On screen, Murphy is saying to me, "A student should feel safe on her campus, especially at an event to get guns off the street."

My face fills the 60" TV. Yeet! I look totally ratchet—bloodshot eyes, red cheeks, my nose dripping and scraggly blonde hair hanging in my face. "That's the last place I'd feel safe," I say. "Just look at the bleep job the cops did protecting us from this wacko."

Murphy: "Don't you think it's unfair to blame the police for this shooting, when they were just doing their best to make our city safer?"

Me: "It's not guns that's the problem. It's crazy bleep! who don't have any respect for other people's lives."

Murphy: "But if those crazy people didn't have guns..."

Me: "They're always gonna have guns!" OMG, I'm totally ranting! "You didn't see the bleep who shot us up standing in line to turn in his gun, did you? The cops will only take guns away from honest people who want to protect themselves. The crazies won't turn theirs in!"

Cut to Murphy with his arm around me, both of us full face to the camera. He looks calm and wise. I look like somebody who just escaped from the locked ward.

"You really think we should let anyone who wants to have a gun?" Darren asks.

I push him away. "You're damn right I do!"

A disembodied voice asks, "Don't you even care about those people who were shot and killed here today?" That's Kiefer.

Me: "You have no right to take my gun from me, or tell me where I can carry it, because some nutjob decided to kill a bunch of people!" I sound like the fucking nutjob!

Murphy: "Do you carry a gun, Natalie? Is that why you came here today? To protest the gun buyback?"

Me: "I just don't want anybody telling me that I'm not allowed to protect myself."

Keifer: "So you admit you carry a gun!"

Woman reporter: "Do you have any remorse for the man you killed in New York City?"

Me: "No! Why the bleep should I? He got what he deserved."

Those were my words all right, but they were edited—edited to make me sound like a raving right-wing nutjob. The scene changes-I'm batting the mike out of the reporter's hand, then running like a scared rabbit across the Commons. Great—they've made me look like a total jerk.

Suddenly, another voice. "Mr. Murphy, I must say that was a disgraceful performance!"

Congressman Bader appears on the screen!

Murphy holds a mike under his chin. "What do you mean, Congressman?"

"I mean that you allowed that young lady to be ambushed by a bunch of loaded questions crafted to cast her in a bad light! That's how you treat anybody who dares challenge your progressive views on the Second Amendment? You should be ashamed of yourself, sir."

"I just allowed her to exercise her first amendment right on television, Congressman. I fail to see how that makes me the bad guy here."

"You knew exactly what you were doing, Mr. Murphy. It's people like you who give journalism a bad name." The Congressman turns on his heel and walks out of camera range.

Yeet! I had no idea that a U.S Congressman defended me to the press. He's sure got my vote next election!

Murphy: "Now, to present the fair and balanced coverage that WTCD TV is known for, we now turn to another student, Betsy Kiefer, a reporter for the campus newspaper, *The State of State*. Betsy, what do say to Ms. McMasters' assertion that anyone who wants to have a gun should be allowed to?

Keifer: "Well, Darren, before I answer that, I want to say that I fully support today's gun buyback and the assault weapons ban under consideration by the legislature. As to Miss McMasters' statement, it shows her total disrespect for our society, which has decided that anyone who wants to should not be allowed to have a gun. That's why our laws are written as they are. McMasters doubles down on that disrespect by carrying a gun on our gun-free campus, emphasizing her contempt for the will of the majority. Then she has her crony, that fascist Bader, make it look like calling her out for it is our fault!"

WTF!

Murphy: "To be fair, Miss McMasters never said she carried a gun on campus." Thanks, Darren!

Kiefer: "She said that no one had the right to tell her that she was not allowed to protect herself. That's alt-right code for I'll carry my gun wherever I damn well please! That attitude actually encourages people like the sniper, by giving them tacit permission to flout the law. She should bear responsibility for this attack too, and be subject to societal condemnation, and even sanctions."

Murphy: "What kind of sanctions do you mean?"

Kiefer: "I don't think expulsion is too severe. She's making my campus a more dangerous place."

I don't believe this babe! I had nothing to do with the shooting! I was nearly killed myself!

Murphy: "Again in fairness, it needs to be pointed out that Ms. McMasters actually stopped an attack much more severe than this one in New York a few months ago."

Kiefer: "Darren, I don't think it's legitimate to talk about the severity of a mass shooting. One death is way too many, especially when it's preventable by passing some common sense gun laws!"

Murphy: "Fair enough."

Kiefer: "I'd also like to point out that Ms. McMasters has a history of inserting herself into situations like this for the publicity. This has affected me personally."

Murphy: "How so?"

Kiefer: "If McMasters hadn't escalated a situation on Roderigo Hernandez's show last year, my sister Andrea might still be alive today."

Now I know who this bitch is! Andrea Kiefer was also a SOS reporter, who attacked me in print when I was the subject of a Title IX investigation by the university. She was killed by the cops after she assaulted a man on national TV—also not my fault. Murphy reminds the audience of the incident, but he doesn't defend me at all. On screen, he touches his ear, then says, "OK. My anchors are telling me we're out of time, so back to you, Tim."

Anchor: "In response to today's shooting, Governor Janes has asked the state legislature to put the proposed assault weapons ban on a fast track..." I grab my phone and kill the TV, then begin ranting, "I can't fucking believe this! They made me sound like a total fascist!"

"I told you that you should not have watched," says Lupe.

I turn on her, ready to clap her back with a scathing remark to her I told you so, but a look at her face stops me cold. Tears are running down her cheeks! She's hurt that they did this to me!

I take her in my arms, then Danny comes and embraces both of us. Eduardo really doesn't get what's happening, but he joins in too. I love my fam, but it's gonna take more than hugs to calm me down after the ass reaming I just got.

After we break up, Danny says, "I love you, Nattie, but Lupe's right. You need to learn to keep your mouth shut, especially to reporters."

I choke back a nasty response. They're both right, of course. Rebecca said it, too. A lot of my troubles are of my own making.

SNIPER!

Chapter 5.

A while later, I get a call from Nurse April. "I'm going off shift," she says. "I just wanted you to know that they haven't brought Dr. Feiner upstairs yet."

"What does that mean?"

"I'm not sure. Call in the morning." This doesn't sound good, squad.

I go upstairs to get ready to go out. Lupe, Danny, Eduardo and I each have our own room. Lupe's is the downstairs master bedroom off the great room, and the rest of us are upstairs. We decide who's sleeping with who on a daily basis. Lupe's room and king-size bed is big enough for the three of us (or sometimes four), so that's where we end up if we decide to sleep as a fam.

It's a warm night, but I put on a pair of sweats and a loose-fitting top. This is my first Krav Maga class—I have no idea what to wear. I strap the little .357 to my ankle, pull my pants leg over it, and I'm ready to face the world. I head downstairs, say goodbye to the fam, grab my backpack and head for the front door. As I get there, the doorbell rings. I open it to Jay Howell.

"Oh, hi, Natalie," she says. "I hope you don't mind. I was out this way, so I came a little early tonight for group."

"I don't mind. I'm headed out," I tell her. "Hey Danny, Jay's here!" I holler.

I close the door behind her and follow her into the great room, keeping her company until Danny comes down. She takes off her yellow backpack and drops it on the floor next to the sofa, then flops onto the cushions with a sigh.

"Rough day?" I ask her.

She looks away from me, toward the curtained windows. "God, yes! Everything's still crazy downtown because of the shooting. Traffic's all jammed up." It's always annoyed me that she won't look at you when she talks to you, but the lady has issues—that's why she goes to the vets' group. So I don't throw her any shade about it.

Danny's combat boots appear on spiral staircase, soon followed by the rest of him.

"Hey, Jay. You're early." Danny says.

35

She looks at him with an expression I've seen on the faces of many women when my husband's around. She'd better not get any ideas...

"Jay says traffic's a bitch, so I need to get gone." I go over to Danny to give him a goodbye peck on the lips, casting a glance at Jay after I do so. She's studying the wall. Good. I sling on my pack and head for the Jeep.

Getting threats from a serial killer a few months ago totally freaked me out. I'm 5'1" and I weigh less than 100 pounds, so just about anyone can do whatever they want to me physically. That's one reason I'm so damn determined to carry wherever I go. But sometimes, shit goes down so fucking fast you can't even get to your gun, so I decided I need some unarmed combat instruction too. Danny has shown me some stuff he learned in the Corps, but that's not the same as actual training. He suggested Krav Maga, a self-defense system developed by the Israeli military to train their citizen soldiers, because it's aggressive, effective, relatively easy to learn, and the closest thing to Marine unarmed combat training that you can get as a civilian. I found an ad for a Karate dojo on Lee Street that offers it two nights a week, with a coupon for a free lesson.

As I approach the Beltway on-ramp, I see bumper-to-bumper traffic on the overpass. Jay wasn't kidding! I drive underneath it instead and follow the back roads to Lee Street, the major thoroughfare that runs from downtown out to State. I struggle not to break the speed limit on the residential roads—guess I'm still wound way tight from the shooting, Rebecca, the news, whatever.

Near campus, Lee Street is full of restaurants, bookstores, and *tschotchke* shops that sell college memorabilia, but it gets pretty seedy the closer you get to the inner city. The dojo I'm looking for is in a storefront about a mile towards downtown from State campus, in a row of two- and three-story brick buildings. The parking lot in back is nearly empty and lit by an ancient light pole with a single bulb that casts a yellowish tinge over everything. The only other vehicle here is a faded green pickup that must be a century old, with a camper shell on the back. Hmmph. Not going to be a big class, is it? An uneasy tingle like I'm being watched courses through me as I get out of the Jeep, and the mingled stench of urine and garbage flows over me—this place is totally a great selling point for a self-defense class! I sling on my backpack and make my way to Lee Street, looking around anxiously as I go, spotting a few condoms and syringes on the ground. The sidewalk out front has better lighting than the parking lot, but it's still relatively deserted—my only company is a drunk sleeping it off in a doorway. The students usually don't venture this far from campus, or maybe everybody is just staying inside because of the attack.

The plate glass in the dojo door and storefront windows is covered for privacy with brown paper inscribed with bright orange oriental calligraphy. I grip the brass knob and turn it cautiously—I'm expecting it to be locked—but the knob turns easily. I push it open and a sweet breath of incense displaces the street funk. Oh no! The place is nearly empty—one big room with mirrors on two walls, and grey foam pads on the floor. A row of lockers in the rear is adjacent to an area curtained off by a bamboo hanging. There's only one guy here, standing next to the curtain. He's dressed in white pants and a matching top that drops below his waist. He's turned away from me, but I can see silver hair falling halfway down his back. He faces me when he hears the door open. OMG, he's ancient! Eighty if he's a day. He's got a round oriental face, a little pointy beard and a long mustache. I'd take him for a janitor except for his traditional Chinese outfit. He gives me a questioning stare.

"Uh, I'm here for Krav Maga?" I say.

"No Krav Maga here." Shit!

I shed my backpack and dig out the ad I saw, with the coupon for the free class. I'm sure I have the right night! I wave the paper at him.

"This says..."

"No care what it say. No Krav Maga here. Teacher quit. Only Tai-Chi Chuan."

Shit shit, shit shit, shit shit, shit! I zip up my pack and turn to leave.

I hear from behind, "Krav Maga suck anyway. You want learn Tai-Chi Chuan?"

I turn back to him.

"You want learn, I give free lesson. You like, you come back. Deal?"

"I need to be able to defend myself," I tell him.

"Gun on leg good for that." He raises his thumb and points his forefinger at me. "Ching-ching, pow! Tai-Chi Chuan good for everything else. You want learn?"

I look down at my ankle. There's a slight bulge from the .357, but it's only slight. This geezer is sharp. I consider his offer. I drove twenty minutes to get here. Danny's got the great room tied up with his vets till nine thirty or so, so if I go home, I'll have to hole up in my room till they're finished, because they need their privacy. WTF, I'm here. If the lesson is free, I have nothing to lose.

"Sure."

He points to the lockers. "Put backpack and gun in there. Next time, leave gun in car."

I do as he says. Turning back, I see him holding out a clipboard.

"You fill out form so Uncle Sam knows I run real business, not hobby."

WTF. I scan the page. It's simple—name, address, phone number. Using the attached pen, I fill it in and give it back to him.

"What I know about Tai-Chi is that it's a bunch of people waving their arms around in a city park on Saturday," I say. "How's that going to protect me from a killer?"

"Come here," he says.

I walk over to him and stand facing him. He's standing with his feet slightly apart and his arms hanging at his sides. Hardly a martial arts pose.

"Hit me," he invites.

Seriously?

"Wassamatta? You don't wanna hurt old man? Hit me."

I swing a half-hearted open hand at his face. It hits with a crack.

"That all you got?" he smiles.

Shit. Might as well play for real. I drive a punch at his nose. His hand flashes up, batting it away like he's swatting a bee.

"You miss."

I try again with the same result.

"Miss again. Come on, girlie, hit me."

Who the fuck you calling girlie, old man? This time, I pop a kick at his nuts like Danny showed me. He simply floats backwards so my kick misses. When I'm off-balance with my leg extended, he steps back toward me and touches my shoulder with two fingers. I tumble over and land on my butt.

He holds out a hand to help me up. I take it in my right hand, and as he pulls me up, I drive a left toward his ribs. He pirouettes aside and keeps pulling on my arm like a folk dancer, slinging me towards the far wall. OMG! If he lets go, I'm going straight into the mirror! But he doesn't, and my shoulder nearly pops out of the socket as my forward motion is abruptly stopped. Then he lets go of my hand, and I struggle not to fall down again.

"Now, want learn Tai-Chi Chuan, girlie?"

"Don't call me that. My name is Natalie."

"OK, Natalie. My name Ye-ye. What you say?"

"I guess so."

He grunts like he doesn't appreciate that answer. "Face me" he says. "Stand like this." He assumes his casual-looking stance once again, hands crossed, pressing on his belly. "First must learn breathe."

Breathing? "I already know how to breathe, old man."

"Name is Ye-ye. Touch tongue to roof of mouth. Breathe in through nose." He counts slowly, "One, two, three, four..." By the time he reaches eight, my lungs are so full I can't inhale any more. "Now drop tongue and breathe out through mouth. One, two..."

I don't get how this will help me take down a bad guy, but the way this old geezer manhandled me says he knows what he's doing. I go along. We breathe for a few minutes, and I can feel the day's stress draining out of me, down my legs, disappearing into the earth through the soles of my feet. He separates his hands gradually raises his arms to shoulder height, his eyes telling me to do the same. He raises his arms over his head, palms up, interlacing his fingers, then brings his arms down slowly, joining his fingers over his belly again. "Don't forget breathe," he says.

After we do this exercise for a few more minutes, I begin to feel an energy moving upwards through my legs into my belly, as my hands reach for the sky. A feeling of calmness slowly comes over me.

He shows me some other movements—drawing a bow, bending my torso forward and rotating it in a circle with my butt stuck out behind. Finally, we re-assume our original stance and just breathe for a few more minutes, before he steps backwards to indicate the exercise is finished.

"Feel better?" he asks.

I nod.

"Touch my hands," he says. He assumes a stance with his right foot forward, one hand at shoulder height, the other at his waist. I place my hands on his, and he moves his arms in a slow circle, encouraging me to follow. "Don't forget to breathe." After we follow this pattern for a while, he reverses it, and I lose contact with him for a minute, but he smiles at me and waits until I'm touching him again, then continues. Soon I'm able to stay with him every time he switches direction. Finally, he says something like "*Bo yo zo gotola*", and steps back, indicating that the exercise is over.

I glance at a clock on the wall. OMG! I've been here over an hour!

"You come back tomorrow night?" he says.

Tomorrow night? "That's a little quick," I answer. "How much does this cost?"

"Fifteen dolla," he answers.

"I can't pay fifteen dollars a day for this!"

"Fifteen dolla a week too much?" he asks.

I was expecting to pay twenty-five a lesson for the Krav Maga, so I guess I can afford that. "This was nice," I tell him, "but I don't see how it will help me protect myself."

"Trust," he says. "Must walk before you can run. You come back?"

I look into those blue eyes of his, and something there just draws me in, making me feel safe. "Okay," I tell him. "I'll come back."

It's dark as I walk to the Jeep, but my earlier uneasiness seems to be gone. I feel a vague emptiness though, a hole in my soul that needs filling. I guess I'll be back tomorrow night.

It's nearly nine, and still warm and humid AF as I pull into my parking space at the townhouse. White light from a nearly full moon reflects off the parked vehicles—three pick-ups and a car are still parked in the guest spaces—the vets' group is still here.

As I open the front door, I'm greeted by raised voices. Danny and Jay are facing each other in the middle of the great room, and Danny's aggressive body posture tells me he's upset. The other group members are ringing them like spectators at a schoolyard fight.

"...sorry," she's saying. "But it's time I've moved on from the group. My campus counselor says I'm too focused on the past."

"It's not just about you, Jay," Danny says. "You help the rest of us by being in the group."

"Damn straight," says Khalid Jones, a tall, young black man in green camo fatigues, who looks like he's in still in the service. "We need y'all with us, Jay-jay."

Jay throws him a grateful smile. "Thanks, Kay. But I've got to do what's best for me."

A short guy with oriental features, in a polo shirt and tan pants, speaks up, inspecting the ceiling as he does so. "Jay wants out, I say let her go. We don't need anybody who doesn't wanna be here." With his stringy hair and scraggly beard, China Mike looks more like a homeless guy than the SEAL he was before he left the Navy. I know he went out under a cloud, but I don't know the details. He and Jay came into the group as a couple, but their relationship seems to have cooled over the past few months, probably because Jay seems to have developed a crush on Danny. I don't really know much more about China Mike, because Danny takes the privacy of the group members way seriously.

The last member of the group is Andy Shores. He looks like your typical soldier—light brown hair in a military-style buzz cut on top, with the sides of his head bare. He's wearing a white t-shirt and gym shorts, so his metal prosthetic right leg is visible. I don't like him, because he's always giving me the eye. He must think he can get some from me because I have a wife and a husband. "You've been a big help to me, Jay," he says, "but you've got to take care of number one. We'll miss you."

Danny is tight-lipped as he surveys the group. "OK people, you win. I'll go with Mike and Andy. We'll miss you, Jay. You can always come back if you need to."

"I know it, Danny." She holds out her hands to the group members. "You guys have been great." Andy gives her a hug, followed by Kay. She steps up to Mike, who stands ramrod straight, not even looking at her. She shrugs and moves to Danny. She says, "I'll miss you, Sarge." and gives him a hug and a peck on the cheek. Danny flinches slightly—Sarge is not a term used in the Corps.

Jay picks up her yellow backpack and heads out, throwing me a smile as she passes. Still won't look me in the eye, though.

SNIPER!

That's the signal for the rest of the boys to pack up, too. "Damn," says Andy, "there goes the hottest babe in the group. Of course, she's the only one..."

China Mike says, "Yeah, and maybe she wouldn't be leaving if you didn't hit on her every fucking time we meet." But he's looking at Danny as he says it.

"Fuck you, Mike! You had your chance with her and you fucking blew it!"

Mike gets a dangerous look on his face. "Watch your mouth, asshole."

Andy drops his backpack and raises his hands. "Come and make me, slant eyes."

Danny steps between them. "Cool it, brothers! The enemy is not here." The two back off, still glaring at each other.

One by one, the guys leave. Andy, the last to go, grins suggestively at me as he heads out the door, then meets Lupe, coming in. He has a leer for her too, but she doesn't seem to notice.

Danny says to her, "Eddie is in his room. I told him lights out at nine."

As Danny locks the door, she goes up to check on Eduardo, and I head into the kitch. "There's no classes at State tomorrow," I say, "so I'm up for a drink. What about you?"

"I'll take a beer," answers Danny, "but hold the bourbon."

I grab two Heinies from the fridge and pour a shot of Turkey for myself. I can use a little help sleeping. I take the bottles by their longnecks in one hand and carry the shot in the other. I sit next to Danny on the couch in the great room, putting the drinks on the low table in front, then put my arms around his neck and give him a long, deep kiss.

"Wow!" he says when I'm done. "What did I do to deserve that?"

"Nothing. I've had a totally shitty day, and I need some love."

He frowns. "Not tonight. I've got to meet Amos early tomorrow morning on a stakeout. I'm off to bed after I finish this beer."

Danny is a partner in my uncle Amos Murdoch's 3M Detective Agency, which does most of its business in insurance work. Danny's stakeout is likely on somebody who filed a claim for compensation, to ensure the injury is as bad as reported. His expression prompts me to ask. "How are things going with you and Uncle these days?"

"Not great," Danny admits. "Ever since I moved in here, he's been all business. Other than that, he won't give me the time of day."

Uncle Amos has been a fundie Southern Baptist his whole life. When Lupe and me got married, he finally accepted the reality of it, but my living with her and Danny as a throuple is just too much for him. I haven't said five words to him since I asked him to come to our wedding with Danny, which he politely declined.

"To tell you the truth," Danny says, "I've been thinking about quitting 3M. Amos and Leon might be better off if somebody else was in my job." Leon is Leon Kidd, a former Marine and police lieutenant, the third partner.

"Oh no!" I reply. "You need to give Uncle some time. Besides, what would you do if you quit?"

"There are plenty of other detective agencies here in the capital," he says. "Maybe I could even get another LEO job in one of the outlying towns." I frown at that. Danny quit his job with the Capital City police because he couldn't tolerate the corruption, as did Kidd. I couldn't see his old bosses giving him much of a recommendation. I tell him so. "Maybe, you're right, but Amos would," he says. "His name still carries weight in this town."

I see Lupe's legs on the spiral staircase, so I drop the argument. Danny's gonna do what he's gonna do. "Grab a beer and join us," I say to Lupe.

She goes to the kitch and returns with a Coors NA. As a recovering addict, Lupe thought it wise to give up alcohol, too. I tried one of her beers once. Yuck! I'd rather quit entirely than drink that mess.

Danny chugs his Heinie. "Ladies, I'm sorry to leave you, but I've got an early one. He gives me a kiss on the mouth and Lupe one on the forehead before heading upstairs. Lupe moves to his space on the couch.

"How are you, *Cariño*?" she asks. Lupe can tell much more than Danny can when I've got issues.

"It's been a totally fucked-up day." I tell her about the canceled Krav Maga class. "The old Tai-Chi guy helped me relax, but I'm still worried AF about Rebecca. Even with the booze, I'm afraid I won't sleep."

She gives me a steamy look with her deep brown eyes. "Finish your beer and come with me. You will sleep afterwards." I do as she says. Like I said, Lupe knows me.

43

Lupe precedes me into the master bedroom. Her spicy fragrance envelops me as I follow and I breathe it in deeply—it's the scent of home and love. I shut the door to keep it inside. The only light in the room comes from the moon shining through the window, bathing the king-size bed in a silvery sheen. I strip off my clothes, hopefully taking off the stress of the day with them, and put on my nightie—a frilly white thing that just covers my butt. Lupe strips and dons a deep red lace chemise. I inspect her body as she pulls it over her head, and I'm happy to notice the chubbiness that she lost while she was using is coming back. Going to the bed, she fluffs the pillows and props them against the headboard, then sits with her back against them, her legs wide. She pats the mattress between her legs. "Come, *Cariño*," she says.

I climb in and sit in front of her, my back against her large, soft breasts, my neck resting on her shoulder. She wraps her arms around me, her cheek pressing against mine. It's a familiar position, warm and comforting.

"That shooting must have been terrible for you," she says.

I feel the tears welling up. "Why does this shit always happen to me, Bae? I was happy. I just wanted to go back to school." The calmness that filled me after Tai-Chi is all gone.

She squeezes me more tightly. "I know, *Cariño*. We do not know why the Lord gives the things to deal with that he does. But you don't have to do it by yourself. He has given you me."

And Danny, I think, but I don't say it.

"The media were totally the WOAT," I say. "I can't even! They made me look like a nutjob. The only reason I carry is to protect myself and y'all. They made it look like I don't care those people got killed and Rebecca got hurt." The damn breaks and I start crying furiously. "Don't they know that I would do anything so those things wouldn't happen?"

"They do not care," says Lupe. "All they care about is how many people watch their show. They say it would be better if the *policia* had all the guns. That is how it was in Mexico. Except that the *sicarios* had them too. The *federales*, the *policia*, and the cartels could do anything they wanted to us, and we could not fight back. That is one reason that I left to come here."

I'm suddenly ashamed. I know that Lupe's life in Mexico was a living hell. She ran to escape the poverty, and the repeated rapes. Things weren't much better for her after she got to the US, but she's persevered to make a life for herself and Eduardo.

She kisses the spot where my neck joins my shoulder. "Relax, *Cariño*," she says. "Let Mama take care of you." She pulls my nightie over my head and tosses it on the floor, and I feel my nipples harden in the cool air. She slides one hand down over my titty, rolling my nipple between her thumb and forefinger, stiffening it more. She places the other one on my thigh, trailing it upward into my curls, parting them with her fingers, finding my sweet spot. I turn my head and begin nibbling at her lips as she rubs me in a circular motion.

Our kisses become deeper and more frantic as her hand moves ever faster. I struggle against her arms, trying to free myself to turn around so I can pleasure her too, but she won't let me. "Relax," she says again. "This is for you."

I give up and lay my head back against her shoulder, letting her work at my breast and my pussy. A familiar yearning grows in my belly and my breath comes faster and faster. Lupe knows me so well that she could do this for an hour, bringing me to the edge and taking me back again, but she does not do that tonight. She locks her lips on mine, her tongue invades my mouth, and her lower hand begins vibrating like a machine. Everything goes black for a second as my release comes, then she's sliding my head off her shoulder, easing me down, placing a pillow beneath my head.

"Sleep, *amor mío*. Tomorrow will be better."

One last thought as consciousness slips away. "How could I ever live without you..."

SNIPER!

Chapter 6.

Music murmurs. Dua Lipa. *Don't Start Now.* I crack open an eye, glare at the bedside clock. Shit! 6:30. No class today, because of the shooting, but I forgot to turn the alarm off last night. Then another thought intrudes. Rebecca! Now I'm totally awake.

I slide out of bed, leaving Lupe sleeping soundly, go into the great room, and call the hospital. They tell me that Rebecca's in ICU and that she's critical. I've got to get over there! Then I remember Eduardo, and school. More shit! I can't leave Lupe to deal with that on her own.

Rattling coming from the kitchen tells me Danny's there. He's dressed in camo pants and a t-shirt, sliding a sandwich into a brown bag. I go over to him and give him a kiss.

"I'm late," he says after we break. "Don't want to leave Leon hanging any longer than necessary."

Remembering our convo from last night, I say, "You aren't gonna put Uncle on blast today or anything, are you?"

"I don't even know if I'll see him today."

"Give him some more time before you quit, Danny. He's an old man in a wheelchair. He needs you."

"That old man's a Marine, Nattie. He'll cope."

My response is cut off by Lupe's arrival—probably a good thing. I must've awakened her, even though I tried not to.

Danny leaves, and Lupe tosses a cinnamon stick and brown sugar into a saucepan of water, puts it on the stove, then cuts on the coffee grinder. I go into the great room and turn on the morning news.

The interim police chief is vowing that the cops will tear the city apart till they get the shooter. A short list of closings scrolls across the bottom of screen. Most institutions and businesses are open, including the public schools, worse luck. State, however, is closed, so the university community can heal, the anchor says. She cautions the public to leave for work early, limit non-essential travel, be patient at roadblocks.

"Senator López and Congressman Bader will be on at noon with comments about this tragic shooting." What's there really to say? But the pols have to have their sound bites.

SNIPER!

The microwave dings, and the aroma of corn and chiles permeates the house. Lupe places last night's tortilla pie on the pass-thru. "You want eggs with this?" she asks me.

"God, no!" I say without thinking. "Toast and coffee is fine." She gives me a disapproving glance, then goes off to rouse Eduardo.

After breakfast, I go upstairs to get dressed for the day. It's only 7:15, but my phone tells me it already 76 degrees and going up to a steamy 95 today. Gotta love fall in the south! As much as I'd love to wear shorts, I opt for jeans instead, so I can strap on my ankle holster and my revolver. Shit. The only pair I have clean is my oldest, which have shrunk to the point where they're a tad uncomfortable. I can't bear to throw them away though. I check to see that the holster is concealed, and I can see a bump, but not the holster or the gun. A bra, my Tool t-shirt and flip-flops completes my attire.

School is a fifteen-minute drive. I take the Jeep, and Lupe and Eduardo go in her car. Thankfully, we don't run into any roadblocks.

Wade Hampton Elementary School is a one-story blonde brick building that occupies an entire suburban block. Lupe drives around to the car-pool line in front, and I head straight to the parking lot in back. All schools are gun-free zones in this state, so after surreptitiously checking for muggles, I snag the .357 from the holster, and lock it in the console between the seats along with my Swiss Army knife. When I get out, I stamp my foot to settle my pants over the holster again, watching for Lupe. When she comes, we both go around to the front entrance to get checked in. It's about as bad as getting into a prison—we have to empty our pockets, go through a metal detector, put our driver's licenses into a machine that generates a stick-on badge with our pictures, and fill out a form stating why we want to be admitted to the sacred halls. There's a blonde, thirtysomething woman behind sliding glass panels who's wearing a name tag—Gemma. I ask her where Mr. Woodley's office is, and she tells me in an Irish brogue that there's a room directory next to the double doors leading into the school. Just like a teacher. Go look it up.

The room numbering system seems to have neither rhyme nor reason. We wander around checking doors, drawing some way sus glances from the teachers in classrooms. Finally, a skinny guy in a white shirt and narrow tie who looks like he's still in high school asks if he can help us, and I ask for Woodley's room.

"I'm headed that way," he says. "Follow me."

The guidance counselor's office is at the end of a dead-end hallway, something so prevalent in government buildings. I see him at his desk through the window in his closed door, gazing at a monitor. I rap on the window, and he waves us inside.

Woodley's office is small and cramped, smelling of sweat and cologne. His metal desk and ergo chair, a file cabinet, and a pair of plastic chairs against one wall take up most of the space in the room. He's got some trophies on a bookcase behind his desk, and about half a dozen framed diplomas and certificates decorate the walls. He looks to be in his twenties, with heavy round glasses, a hint of a mustache, and long, curly brown hair cascading halfway down his back. He's dressed in a plaid shirt over blue jeans, brown jacket and a knit tie. His bushy eyebrows cock inquiringly.

"I'm Natalie McMasters-Ibáñez, and this is my wife Lupe. We're here about Eduardo Ibáñez."

Assuming a serious demeanor, he says, "Of course. Please close the door and have a seat."

We bring the chairs up in front of his desk. They obviously weren't made with the comfort of humans in mind, because my tight jeans get even tighter in my crotch and ride up my legs as I sit. I look at Lupe and see her struggling to get comfortable, too.

Woodley asks me, "And Eduardo's father..."

"Our husband couldn't make it. He's working." Was that a smirk that just flickered on his face?

"I see," he says in a disappointed tone.

"Where is Eduardo?" Lupe asks.

"He doesn't need to be here for this," Woodley answers, then pauses before continuing. "I want to say that I admire y'all for having the courage to live as you do. Society will never progress if we are afraid to challenge its norms. However, there are some rules that we always have to obey. Refraining from violence is one of them."

He goes on. "Here at Hampton Elementary, we have a zero-tolerance policy for bullying. The first infraction brings a two-day suspension, and a reoccurrence can trigger expulsion." I glance at Lupe and see her flinch at that last word. "I wanted you all here this morning to make that perfectly clear. Eduardo will be in detention all day today and tomorrow to impress the seriousness of his violent behavior on him."

Jesus! This nerd makes it sound like Eduardo committed felonious assault or something! I say, "All due respect, Mr. Woodley, Eduardo's eight, and he's a little guy. I'm sure he didn't do much damage to the other kid." I hesitate, then out comes what shouldn't. "And truth be told, if somebody called my mama a whore, I'd pop him one too."

Lupe gives me her STFU look. "Señor Woodley, I am Eduardo's mother, and I will tell you that this won't happen again."

"It better not," he says. Looking straight at me, he says, "If you keep encouraging Eduardo to be violent, his future at this school is in serious jeopardy."

I clap back. "I don't encourage him to be violent, but I understand why he was. And what is your school going to do to make sure that Eduardo isn't bullied by the other kids again, so he doesn't have to strike back?"

"One is never forced to strike back, although you don't seem to agree with that, Ms. McMasters. I caught your interview on the evening news."

Oh-oh! "And..."

"And I'd like to remind you about the laws in our state regarding guns in homes where there are children. It is unlawful to store or leave a firearm that can be discharged in a manner that a reasonable person should know is accessible to a minor," he sounds like he's reciting from memory. "All guns should be secured either in locked safes or cabinets, or with trigger locks, kept unloaded and any ammunition locked up in a separate room."

"Now that last part is just not true. The law doesn't say that." I know, because we reviewed the firearms storage laws in my concealed carry class.

"It's a misdemeanor in this state to allow a minor access to a firearm in a condition in which it can be discharged," he says.

"That's right. And we don't." My gun is kept in my bedroom when I'm not carrying. And Eduardo knows not to touch it. That's how my Mama and Daddy raised me.

Not missing a beat, Woodley claps back, "And I wonder if Eduardo's predilection for violence doesn't stem from seeing all these guns around the house?"

How dare he? I feel the rage rising in my gorge, and I get ready to blast him, but I stifle it. God knows how much trouble this a-hole could make for our fam if he wanted to. I try to keep my tone measured and level. "We don't encourage Eduardo to be violent at home, Mr. Woodley. We try our best to live by the Golden Rule." That's the damn truth. I've never done unto anybody unless they done unto me first.

Woodley frowns and squints at me. I can tell he doesn't believe a word of it.

Lupe tries to mollify him. "Nattie is right, sir. Eduardo knows it is wrong to fight. He will be punished for this. I will take away his video games for a month!" Woodley's expression softens a little.

The best thing for everybody concerned is for me to get my ass out of here ASAP. "Will that be all, Mr. Woodley?"

I can tell he wants to keep the argument going—petty dictators like him don't care much for strong women. But he finally says, "Yes, that's all. Just remember that no reoccurrence of this behavior by Eduardo will be tolerated."

Both me and Lupe chime dutifully, "Yes, sir."

We struggle out of the uncomfortable chairs, and I try to straighten my clothes. On leaving the room, I hear a sharp intake of breath from Woodley. What's his prob, now? Just get yourself gone, Nattie. We go out in the hall, closing the door behind.

As we're approaching the school's front door, I hear running footsteps from behind, and a voice barks, "Just a minute, Miss."

I turn to see a uniformed school resource officer approaching. He looks like he used to be a pro wrestler—he's a humongous, bald white guy with a beard and walrus mustache. He must weigh 300 pounds! He's got one hand on his weapon, with the other arm outstretched. "Please come with me," he says, taking me by the elbow.

Alarms bell ring in my head. "What's going on, officer?"

"Please come with me," he repeats, his voice low and tense, his grip on my arm tightening painfully. He steers me outside, then on to the lawn, perp-walking me up to the school building wall.

"Place your hands on the wall, Miss." His tone has become even harder. His hand on my right arm is like a vice, and the other one has never left his pistol. WTF? I know! Woodley must've called him. He saw the ankle holster peeking out of my jeans! I do as the cop says, then he tells me, "Now kick your legs back and put your weight on your hands."

I glance at Lupe as I follow his orders—her skin is three shades lighter than normal. She's visibly shaking, and her expression is horrified.

I say, "Officer, I'm not..." I want to tell him I'm not carrying, but he cuts me off.

"It's a felony in this state to possess a firearm on school property, Miss," he says. He reaches down and pulls up my pants leg, to remove the revolver from the holster. He jerks, seeing it's not there, and his face reflects his disappointment. Then, in an accusatory tone, "Where is the weapon?"

OMG, now I'm pissed! It's pretty clear that Woodley sicced his dog on me. People who hate guns have no prob calling on people who carry them for protection. It takes all I've got to respond to officer calmly.

"It's in my car, Sir."

"Let's go to your car."

We walk around the school to the parking lot. He holds my arm the whole way, and it makes my flesh crawl, but I don't dare pull away. I know that I have done nothing wrong here, but I'm still scared AF.

We approach the Jeep. "Open it," he orders.

It occurs to me that he's got no right to do this, once he found out that I wasn't carrying. And he never even asked me for a permit. OTOH, from the news this morning, I know the cops are wired tight today because of the shooter. I decide to comply.

I unlock the driver's door and open it, then stand back.

"Where's the weapon?" he asks again.

"In the center console," I tell him. He reaches in and tries to open the lid, finds it locked.

"Unlock it," he says.

"No."

He glares at me. "I gave you a direct order. You want to be charged with resisting an officer?"

I've had enough of this dickwad. "Better that, than to be charged with possession of a firearm on school property. We're still in the school parking lot. As long as that console stays locked, the law says I'm not in possession." I listened at that concealed carry class! "May I get my id and my permit?" I ask him.

His face says he doesn't like it a bit. "Do it," he grates.

I dig out my wallet and give the cards to him, and he examines them minutely, making a point of comparing my face to the pic on the license, and the names on both.

"Am I being detained?" I ask.

Cops hate that question. It means you know your rights.

He hands me back my cards. "No," he says. "Get out of here."

I don't argue with him. "I'll see you home," I say to Lupe. Poor kid has to go to work after all this—she's gonna be a basket case all day.

After I pull out of the parking lot and get on the road, I breathe deeply and steadily to calm my racing heart, which is pounding in my ears. The last couple days have truly sucked! I think briefly about running by the hospital to check on Rebecca, but that's school property, too. It's just not smart to have a gun anywhere near me on that campus, even locked up, after I was warned. I can call the hospital for an update when I get home.

Once home, I take my pistol from the console and slip it into the ankle holster. Inside, I get Nurse April on the line, and she tells me that Rebecca has been taken for more surgery. She won't go into details. "You'll really have to talk to the doctor about that," she tells me.

"Who's her doctor?"

"Dr. Arthur Hall—one of our best vascular surgeons. I'll give you his number." She does so. "The best time to get him is early in the morning, before he starts work for the day."

Shit. More waiting.

I'm not used to being home during the day with nothing to do. I think about lunch. I'm not hungry, but I grab a beer and heat up some of Lupe's tortilla pie to soak it up. I cut on the noon news for the noise.

"A reporter at *The State of State* tells WTCD news that she has allegedly received a letter from the sniper."

Betsy Kiefer's face fills the screen, grinning like she's accepting a Pulitzer prize. "The letter says that the attacks will continue unless the State legislature immediately ceases debate on the proposed assault weapons ban, and kills the measure. We at SOS consider this a totally despicable act of terrorism, and intend to say so in an editorial to be published tomorrow!"

Cut to a split screen with the anchor between Senator Sam and Congressman Bader. "WTCD has tried to reach Governor Janes for comment, but his office has said only that the state will not negotiate with terrorists, and a statement from him is forthcoming. Senator, can you give us your reaction?"

The Senator's voice would cut glass. "This sniper is holding the citizens of this city hostage to further a political agenda! We cannot and will not allow such outrageous actions in the United States of America!"

Anchor: "Congressman?"

"For once, the Senator and I completely agree. While I have made no bones about my position on this legislation, it's vital that it be permitted to play out according to our American democratic system. Anything less relegates the United States to the status of a third-world banana republic."

Anchor: "The police have asked all citizens to limit their travel, spending as little time out of doors as necessary until this shooter is caught. They have assured WTCD that an arrest is imminent."

I cut off the TV. Holy shit! The government could never agree to quash legislation under debate because of a threat! Doing so would bring every nutjob with an agenda out from under their rocks.

I want to be doing something, but I can't and it's driving me cray. Since Lupe went to work late this morning, she can't be here when Eduardo gets home from school, and Danny's on stakeout, so I've got the duty. I told Dr. Marks that I'd make an appointment with him. I do that now, setting it up for tomorrow at 10:30. It's excellent that the campus closure doesn't affect the counseling center, which is considered to supply essential services.

I spend the time until 3:30 cleaning—not my fave. Then I head out to meet the school bus on the main road. The bright yellow bus is just pulling up to the stop as I get there. About a dozen children in the complex use it, so

I don't see Eduardo immediately after the doors open. A crowd of kids forms on the sidewalk, the bus doors close and it heads off down the road. As the crowd disperses, I see that Eduardo is not there. Shit! I run after the bus, but it's going too fast, so I double back to the Jeep. Eduardo has missed his stop a couple of times before, and just gotten off at the next one.

I catch the bus as it's just leaving the next stop. Still no Eduardo. WTF? Is he asleep or something? The drivers are supposed to watch out for the kids, make sure that they get off at the right place.

I hit the gas to get ahead of the bus before the next stop, and as he's slowing down, pull in in front of him so he can't get by me without backing up. When the door pops open and the kids come out. I stick my head inside.

"'Scuse me? I'm looking for Eduardo Ibáñez?"

The driver is a large woman in a blue-and-white striped top, shorts and flippies. "I know Eduardo," she tells me. "He never got on the bus."

WTF?

"Now move ya car 'fore I call the law."

Fuck you too, bitch. Worried sick, I jump back in the Jeep and head for home to call school.

When I get there, I see a car in Lupe's space, but it's not her little Chevy. A woman in a grey business suit, carrying a briefcase, is standing at our front door. The heat slaps me as I jump out of the Jeep. How can she stand that outfit in this weather?

She moves to meet me as I approach. She's a fortysomething, with skin the color of coffee with a spoonful of milk added, short black hair glazed blonde on top, and broad, plain features. Her white blouse has a ruffle down the center and a gold cross dangles from her neck. "You must be Ms. McMasters," she says. OK, how does she know me when I don't know her? "I'm Pamela Puryear, from Child Protection Services. I need to speak with you and Ms. Ibáñez about your son Eduardo."

SNIPER!

Chapter 7.

Fucking CPS? **"What does Child Protection Services want with us?"** I ask.

"I need to inspect your residence to ensure that it is safe for Eduardo."

My stomach feels like it's lying on the sidewalk. "Where is he?"

"He was taken to our offices from school," she says.

OMG! They have my son! "Why?" is all I can croak out. I think I know.

"Because we received a report that an unsafe situation might exist in your home. When that happens, our policy is to remove the child from the home immediately until we can verify or refute the allegation."

Fucking Woodley again! He saw the holster, reported me to the law, then called CPS. That motherfucker!

"I would also like to have Ms. Ibáñez here," she says. "She's Eduardo's parent, correct?"

We both are, but not legally, I guess. I nod. "She's at work."

"How long would it take to get her here?"

"Twenty minutes, half an hour."

"Then why don't you call her. We can spend the time while we're waiting gathering some basic information."

What I want to do almost more than I want to live, is to tell this bitch to take a royal, flying fuck at a moving bus, then go and bring Eduardo home. But I know I can't. I've heard the horror stories about CPS on the news. If they get their hooks in you, there's virtually nothing you can do.

I open the townhouse door and I shiver as a blast of air-conditioning rushes out. I hang my keys on the hook beside the door, lead Puryear into the great room and wave her to the sofa, then take the easy chair, facing her. I pull out my phone and hit speed dial for Lupe. When she answers, I tell her to come home right away.

"Is something wrong?" Lupe does not handle surprises well.

"Everything's OK," I lie. "Just come home and I'll tell you what's up when you get here." I don't want her driving knowing the government has kidnapped her son. I kill the call before she has a chance to ask any more questions.

I look at Ms. Puryear expectantly.

"Before we begin," she says, "I must ask, are you armed?"

I grit my teeth. I want to tell her nunya, but I know I can't. "Yes. I have a permit."

"Being in the presence of an armed civilian makes me nervous," she says. "Could you please put the gun away before we begin?"

I don't fucking care if you're nervous or not, lady. This is my home! But she has my son. If I refuse, I may never get him back. I get up and walk toward the spiral staircase to go up to my bedroom. As I mount the first step, I see that she's following. I stop and look at her.

"I want to see how you're going to store your gun," she says.

I think fast. Normally, I would just put it in my sock drawer in my room. Eduardo hardly ever goes in there, and he's been told never to touch a gun in any case. But I know that doesn't conform with state guidelines.

"OK, come on," I say.

When we get to my room, I open the door. A sour odor fills the hallway. "Excuse the mess," I say. "I haven't had time to do laundry." She doesn't respond. I'll bet my messy room is going into her report.

We enter, and instead of going to my bureau, I open the closet. I hope I remember where the pistol case is. I move some junk on the high shelf above the hanging clothes, standing on my tiptoes so I can see what I'm doing. My fingers brush hard plastic. Yes! I grab for it, way far back on the shelf, so I have to totally stretch to get it. I take it over to the bed, flip the locks and open it. It's here!

There's a law in this state that says, when you buy a handgun, the manufacturer must provide a gun lock. The one that came with the .357 is still in its plastic bag in the case. I may just get out of this yet!

I extract the little revolver from the ankle holster, flip open the cylinder, eject the cartridges into my hand, and lay everything on the bed. Hoping she doesn't notice, I tear open the plastic bag containing the lock, remove it, and turn the key already inserted. The long shackle pops open. I thread it through the barrel of the revolver from the front, swing the body of the lock into place, then close it so the cylinder can't go back into the gun. I put the .357 in the case, drop the shells in too, and close the lid. I have a bad moment when it looks like the locked revolver won't fit, but I shift things around so the lid can close and the tabs can lock. Then I replace the case on the top shelf of the closet.

I can hear the disbelief in her tone. "And that's how you normally store your pistol?"

I can't help myself. "It's a revolver, not a pistol," I tell her. "And yes, that's how I normally store it since there's a kid in the house."

"That case is not locked. The bullets are dangerous too, if the child got ahold of them. You should store them separately in a locked container."

God, I want to clock this bitch! "We can make that happen," I say. Her expression says *Suure you will*, but she doesn't comment.

We go back down to the great room. Puryear sits on the couch, opens her briefcase, extracts a black leather portfolio and opens it to a fresh page. After getting the townhouse address, she asks, "Now who's living here?"

"Me, Lupe, Eduardo and Danny Merkel."

"Who is Mr. Merkel?"

I start to say that he's our husband, but even though we consider him so, he's not in the eyes of the law.

"He's my partner at work," I tell her.

"So he's a roommate?" Her tone is snide, and plainly indicates that she thinks that he's something else.

"That's right."

"How...," she continues, then the front door rattles, and Danny enters. He stops and stares at the two of us.

"Mr. Merkel, I presume," says Puryear. "Come and join us." Like Danny needs permission to in his own home.

"What is going on?" Danny asks, his expression puzzled.

Puryear gives him the same CPS spiel that she gave me, about a home safety check.

"Where is Eduardo?" Danny's tone is dangerously low.

"He's at our offices, where he will remain until I have completed my assessment," Puryear says. "Are you armed, Mr. Merkel?"

Danny's quiet for a second, his expression questioning whether she even has a right to ask that question, then he replies, "Yes. I am a licensed private detective and I have a permit to carry."

59

"Weapons in my presence make me uncomfortable, Mr. Merkel. Could you please put your weapon up before we continue?"

Another beat, then, "No ma'am. I assure you that you're in no danger from me."

"That may be," she replies, "but I must ascertain how the weapon is stored, so I know the child is in a safe environment."

Pretentious people who tell him what to do, do not sit well with Danny. "I can guarantee you that he is, ma'am. When not on my person, my weapons are locked in my room." That's a lie. I know he doesn't lock them up.

"Nevertheless, I am required to inspect them in storage, so I can ascertain whether they constitute a threat to the child. If you refuse to comply with my request, I simply cannot authorize Eduardo's return to the home."

The front door opens again, and Lupe comes in. She freezes as she sees us.

"Ah, the child's mother," says Puryear. "Now our party is complete."

"Where is my son?" Lupe asks, her tone frantic.

Puryear launches into the CPS spiel yet again, finishing with, "I was just asking Mr. Merkel to show me how he stores his guns." She cocks an eyebrow. "I don't suppose you carry weapons, too?"

Now fearful, Lupe shakes her head.

Cruella de Vil turns her attention back to Danny. "Well, what'll it be, Mr. Merkel?"

Danny knows when he's licked. "OK, so maybe I wasn't quite honest with you. My guns are on my person whenever I'm awake. They're in a drawer in my nightstand when I'm sleeping."

"Locked?"

"No ma'am. But Eddie doesn't come in my room."

"The point is that he could," she all but smirks, closing the portfolio with an audible crack. "I have what I need. For now, Eduardo will remain in CPS custody."

"No!" Lupe shouts. "You cannot do this! He is an American citizen!"

"We're not immigration, Ms. Ibáñez," Puryear says. "I'm going to draft an order to require you to either get all weapons out of this home, or store them in a safe manner. Once you're in compliance and have been inspected, we can revisit returning the child to the home."

Lupe is plainly terrified. "What are you going to do with my son?" she croaks.

"He'll spend tonight in a shelter," Puryear says. "Tomorrow, we'll try to get him space in a group home until you comply with my order. If you do so expediently and everything checks out, he could be home by the end of the week."

The end of the week! Lupe now looks like someone has a gun to her head.

Puryear packs her portfolio back into her briefcase, then extracts a business card and gives it to Lupe. "Just contact me when you're ready for that inspection, and we'll see about getting the child back into the home." She moves to the front door and places her hand on the handle, then turns her head. "Of course, we'll also have to verify that the lifestyle here is conducive to a proper upbringing." She opens the door and leaves.

When the door closes, Lupe looks at me with burning eyes. "See what you have done now!" she snarls.

I clap back, "What do you mean, what I have done? I didn't do this—Woodley did!"

"Only because you have to take that stupid gun everywhere!"

I reply without thinking, "You didn't seem to mind when I used it to save your ass!" I'm immediately sorry when I see the pain flash across her face.

Danny steps behind Lupe and puts his arms around her, but she shakes him off. "That was really unfair, Nattie," he says.

I'm still hurt. "She wasn't fair to me either," I tell him.

"What the hell did she mean by 'a lifestyle conducive to a proper upbringing'." Danny asks.

"You know damn well what she meant!" I say. "The throuple."

"Maybe I need to move out of here," Lupe says.

Where the fuck did that come from? "So, you're going to run away again?" I say incredulously. "Look what that got you the last time!"

"I don't care," she cries. "I want my Eduardo back!"

I can't even! I feel the bile rising into my throat and I just know that I'm going to blurt out something devastating. I run across the room, grab my keys from the hook and tear open the door.

61

SNIPER!

"Where are you going?" Danny shouts.

"Out!" I holler, slamming the door behind me.

Chapter 8.

Later, stuck in rush hour traffic on the freeway, I'm cursing myself for an idiot for going this way in the first place.

How the fuck can Lupe blame me for this shit? I totally don't get why this keeps happening to me. I'm just trying to keep my head down, get through school and stay out of other people's shit, but I'm constantly being thrust into the media spotlight. Even though it hurt her, I totally meant what I said to Lupe about running away. There's got to come a time when you stop letting people fuck with you!

I open the center console, reach inside and rummage around. Ah! Got them! I come out with a red and white cigarette package, about half full. I shake it and pull out a non-filtered Lucky Strike with my teeth. I put the pack back into the console and push in the cigarette lighter in the dash.

My phone dings—a notification. Tai-Chi—1 hour. Shit, I totally forgot! My first thought is to blow off Mr. Miyagi. Then I think some more. I'm still as ratchet as a cat in a room full of rocking chairs, as Uncle Amos would say. If I go home and Lupe's still po'd, I will prolly say some shit I shouldn't. OTOH, last night's Tai-Chi session really calmed me down. My eyes flick up to the overhead exit sign. Yeah, I can get there from here.

The lighter clicks as it pops out, but I reconsider the smoke. I'm going to an exercise class—do I really want to get started smoking again? That would be no. I retrieve the cigarette pack from the console and get the cig back inside the package with some difficulty, all the while watching the road so I don't rear end somebody. I think about slinging the whole mess out of the window, but there's no need to go that far. I put the pack back in the console instead.

At the dojo, I drive around back to park in the same spot as yesterday. As I get out of the Jeep, I see that, unlike last night, the parking lot isn't unpopulated. The old pickup is here, along with four guys huddled under a tree near to it. Looks like a drug deal going down. Silently wishing for my revolver, still locked up at home, I walk quickly out of the lot without looking at them. They pay no attention to me. I hope they're gone when it's time to go home.

When I go inside, the *dojo* is much as it was last night. Ye-ye is standing in front of the mirrored wall with his top off, assuming a series of martial stances. OMG! He may be pushing eighty, but he has a torso like a Greek statue, his muscles rippling under his skin as he shifts from pose to pose. Without turning around, he says, "Stand behind, and follow me. Don't forget breathe." I do as he says. He's watching me in the mirror, and after a minute, he says, "Never mind the arms. Just follow from waist down." Yeet! I was doing all of the arm movements with no legs. At first, I find it difficult to take long strides like he's doing, until I figure out that I have to take my weight off the leg I'm stepping with first. Then it becomes easier to follow him. We keep this up for quite a while, until a thin sheen of sweat coats my body under my clothes. Ye-ye finishes the exercise by bringing us to a stance with feet together, arms at the side, then says, "OK. You need break?"

I start to say no, then I realize there's dull ache in my hips and my legs quiver slightly when I move. I nod instead.

He runs his eyes over my body. Normally, it brings back my days as a stripper when a guy does that, but something tells me this old man's not assessing me as a sex partner. He steps toward me, holding his hands apart on either side of my head, then he asks, "Can I touch you?"

I nod.

He puts his hands on the top of my head, then slides them down so they're covering my ears and touching my temples. A tingling sensation courses through my head, then runs down my spine, gathering in my lower abdomen.

"Your *chi* flow is disturbed," he says. "Something has upset you today?"

I'm not about to start discussing my personal issues with my Tai-Chi guy. "Not really," I tell him. His expression plainly says he doesn't believe me, but tough titty.

"Okay," he says, stepping back and raising his hands for the push hands exercise. I find it much more difficult to follow him than I did last night, continually falling off-balance, forcing us to restart. Finally, he stops, says "We do *qi gong* instead. Stand in *wuji-bu*," taking a stance with his legs at shoulder width, knees slightly bent. "Just breathe," he tells me, "eight seconds in, eight seconds out. Find *chi* in the earth, draw up through legs into the *dantian*." He grips his lower belly in both hands.

64

We do the breathing for what seems like an hour. It's hard. Even though I'm inhaling for a full eight seconds, I feel like I'm not getting enough air, so I have to breathe in fits and starts. But eventually, I find a rhythm, and soon I feel tingling in my feet, rising to my knees, then to my groin before settling in my belly. A sense of peace comes over me.

"Okay," he says finally. "Enough for tonight. Come back tomorrow." He pauses, then, "It's hard to train when you out of balance. I can help you get balance back, but you must allow."

Not happening, Hunty. I say good night and head to the Jeep.

A whiff of motor oil and garbage in the tepid air come to me as I exit the *dojo*, and it's fully dark. I wonder if this Tai-Chi shit is totally worth my time. Sure, it seems to calm me down, but a beer and a shot will do that. What I need is to learn to defend myself, so every big-ass man can't push me around. I'm not getting any of that from Ye-ye.

As I come around the building into the rear parking lot, I stop suddenly. Those asshats are still here, and they've moved over by the Jeep. Shit. There's no way I'm getting into my car without dealing with them. This is what I need a self-defense class for! I briefly think about going back to get Ye-ye, but what's an eighty-year-old dude going to do with four thugs? I pull my keys from my pocket, take a deep breath and walk straight to the Jeep. Show no fear, Nattie!

Sure enough, one of the sleezeballs moves to block me from the driver's door. He's fortyish, dressed in a filthy tank top and cut-offs, with scraggly blond hair, a patchy beard and sores on his face. His half-vacant look and emaciated arms tell me he's no stranger to a crack pipe. "Hey sweetness," he says. "Wanna party?"

I grip the keys tightly. Maybe I can get one of them in the eyes, but there are three more. Somehow, I've got to get them to move away from the car.

"Maybe," I say. I can tell from the fucker's face that he wasn't expecting that. "Whatcha got?"

He grins with missing teeth and looks at his buds, who are moving to get on either side of me. He reaches in a pocket, pulls out a pipe and a small bag. "Got Tina," he says, offering them to me. "You want some?" Two of the tweakers are now behind me, cutting off my retreat.

SNIPER!

This ain't gonna work—I am fucked if I don't get outta here right now! Stepping toward the dude with the pipe, I wait until I see his face relax, then I abruptly whirl and dash towards Lee Street. One guy dances towards me with outstretched arms and I pivot away from him, but another goon extends a leg, sending me to the asphalt. Strong arms grip my shoulders and haul me to my feet.

I shrug off the clutching hands and spin around, stabbing my keys at one thug's face. He tries to back off, so I miss his eyes, but I open a long gash on his cheek. Then arms like iron bands clamp around my waist from behind.

"Leggo, goddamnit!" I scream. "Help! Help!"

The animal in front of me grabs the neck of my t-shirt and pulls, ripping it open, leering at the sight of my bra. I try to bite him as he grabs it, but I can't reach. He yanks, the straps pop and my titties spill out. I struggle furiously against the guy holding me as the other one mauls my breasts, a shit-eating grin decorating his ugly face. People, I'm in trouble!

The arms holding me suddenly relax as the eyes of the guy in front of me widen in surprise. Suddenly off-balance, I fall on my knees, a bolt of pain shooting up my legs as I hit the tarmac. Someone steps past me, thrusting two hands into the center of my would-be rapist's chest. The dude flies up and backwards, landing on his back.

Ye-ye!

The guy who originally blocked me from the Jeep charges him, but Ye-ye simply turns his body while catching the thug's arm with one hand and placing the other on his lower back, directing him away and sending him sprawling too. That tweaker struggles to his feet, and the rest of the thugs regroup. Boss shithead pulls out a knife and flips it open. "You just bought a mess of trouble, grandpa," he says.

The four of them charge Ye-ye as one. Ignoring the others, Ye-ye steps toward the knifeman, slapping at his hand, and sending the blade spinning off into the night. Unfortunately, that move allows the other three to get hold of him.

I expect to see the old man taken to the ground, but he slides his legs apart like he's straddling a horse, letting the thugs strain against him, weaving back and forth so he doesn't go down. Suddenly he twitches, and all three assailants are staggering away from him like a grenade just went off in their midst. Two of them go ass over teakettle while the third stands there stupidly, trying to figure out just what the hell happened. Ye-ye steps up and kicks him square in the nuts, so he's no longer interested in the fight.

Head meth head has retrieved his knife and charges the old dude with his hand high, bringing his blade downwards in a chopping motion. Ye-ye freezes. OMG! He's gonna take a knife in the head! But just as steel is about to meet flesh, Ye-ye steps backwards, grabs the dude's wrist, and pushes the blade downwards, burying it to the bone in his opponent's thigh. The thug wails like a scalded siren and collapses.

The fourth guy takes one look at all the carnage and bolts like a cat running from a bulldog. The other two soon follow. The guy with the knife in his leg is left rolling on the ground, blubbering like a baby. Ye-ye ignores him.

He helps me to my feet. "You can't go home like that," he says, looking at my titties hanging out. "Come with me."

He takes me back to the *dojo*, sits me on a bench then goes to the rear, returning with a cup of water in one of those cheap paper cones. As I drink it, he holds out a white, Chinese-style jacket.

"This is much too large, but it will preserve your modesty until you can get home to change." He places it over my shoulders, allowing me to button it in front. I'm still shaking from the adrenaline rush, so my fingers fumble with the big woven buttons. He holds his hands out. "May I?" he asks. I nod, and he buttons the jacket around me.

Abruptly, I notice something. "Your English is way better than it was a little while ago," I tell him.

"Sometimes I must show people what they expect to see," he says. "I don't need to do that with you anymore."

"How come?"

He smiles. "Because now, I know you will come back tomorrow."

I can't help myself. Smiling, I say, "Oh, you think so? You didn't hire those dudes to help you sell Tai-Chi classes, did you?"

"Sure," he says, grinning too, "but I've simply got to find a better way. A knife in the leg every time makes it hell to find replacements."

I frown. "I thank you for helping me, but I don't know that I will come back. I came here to learn to defend myself, not how to breathe. You're not teaching me anything useful."

He looks at me for a minute. "You're right," he says. "Stand up. Face me."

I do it. He looks into my eyes with his blue ones, then suddenly flicks a hand at my face. I instinctively move to block it, and I feel a slight thump on my leg.

"Again," he says. "Watch my feet this time."

He feints at my face—I have all I can do not to react. I watch his foot snap upwards to touch the side of my leg. "I'm hitting your calf instead of your knee because it's dangerous to kick a knee" he tells me. "But that is what you must do." He stands back a little. "You try it. Put your weight on your back leg, leave the front leg empty. Rotate your hips when you snap the kick."

I try a few times. It's not hard.

"Practice in front of a mirror at home," he says. "Snap the kick into the side of the knee and your man will go down. Then run like hell."

He fishes in a pocket, then hands me a little plastic bag. "Brew this like a cup of tea at home. It will relax you and help you sleep."

I don't take it. "A beer and a shot will do that," I tell him.

"But this won't give you a hangover in the morning." He extends his hand again. "Please."

I take it, but the jury's out on whether I use it or not. I stand, then step up and give him a hug. He smells of sweat and incense. "Thanks for helping me with those guys. I'll see you tomorrow night." He hugs me back, and I feel tears welling up. I've got to go—I won't cry in front of him.

The guy with the knife in the leg is gone when I get back to the parking lot. The townhouse is dark when I get there, with only the night light on in the great room. Lupe and Danny must've gone to bed early. That's good, because I totally don't feel like explaining why I'm wearing a Chinese jacket three sizes too big. I start to go up the spiral staircase to the safety of my room, but I hesitate. Something's nagging at me. Like a robot, I turn and head for the front door, open it and go outside. I walk to the Jeep, unlock it and pop the top to console. The red and white pack of Luckies peeps out at me. I take it, shake one out and put it in my mouth, then reach into the console for matches. I come out with a little plastic bag instead. Ye-ye's tea.

I spit the cigarette out, throw the pack on the sidewalk after it, and stomp both repeatedly until the mess is unsmokable. I go inside to brew the tea.

Tomorrow's just got to be a better day!

SNIPER!

Chapter 9.

I t's 0300—oh dark thirty if I've ever been there. I'm driving down a two-lane road on a ridge. One side is a forest, the other overlooks a valley which is packed with homes. Suburbia, U.S.A.

Rounding a curve, I come to a place where the shoulder widens and tire tracks indicate that many have pulled off to enjoy a smoke or neck a little while looking down on the pastoral scene below. I follow suit, then shut off the engine and get out of the truck. This is my final firing position today. Going to the rear, I open the tailgate, flip up the bed cover, and climb in. I reach up and close the bed cover again, leaving the tailgate down.

I open the backpack I find inside and take out the pieces of my weapon system. It only requires a minute to assemble the rifle—insert the bolt into the receiver, screw the barrel on in front, followed by the suppressor, the bipod, then slap a mag of 7.62s into the bottom. I remove the lens caps from the scope, put the rifle to my shoulder, and rest the bipod on the tailgate. Only about an inch peeps out from under the bed cover, so it's highly unlikely anyone driving by will even notice.

There's only a quarter moon tonight, so it's still too dark to survey the killing ground, but that's OK. The most essential quality that a sniper must possess is patience. Lying as still as a corpse, I mentally review the mission parameters— insertion is complete, camo in place. All that remains is recon, carrying out the mission itself, and exfiltration from the FPP.

As the sun rises, the homes transform from a uniform grey to a colorful palette on a green background. This is an older neighborhood, so no two adjacent houses are alike. I begin my survey—ideally, I'd like to take out a target after they get into their car. That will be less obvious than dropping them in the driveway, allowing plenty of time to elapse before the body is discovered so I can be long gone. The streets of the subdivision begin to fill with traffic, but I don't want to take out anyone who's made it out to the road. The longer it takes people to realize what's happened, the greater my chances of a clean exfil.

I catch a glimpse of movement in a driveway. A side door opens, and a boy about ten comes out. I capture him in the reticle, framing his head and shoulders. It's short range—only about 100 meters. I take one more check of the surroundings and it's a good thing. The door opens again and mom and little bro exit the house—I guess she's driving everyone to school. I abort the target and look for another.

SNIPER!

A few blocks away, a garage door opens and the rear of a car appears. Placing the reticle on the passenger window, I can see the silhouette of the driver inside, but the body of the auto provides enough concealment to make a precise shot impossible. I'm not looking to wound. I abort again.

Finally, patience pays off, as it always does. A guy comes out his front door and goes to his car in the driveway, parked with the front facing the street. It's a red Mustang, and he caresses the hood as he passes in front of it—he really must love that car. He unlocks the driver's door and slips inside as I put the reticle on him and make the range about 400 meters. I let him pull the door shut before I squeeze off a round, and I see him slump toward the passenger seat. Perfect left temple kill shot.

I open the bolt and eject the round, push forward to load another, and survey the scene once more. Shit. Here comes wifey, out the front door, holding his briefcase. She must be calling out, but he doesn't hear her of course, so she walks over to the car to give it to him. It takes her a second when she bends down by the passenger door to realize something's wrong. When she straightens up to scream, I squeeze off a round and drop her. Now I survey the area again, looking for witnesses. Back on the front door, a teenage girl is framed in the opening. She looks toward the driveway, and her mouth pops open in horror. She disappears back inside the house before I can get a round off. Shit! It was time to get the fuck outta Dodge two minutes ago.

I lay the rifle down on the towel I've placed there for it, climb out of the load bed, close the tailgate and hop in the truck. A car coming towards me passes as I fire the engine up. Good thing this state doesn't require a license plate on the front. I put her in gear, check my mirror, then pull out in the road. I head for the highway where there'll be lots of traffic to lose myself in.

Mission complete.

Chapter 10.

As I come downstairs in the morning, twin aromas of coffee and corn tell me Lupe is up making breakfast. Danny is sitting on a stool at the pass-thru, and I slide onto the stool next to him. He gives me a peck on the cheek as Lupe pours me a cup of her strong *café de olla.*

"How are you this morning?" he asks uneasily.

I think about my answer before I say anything. "Not great," I finally reply. "What are we going to do about Eduardo?"

"Lupe and I have been talking about it," he says. "She thinks she should move out and get her own place. I've been trying to discourage her."

I feel my cheeks flushing as anger wells up. Don't go off on her, Nattie! I swallow, then say, "Good." I look at my wife, who's studying the kitchen floor. "I don't want you to go, Bae. We'll do what they want and lock up the guns. Then they'll let him come back."

She still won't look at me. "And what if they do not?" she says. "What if they say you must get rid of your guns?"

"Then we'll fight them," I say. "They have no right to do that."

She raises her head and glares at me. "Oh, you are a child!" she spits. "You Americans do not understand that the government does whatever it wants to, because it can! I could tell that this woman, she does not like the way we live—two women with one man. Even if the guns are locked up, she will find another reason to keep Eduardo."

"You don't know that..."

"Yes, I do!" she yells. "You heard what she said before she left here!"

I choke back a yell in response. "Look," I say finally, "it's Wednesday. Please give me until Monday to see what I can do." I turn to Danny. "Let's get the guns locked up like they want, then call CPS this afternoon and tell them we're ready for that inspection."

"I'll buy a gun safe for my room today," he says. "I can get the kind that reads your fingerprints, so I'll still have rapid access. I'll get you one too, if you want."

"Great." Back to Lupe. "Will you please give us a chance to fix this?"

She's still looking daggers at me, like this is all my fault. "OK," she relents. "I must look for a place to go anyway, and that will take a few days. But if my son is not back by Friday, I am moving out this weekend."

I nod, but my mind is whirling. Puryear can't do this! Our home was safe for Eduardo before she got involved. And Lupe is right—even if we lock up the guns, the whorebitch is probably going to try and make something dirty out of our family, and that I'm not going to tolerate. I need help! God, I wish I could talk to Rebecca.

OMG, with all the drama, I almost forgot about her. I pick up my cell and hit speed dial.

Nurse April comes on the line. "Natalie, I was hoping you'd call. Dr. Feiner is in her room now. She's still critical, but she's stable. You can come by and see her when you want."

"I'd like to talk to her doctor. When will he be there?"

"Oh, Dr. Hall is an early bird. He's already come and gone."

Shit. I look at my phone screen. It's 8:30. My appointment with Dr. Marks is in two hours. Maybe he can help me sort this mess out. If I hurry, I can get by to see Rebecca before I see him.

I punch the button to clear my screen, but the phone dings again, bringing up one of those super-annoying news notifications. I start to get rid of it, but read it involuntarily:

Sniper attack in suburbs leaves 2 dead

OMG! I grab the remote and turn on the TV news.

"...Charles Frierson and his wife Marjorie were ruthlessly gunned down in their front yard this morning as Mr. Frierson was leaving for work. Their daughter, Lisa, 15, saw the whole thing and called the police. Police have not confirmed that the Frierson shootings are the work of the shooter who killed four at the gun buyback on the State campus on Monday, but a letter to the campus newspaper, *The State of State*, allegedly from the sniper, promised further killings if the state legislature did not immediately quash the assault weapons ban it is currently considering. The bodies were discovered at 7:45 this morning and shortly thereafter, police set up roadblocks on all roads leading out of the Rosewood Valley subdivision

74

where the shootings took place. A police spokesman has just informed WTCD that the roadblocks are being expanded in an all-out effort to capture the sniper. Acting Police Chief Leslie Porter had this to say:

'We strongly urge everyone who can to stay off the city streets this morning in an effort to reduce traffic congestion while we hunt this vicious killer. If you can work from home or go into the office later, please do so.'"

I kill the TV. Dammit! I totally need to get to the hospital!

Danny says, "I've got to go and relieve Leon—he's been on stakeout all night." He drains his coffee, kisses me and Lupe goodbye, and heads out.

"And I must go to work this morning also," says Lupe. "If the gym has to give my client her money back because I am not there, it comes out of my pay."

Later, in the Jeep, I decide to stay away from the beltway and stick to back roads to avoid traffic. The roads are clear until I reach Lee Street, where a solid line of cars inches towards campus. Sitting at a red light, I see that the cars are blocking the intersection, so I can't turn right to join the parade. When it goes green, I inch out into the intersection, attempting to force my way into the line. I put my right bumper directly in front of the headlight of an oncoming car, take my foot off the gas, letting the Jeep creep forward as the car in front moves. The driver of the car I'm blocking leans on the horn. I glare at her. Give me a break, bitch! She raises a middle finger skyward. I want to reply in kind, but I have a gun in the car. One of the first things I learned in concealed carry class was not to escalate a situation when carrying—don't create a situation where you have to use the gun. Eventually, I merge into the lane, and the driver behind pounds on the horn a few more times before giving up. It's all about position and power, bitch.

It's nearly 9:30 when State campus comes into view. Shit, there's a roadblock! No way I'm gonna make to the hospital, then to my 10:30 with Dr. Marks. Oh well, I can always see Rebecca after my session—*if she's still there*, says a little voice in my head. STFU!

To their credit, the officers don't detain us long. As I pull up, the cop says "License and registration, please." I hand them to her, and she scans them briefly before giving them back. "Student?" she asks.

"Yes ma'am." Uncle Amos taught me a while ago never to say anything more than required to a cop. I certainly don't mention I have a gun in the car.

After she waves me on, I turn right on Kershaw, heading for the fringe lot. A few minutes later, I finally find a space for the Jeep. It's only a fifteen-minute walk to the Counseling Center from here, so I should make it on time.

I automatically pop the console top and reach for my revolver, then I realize where I am. Do I dare carry on campus after being caught? I'm way shook when I'm without it, but now I'll be equally nervous carrying. That decides me—they can't put me in prison for anxiety, but they totally can for carrying in a gun-free zone. I lock the console with the gun still inside.

Walking along Kershaw, which runs along the edge of campus, I pass bumper-to-bumper traffic—doubtless people trying to escape the mess on Lee Street to no avail. After passing under the railroad bridge, I swing right onto North Campus. As I start up the brick stairway leading to the New Commons, a shout rings out behind me.

"Natalie McMasters! Stop!"

I turn and see a man in blue. He shoves something in his pocket (a cell phone?), then jogs towards me. Shit! It's that same cop that almost arrested me in Rebecca's office.

"What do you want now?" I say.

"Don't you take that tone with me, young lady! Put your hands on that railing and kick your legs back–you know the drill."

"Why?"

"Because you've been known to carry a firearm on campus. And today, there's no amnesty."

I'm totally pissed, but I have no choice. I do as he says. Once I've assumed the position, he pulls up the right leg of my jeans, exposing my ankle holster. My empty ankle holster.

Sometimes I just can't help myself. "Fucked up on that one, didn't you, Barney?"

A voice from my left: "Hey McMasters!" I look that way and see a woman holding a cell phone in front of her face. "Say cheese!"

Betsy Kiefer!

"That'll look great in tomorrow's paper," she says.

"Fucked up on that one, didn't you, McMasters?" the cop smirks.

***

I'm still salty AF going up the front steps of the counseling center—the last thing I need is to become campus poster girl for the right-wing nutjob fringe. But I totally can't blame the cop, either. The sniper's got everyone way shook, and the officer did have probable cause to suspect I'd be carrying. It was just my bad luck that Kiefer was around for the photo op.

Or was it? I saw the cop put his cell phone in his pocket before confronting me. Could he have called Kiefer? He was certainly smug enough about the picture.

Way to be paranoid, Nattie...

Once in the waiting room, I give my name to the receptionist, and he calls back to tell Marks I'm here. A minute later the doctor appears. Today he's got on a seersucker jacket over a navy golf shirt and a pair of white linen slacks. Doesn't look like mourning attire to me, but I guess everybody handles grief in their own way.

He takes my hand and presses it softly with both of his. "I'm so happy you could make it this morning, Miss McMasters." He lets go, steps aside and beckons toward the open door leading to the offices in the rear. "My office door is open."

I find it and go inside. Marks office couldn't be more different than Rebecca's. Instead of steel, glass and vinyl, his den is done in dark wood and leather, smelling of subtle spice. Following me in, he closes the door. The obligatory daybed and therapist's chair have been strategically placed near a tall, multipaned window that overlooks a rear garden full of late summer flowers. I settle on the couch without an invitation, and he takes the chair, picking up a notebook and pen from a small table alongside.

"Now Miss McMasters," he begins.

"You can call me Nattie, Dr. Marks," I tell him.

"Only if you call me Leland," he responds, obviously pleased. "Now Nattie, how have you been since we last spoke?" His voice is smooth, low and level, soothing like a tablespoon of honey in a shot of Wild Turkey.

I open my mouth to answer him, and I'm suddenly in tears. "I'm totally clapped!" I tell him everything—about my interview with the media trolls and its aftermath, Eduardo and CPS, the stop-and-frisk on the way here, all of it. "And the WOAT is that my wife Lupe says she's gonna leave me again so she can get Eduardo back..." I finish.

He snags a box of Kleenex from a convenient shelf and hands it to me. Once I get myself under control, he says, "It seems you've had quite the time. Your wife wants to leave you! Of course, it could be worse..."

Crimson shame flushes my cheeks. "You're right. I'm sorry. I forgot about your wife."

"That's as it should be, Nattie. We're here to help you, not me." His utter selflessness makes we want to cry again, but I choke back the tears. "What is your plan going forward, to get Eduardo back?" he asks.

"Other than locking up the guns like CPS wants, I don't really have one," I admit. "And I'm way worried even that won't be enough! That caseworker put out a vibe that she totally hates guns, and that she really wants all of them out of the house. And that just can't happen."

"Why can't it happen?"

"Because Danny's a private detective, for one. He carries as part of his job."

"Ah, it's part of his job," he repeats. "But couldn't he leave his gun at the office when he goes off duty?"

"I guess, but he's a Marine. He'd never agree to do that."

"Never? Even if it was necessary to get Eduardo back?"

A cold ball grows in my belly. I totally don't want to have to ask Danny to do that. "And it would mean I'd have to get rid of my gun, too."

"You might have to get rid of your gun, Nattie," he says, "but is that really so bad? When have you ever actually had to use it to protect yourself?"

Yeet! He obviously doesn't know about the people I've killed in defense of myself and my fam, and I'm not about to tell him. Now I'm really missing Rebecca. She does know.

"That's what I thought," he says, taking my silence as a sign that his last comment was true. "Is there anything else you could do to get help with Child Protection Services? You did say that Congressman Bader stood up for you on television, and he's a well-known Second Amendment guy. Perhaps he could talk to them for you."

"I guess I could call his office..."

"Why don't you try that and see if he can do anything?" He looks at his watch, then back to me. "Maybe you should come in again tomorrow. As a matter of fact, I don't think daily sessions are a bad idea, at least until we get a handle on your issues. What do you think?"

"I think that's an excellent idea. I totally appreciate the time you're spending with me, Leland."

"It's what I do Nattie," he says, checking his watch again. "Now I've got another appointment in a few minutes, but why don't we set you up for the same time tomorrow?" He stands, extending his hand to help me up from the daybed. When I'm standing, he places his other hand on top of mine, pressing gently and gazing into my eyes with his pale blue ones. "We're going to beat this, Nattie. We'll get Eduardo back to you, and Lupe won't have to go anywhere. Do you believe that?"

His sincerity takes my breath away. "Yes, I do," I tell him, and mean it. "Thank you so much..."

"Tosh," he says, removing his top hand and leading me to the door with the other one. "Come, I'll walk you out." We proceed down the hall hand-in-hand. When we reach the door to the waiting room, he lets go and reaches over my shoulder to push the door open. "See you tomorrow," he says.

I take two steps into the waiting room before I see Jay Howell getting up from a chair, her mouth opens and her eyes widen as she sees us. From behind. Leland says, "Welcome, Jay, it's so good to see you," in that expressive voice of his, and a brief flash of anger passes through me.

I try to keep it out of my face as I say, "Hey, Jay."

She doesn't look at me as she follows him back to his office, and the door closes. What is your problem, bitch?

SNIPER!

Chapter 11.

S tanding on the high porch of the Counseling Center overlooking the courtyard below, I'm thinking about heading to the hospital to see Rebecca. I check my phone. 11:39. If I'm going to make an appointment with the congressman, shouldn't I do it now? No telling how long it will be before he can make time for me.

I Google his office number, tap on it and the call connects.

"Congressman Bader's office."

"Hi, my name is Natalie McMasters, and I have an issue that I'd like to discuss with the Congressman."

"There's a page on our website where you can fill out a form for that, Ms. McMasters," the receptionist says.

"I'm not in a place where I can do that right now," I begin...

"Hold on," he says. "Here's the Congressman."

Bader comes on the line. "Miss McMasters. I was just going to lunch and I heard Toby mention your name. What can I do for you?"

I give him an elevator pitch about my troubles.

"Say no more," he interrupts. "Where are you right now?" I tell him. "How would you like to join me for lunch?"

"That would be great!"

"If you'll go and stand on Lee Street, I'll be by in about fifteen minutes to pick you up."

"I'll be in front of Max's," I say. "You know where that is?"

"Of course! I'm a State alum, Miss McMasters," he says in a hurt tone. "We can have lunch there if you'd like."

"OK! I'll go up then, and get us a table."

Everybody at State knows Max's—there used to be an overhead sign, but it blew down in a hurricane decades ago and was never replaced. Max's is your typical college bar, on the second floor of a couple of red brick buildings on Lee. My feet cling to the treads as I go up the narrow stairs, and I'd rather not get into what's making them stick. Opening the metal door at the top, I enter a large room buzzing with conversation and redolent with yeast, booze and food, with a square central bar and tables scattered around the sides. It's lunchtime, so the place is fairly packed, but I'm in luck—a couple is getting up from a table for two in a corner, by a window overlooking Lee. Max's doesn't have waiters, but I push my way through the crowd and snag the table anyhow. We can go up to the bar and order after Bader gets here.

In a few minutes he comes in, and I stand and wave. He spots me, and maneuvers around students to make his way to me.

Ralph Bader is an overweight fiftysomething with a square, jowly face and steel-grey hair cut in a flat-top. He's not exactly handsome, but he's got one of those faces that make you smile when you see it—hardly a detriment for someone in public office. He's wearing the obligatory blue suit, red tie and an American flag pin in his lapel. His deep blue eyes fix on mine and he gives me a car salesman's smile, but it produces a mild tingle inside me nonetheless. Another reason he's a good politician.

"So nice to see you again, Miss McMasters," he says as he sits. "I do want you to know how much I appreciate that brave stand you took with the media the other day."

"You can call me Nattie, Congressman. And it wasn't really brave. I was just telling the truth."

"A rarity in these days of fake news, Nattie."

"Facts. I totally appreciate your going to bat for me on TV."

"Had to. Couldn't let them disrespect you that way for supporting our Second Amendment," he says mechanically. "Now what would you like for lunch? It's on me."

I'm just poor enough these days that I don't complain. "Just one thing to get at Max's. Chili!"

"My God, I haven't had Max's chili in way too long! Let's make that two, and I'll have a draft. Do you mind ordering? I'm not as young as I used to be..." He grimaces as he mimes rising from his chair.

"No prob." I get up, fight my way to the bar, and give the order. After a few minutes, I return, carrying a tray with two bowls of chili topped with cheese and onions, four packs of saltines, two drafts, a shot of Turkey, two large spoons and the cash register ticket that serves as the check. I set it down at my place, and pass one bowl and a beer to him. I'll eat off the tray.

He eyes the shot but doesn't say anything. I down it and shut my eyes as liquid fire spreads through my belly, open them again and take a long drink of beer. In response to his raised eyebrows I say, "It's been a day."

"What's been going on, Nattie?"

I don't look at him as I'm stirring cheese, onions and hot sauce into my chili. "Child Protection Services took my son away because we've got guns in our house."

"What! Tell me what happened."

I tell him the whole sad story, mentioning that neither me nor Danny routinely lock up our guns. "But Eduardo never goes in our rooms, and he knows not to touch the guns."

"Danny is your husband?" he asks, eying my wedding ring.

"Yes. Well, not exactly. I'm legally married to my wife, Lupe. We both consider Danny our husband, but of course, we can't be married in the eyes of the law. I think the CPS lady didn't like that either."

Bader spoon is poised in midair; he's staring at me like I've just sprouted another head. He recovers quickly, but now his smile is totally forced. "Well, that's too bad, Nattie." A beat. "I don't know that I can really do anything for you. CPS is a local agency, not under federal jurisdiction. Maybe you'd just better lock up your guns."

"We're going to. But I'm afraid that won't be enough. I think the caseworker's gonna insist we get rid of them before she'll let Eduardo come back."

"Well, as I said, I don't think there's much I can do..."

I talk right over him. "Doesn't that piss you off, Congressman? You say in your speeches that our right to self-protection is God-given. Can some bureaucrat just take mine away because I happen to be a parent?" I give him my doe-eyes and my mild southern accent. "Please, Congressman. If you could help me, I'd be ever so grateful..."

He looks at me, then at my ring again, and a light comes on in his eyes. He shows me a row of perfect teeth, saying, "By God, you're right! Let me make some calls this afternoon. Can you come by my downtown office at six or so, and we can talk about it some more?"

Gotcha! "I've got my Tai-Chi class tonight at seven, and downtown isn't far from the dojo. Sure, I can make it."

"Great! Now tell me more about this unusual family of yours..."

I do so as we're eating our chili. I'm getting a vibe that he's not really interested and maybe even a little freaked out, but I go on anyway because he's one powerful dude and I totally need his help. When we're finished, he picks up the register ticket and looks at it. Reaching in his pocket for his money clip, he extracts a hundred-dollar bill, and passes it to me. He eyes the line at the bar, which has become a lot longer since we got here, and says, "I need to run, Nattie. Can you please pay the bill? You can give me my change when I see you tonight." He wipes his lips on a paper napkin, gets up and leaves.

The bartender glares at me when I give him the hundred for a twenty-dollar lunch. I put the change in my back pocket to keep it separate from my money, so I can give it to Bader tonight.

Now I can finally get to the hospital to see Rebecca. The heat slaps me in the face as I exit Max's. It's gotta be over ninety! The hospital is about a mile from here, and it's as far again to the fringe lot where the Jeep is parked. I'm going to smell like a goat when I see Bader this evening, unless I can make it home to shower and change beforehand. I decide to walk to the hospital so I don't have to fight the traffic and roadblocks.

Campus is still closed, so it's like walking through a ghost town. The energy I normally feel is totally absent, making the heat more oppressive and the walk seem longer. I linger in the tunnel under the tracks to get a break from the sun. Not surprisingly, it seems like more anti-gun propaganda has sprung up since I was last here. When I get to the pedestrian bridge, the highway that separates campus from the hospital parking lot is still jammed. Waves of heat radiate upwards, making it feel like I'm crossing a hot stove. Under my clothes, sweat pours off, prompting the thought that I don't need to be wearing these heavy jeans in this kind of weather if I'm not carrying.

As I approach the hospital entrance, there's a cop there again. Shit! I've still got Daddy's knife. I can't count on every officer I meet to be as accommodating as Ms. Gomez. Walking to the Jeep in the fringe lot and back again will take another half hour, at least, and turn me into a hot mess, but what choice do I have? Why can't they see that their goddamn stupid rules just make our lives miserable? If they actually protected us, Rebecca wouldn't be in ICU.

I'm damn near cooked well done when I get to the Jeep. I unlock it, get in and turn on the AC full blast, close my eyes and bask in the cold air. I'm shivering when I wake up and I feel sick. Now I regret the whisky and beer at lunch. I turn down the AC and open the window to bring the car to a comfortable temperature, then roll it back up. I'd like to just go the fuck home, but I have to see Rebecca.

I encounter another roadblock on the way to the hospital, so it's nearly 4:00 when I arrive. I drive around in the parking lot for ten more minutes until a space opens up. I take all the metal out of my pockets—knife, money clip, coins—and lock them in the console with the Ruger. I open the door of the Jeep to a blast of broiling air.

The badge I got last time lets me breeze through the checkpoint. I look for Nurse April when I get to ICU, but don't see her. I ask another nurse, who tells me April's on break.

"I've come to see Rebecca Feiner." He shows me to her room.

All of the rooms in ICU have glass walls, so the patients can be constantly observed. Rebecca's uncovered, wearing a short blue hospital gown and lying in a spiderweb of tubes and wires. Oh no! They've cut off all of her beautiful hair and put a tight-fitting blue cloth cap on her head.

I slide open the door and step inside. My skin is still damp under my clothes so I'm freezing in here, and the medicinal odor is nauseating. I sit in the uncomfortable vinyl chair by the bed and look sadly at my friend and mentor.

Rebecca seems at least ten years older. Tears stream down my cheeks as I see her pale, wrinkly skin. I reach to touch her forehead, then abruptly get up and bend to kiss it instead. It's hard and cold against my lips, and I check the monitors next to her to reassure me that she's still with us.

I met Rebecca two years ago after the brutal murder of a dear friend. The killer attacked me as well, giving me a raging case of PTSD that's still a problem. Rebecca gave me the courage to get rid of years of Catholic baggage and admit that I was in love with Lupe, stood up for me when I was nearly expelled from college, and helped me realize that it was okay to love Danny too. She's so strong and wise that I guess I never realized that she had her own issues, which came boiling to the surface at that relationship retreat last spring. She got back into a toxic relationship with a man she did not know was a monster—Barrett Tybee, aka Leonard Ashworth, a serial killer dubbed the Marquis by the newspapers because of how he tortured his victims—and actually agreed to marry him. No wonder she was so cray-cray at our last meeting! And I was so wrapped up in my own shit that I couldn't even see what was happening to her.

Watching her clinging to life after the bullet tore into her, I'm ashamed. I'm gonna be there for her like she was for me, politics be dammed!

I've been with her nearly an hour when there's a tap on the glass. It's Nurse April, beckoning me to come outside. She steps back to give me room as I enter the hall.

"How is she?" I ask. "She looks awful! Why'd y'all cut her hair?"

April looks like she's gonna cry. "I know, right? But we just couldn't do what we needed to with all that hair flying around."

"How is she?" I ask again.

"Stable. Still critical, but stable. Dr. Hall said she lost nearly 40 percent of her blood volume before she got here and was in hypovolemic shock. They pumped fluids into her for hours before Dr. Hall got her arteries repaired so her volume could be brought back up."

"So, she's gonna get better?"

"Dr. Hall said she'll probably be OK."

I don't like the look on April's face. "What do you mean, probably?"

I see on her face that she doesn't want to say anymore.

"OK." Turning to leave, I continue, "I'll be back to see her tomorrow, and every day while she's here."

I've got a way bad feeling about this.

Chapter 12.

Back in the Jeep, I totally don't want to do anything but go home to bed and pull the covers over my head. But that won't solve anything. I promised Congressman Bader I meet him at his office at about six, and it's nearly five now. It will probably take an hour to make the fifteen-minute drive downtown. I pull up his office address on my phone and tell Siri to take me there, then take off.

I'm not wrong. I have to go through yet another roadblock on the way, so it's five thirty when I arrive at the building where Bader's office is, then it's another ten minutes finding a place to park on the top level of a parking deck two blocks away. It's still hot AF when I exit the Jeep, and I'm totally ripe. Normally, I'd call and cancel if I was in this condition, but getting Eduardo back is just too damned important. I'll have to suck it up, and so will Bader.

I look at the console in the Jeep, where my .357 is, as I'm closing the door. Should I take it with me? It's way likely that the congressman's building is a gun-free zone too, and I've totally had enough of assuming the position. I lock the door and head down to the street.

The address is in the heart of downtown, just a block from the capitol. It's a modern building of white brick and glass that looks out of place among the older brick structures that occupy the area. The lobby goes all the way to the roof, with balconies on each floor overlooking the reception area. The front door is locked, but there's a security dude inside who sees me and buzzes me in.

Walking up to his station across a gleaming black-and-white tiled floor, I tell him, "I'm Natalie McMasters, here to see Congressman Bader. He's expecting me."

Dude wrinkles his nose and looks at me like I've got leaves growing out of my ears or something. He points at the metal detector. "Go on through." I do, and the little green light indicates that I'm clear. The guard presses a button on his walkie-talkie, waits a second. "A Natalie McMasters to see Congressman Bader."

A fuzzy voice from the speaker: "Send her up." His lips go into a smirk.

Putting the radio back in his belt holster, he says, "OK, go on up. Top floor." He's still giving me an odd look as I head for the elevator.

The elevator doors and the shaft are glass too, so I get a panoramic view of downtown as I ascend. Doors hiss open behind me at the top, and I exit to the balcony. The congressman is coming down the corridor across from the elevator. He's in his shirt sleeves, his tie is loosened and his collar open.

"Natalie, great to see you again," he says like we've been apart for years instead of hours. Come on down to my man-cave, and I'll update you on the progress I've made."

I follow him through an open door into an office with a receptionist's desk and cubicles, all unoccupied. Stupid pictures of beach and mountain vistas hang on the walls, overlaid with ridiculous inspirational sayings. *You can never cross the ocean until you have the courage to lose sight of the shore. – Christopher Columbus. Believe you can and you're halfway there. –Theodore Roosevelt.* Suure! Then some bureaucrat comes along and takes your kid away.

He waves me through another open door into an office lined with mahogany bookcases filled with leather-bound lawbooks. The far wall is a giant window that frames a postcard of the city with the Capitol in the center. He waves me to a brown leather sofa, and goes to a full bar along one wall, saying, "Can I get you anything? Heineken and bourbon, right?"

I'm still feeling a little shook from the drinks at lunch. "No thanks Congressman, not on an empty stomach." I take a seat on the sofa. "By the way, you forgot your change earlier."

He smiles. "Call me Ralph. And you can donate it to a worthy cause." I open my mouth to protest, but he cuts me off. "I have soft drinks, too."

"All right, a Coke then." It will settle my stomach.

He goes behind the bar and bends down, disappearing for a sec, then reappears holding a familiar red-and-white can. He snags a tumbler and fills it with ice from a bin in the bar, and places it on a tray. He spends a couple of minutes making a complicated cocktail in a shaker, finishing by shaking it with a flourish while smiling broadly at me. I'm not impressed. He puts his drink on the tray and adds a couple of maraschino cherries, then another on top of the ice in my glass. He brings the tray over to the

88

sofa, setting it down on a low table in front of me. Then he comes around and takes a seat next to me. His nose wrinkles. I tense up, but he smiles, keeping his distance, so I relax again. He pours my Coke, stopping precisely when the brownish foam just reaches the rim of the glass.

"So, have you spoken to anyone about my problem?" I ask him.

"I have," he says. "As I told you, as a U.S. Congressman, I don't have jurisdiction over a local agency like CPS. But I did tell Toby to call them and put them on notice that my office is going to be reviewing the matter."

"What will that accomplish?"

He leans forward and looks at me earnestly. "It will let them know they're being watched. CPS has a lot of power, but like any government agency, they still have to worry about bad publicity."

"Sounds good. How about we give them some?"

He smiles again, reaches towards me and takes my hand. I tense again, but his expression is one of concern, so I relax once more. "Great minds think alike," he says. "Tomorrow, I'll have Toby put in calls to the NRA, Fox News and a couple of local groups who support our Second Amendment. I'm sure none of them will appreciate some petty, local bureaucrat holding a child hostage to support her own gun control agenda." His thumb makes circles in my palm, sending little tingles up my arm. It makes me uncomfortable, so I try to withdraw my hand, but he increases the pressure ever so slightly and moves with me, sliding a little closer on the sofa.

I'm not sure if this guy is trying to put the moves on me or he's just the touchy-feely type. Everything about his demeanor suggests the latter, but he's still creeping me out. I need to be careful—I totally need his help to get Eduardo back, so I don't want to accuse him of something he may not be intending. I look at him, then at my drink, and try to withdraw my hand again. He gets it this time and lets go. I pick up my glass and take a long drink of Coke. I'm usually not much for soft drinks, but I must still be partly dehydrated from running around in the heat all day, so the icy sweetness feels way good going down. I suddenly realize that I'm really thirsty, so I take another long swing, draining the glass. When I set it down, Bader picks up the can and fills my glass again, this time only about half-full before the can is empty.

That avuncular smile again. "Would you like another?"

"Yes, please."

He goes back to bar and fetches it, pops the top as he brings it back, sits down and fills my glass. Now his leg is just barely touching mine.

"Natalie, as I said, it will be tomorrow before we can contact these people, and probably a couple of days before CPS finds out there are other interested parties. I know it will be hard to have Eduardo gone a minute more than necessary, but good politics does take time." Now his hand is on my knee. "While we're waiting for my efforts on your behalf to bear fruit, I wonder if there's anything you could do for me?" The hand moves up to my thigh.

A cold ball erupts in my belly—I've seen a light like the one shining in his eyes a thousand times doing lap dances in a strip club. Now I totally want to throat punch this shithead, but dammit, I need him! I sidle back, giving him a sexy smile at the same time. "But you haven't really given me much yet, have you Ralph?"

That jerks him up straight, an angry expression on his face. "What do you mean?"

"What I said. Eduardo's still gone, ain't he? Maybe if he was back home, I could be properly grateful." I take his hand and replace it on my knee, batting my eyes at him. "You don't get the lap dance if you don't pay up front, sugar." His face says he's pissed, but he's confused, too. This could go either way. Back in the club, I had a panic button on the wall that would bring a couple of hunks if a customer got out of control. Not so here in his crib.

The hand goes away again. "Okay. *Quid pro quo*—I get it. You know that I can't control what CPS will do, I can only provide an incentive to get them to do the right thing. If you want that, I'm gonna need a little down payment."

Now it's my turn to ask, "What do you mean?"

He smiles, and it's as far from avuncular as you can get. He reaches for me. "C'mere."

Holy shit, do I really want to do this? Fuck no! But that's never stopped me before. I take his hands and slide into his arms. He's putting his face up to be kissed, and I oblige. Unsurprisingly, he slips me some tongue. The taste of booze and cherries makes me want to gag, but I hold it back. He pushes my hand downward toward his crotch—I resist a sec, then I go with the flow. Sometimes you can get control if you can get them worked up enough. I stroke his hardness with my fingers, driving my tongue deep into his mouth. Guys hate it when they come in their pants, and this jerkwad seems to be a totally good candidate for that. I crawl up on top of him, take my hand away and start grinding my crotch into his, pinching his nipples through his shirt. That does it! He exhales sharply into my mouth and I grind all the harder just to make sure that every last drop is running down his leg. Sure hope he's got a spare suit at the office. Not!

He's sinking back onto the sofa, his eyes closing, so I push against his chest to get to my feet. The wet stain spreading across the front of his pants brings a smile to my face. "That's just a sample," I tell him. "Get my boy back for me and I'll totally show you what I can do."

I get the fuck out of Dodge before he gets his second wind.

SNIPER!

Chapter 13.

On the way to the parking deck, what just went down totally starts to sink in.

I just got sexually assaulted. By a motherfucking congressman! Sure, I used some skills to prevent getting raped again, but that doesn't mean that I wasn't violated.

God DAMN it! I totally need this asswipe—I can't fight CPS on my own. His idea of getting some 2A groups involved is a good one, but will he even make any calls after what I did? And if he does, he's gonna expect some serious payback. We all know what that will have to be.

My phone dings. I check the screen. Tai-Chi, 7 p.m.

Ye-ye? Should I tell him about Bader? Fuck no! He's old enough to be my peepaw, or even my great peepaw. He'll totally never get what something like this does to a woman.

But if I don't tell somebody, I sure won't be sleeping tonight...

A while later, I'm parking behind the dojo. The assholes from last night are absent. I automatically check the console for the Ruger—I realize that I haven't had it on me all day. I pull my leg up on the seat, undo the ankle holster, and toss it on the passenger seat. No sense in being uncomfortable if I'm not gonna carry. I reach in the back to grab the jacket that Ye-ye gave me last evening, then exit the car and lock it up.

The bell tingles when I open the dojo door. Ye-ye is standing in the rear in front of an easel, his back to me, working on a piece of parchment with a brush. A string of black Chinese characters is slowly appearing on the light brown surface. He doesn't acknowledge me.

"Whatcha doin'?"

"Calligraphy."

"What does it say?"

"Nothing. Sign no talk."

Wiseass. Back to pidgin too, I see. What's up with that? He lays his brush on a stool next to the easel, turns to face me. I hold out the jacket.

"Just drop it on the floor. Ready?"

"I guess."

We start with breathing exercises—*qi gong*, he calls it. There are associated movements, too. "When I go left, you go right," he says.

"Why?"

"Because you're a woman."

I don't know whether to be insulted or not, but it doesn't matter, because he begins the routine and I'm scrambling to follow. He's watching me in the mirror with his back to me. I just can't seem to get my brain to understand that when he lifts his right arm, I must lift my left. He makes a sound of disgust and turns around, facing me. "Now move on same side as me." This is easier, but try as I might, I can't keep my mind out of Bader's office, feeling his stiffness invading my crotch and tasting cherries and booze in his mouth.

I see the disapproval on Ye-ye's face as he watches me. He stops the routine. "Okay, Natalie. One of the reasons that Tai-Chi is so effective for promoting emotional stability is that you can't do it properly unless you concentrate totally on your body, your breathing, and your movements. You are not doing that. What's wrong? Do we need to stop for tonight?"

I want to tell him what happened, but I can't even. Why not? I didn't do anything wrong. I was the victim, goddamnit. I open my mouth to speak, but the words won't come. Instead I say, "You know what? It has been a rough day. Maybe we should try again tomorrow."

"Fair enough," he answers. He turns his back to me and begins another routine.

I turn and head for the door. I hear from behind, "If you won't talk to me about it, talk to somebody before you come tomorrow."

My mind keeps whirling on the drive home. I stick to the back roads to avoid roadblocks, so traffic is less. Good thing—I'm so preoccupied with what happened with Bader that I nearly run a red light. Ye-ye's right. I gotta talk to somebody. I'm not seeing Leland until tomorrow—I hope I can wait that long. I could try to call him, but he didn't give me his personal number—our relationship isn't at that level yet. I don't dare tell Danny. He'll go to see Bader to bang 30s and prolly end up in jail. Lupe is way too wrapped up in Eduardo's abduction to wanna hear my shit. I'll just have to hold on till tomorrow.

Making the decision to spill my guts to Leland has steadied me by the time I get home. But as I open the townhouse door, loud voices make me jump.

"I don't see how you can say that one of ours could be this sniper, Mike!" a female voice shouts. Jay? WTF is she doing here? I thought she quit the group.

"I'm just saying that this dude has got to be ex-mil," Mike says. "He's just too good. He's like smoke, man, the cops can't touch him." I can hear the admiration in his voice.

"Mike, he's killing innocent people," Danny says. "Even if he was in the service, he ain't no brother of mine."

"He's just neutralizing targets, man, like they trained us to do," Mike persists.

"They don't train us to prey on our own," says Danny. "They train us to protect them."

Mike just won't let it go. "All I said was that the dude's a hell of a sniper, man," he says "It's a fact and I ain't takin' it back."

The vets' group members are all standing in a circle, Jay and Mike facing off with Danny between them. The others are looking on—Kay with a disgusted expression and Andy with a smirk. Jay looks totally ratchet.

"C'mon guys!" says Kay, sounding stressed. "We come here to talk about our issues, not about some psycho who's taking out noncombatants. We need to stick with the program."

"Whatsamatta, Kay?" says Andy. "Mike hittin' close to home? I heard you say that you had some sniper training. What you been doing on your off time?"

"What the fuck you mean by that, Andy?"

"Oh nothin', man, nothin..."

Kay steps in on Andy, grabs him by the collar. "It better be fuckin' nothin', motherfucker! You sayin' I'm the fuckin' sniper? Huh?"

"Get your fuckin' hands off me bro..."

"Belay that shit, gennelmen!" Danny barks. Andy and Kay snap to attention in spite of themselves. "Did you motherfuckers forget we're here to help each other?"

"Sir, no sir!" Kay yells. Andy now has a disgusted look on his face.

Danny continues, "We'll have no more of that shit in this group. You will treat each other with respect. And no more of this kind of talk about the sniper. We need to let the LEO's do their job." He spots me across the room, turns back to the group. "Why don't we call it a night, start fresh tomorrow. If y'all want to talk about how this situation is affecting your lives, fine. But let's eighty-six the rest."

"It's hard enough for us to get back into normal life without people looking at us like we're killers," says Jay, pointing her finger at Mike. "Talk like that don't help any!"

Danny silences Mike's retort with a drill sergeant's glare. "I said we're done, Mike," he barks. "Jay, put a lid on it."

She throws him a hard look, but he bores into her with his eyes and she finally looks down at the floor. The others begin packing up backpacks in preparation for leaving. I run over to Danny and give him a hug. He hugs me back for a sec, then pushes me away. His look says he knows something's off. I smile to reassure him, but I can tell he's not buying it.

"I guess I'll see everybody tomorrow night," Jay says, watching me and Danny like we're screwing on the living room carpet. What is your problem, lady?

Danny lets me go and sees everybody out. Jay hugs and thanks him before she goes while Mike gives her a dirty look. Kay and Andy are still glaring at each other. After Danny closes the door, he turns back to me and says, "OK. What's going on?"

That's the problem with people who love each other. It's way hard to lie to them without them picking up on it. But I just can't talk to him about what happened with Bader. I can't!

"Just one big happy fam?" I say, referring to the vets.

"Don't dodge the question, Nattie," Danny says. "Wassup?"

"It's just been a totally fucked up day," I tell him truthfully. "I feel like it's my fault that they took Eduardo away from us."

"You know it's not," he says. He gives me a questioning look. "Are you sure that's all there is?"

I stand on tiptoes and slip my arms around his neck, pulling his face to mine. He resists a little, then gives in. I brush his lips with mine, then kiss him softly. "Maybe I'm a little horny, too," I tell him. He opens his mouth to speak, but I cover it with mine again, slipping my tongue inside. At first, he doesn't respond, but hey, he's a guy. His tongue begins to move against mine, and I reach down to stoke his rapidly swelling crotch.

Our mouths separate with a pop. "Not here," he says. "Lupe will be home from NA any minute."

I slide my arms down his body to take his hand and lead him to the spiral stairs. "Your room or mine?" I ask him.

"Mine's closer," he says.

We head upstairs. Our throuple doesn't have strict rules for sex—we just let things happen, and rely on each other to say something if anybody feels left out. Of course, Lupe and Danny don't fuck because she's a lesbian, but sometimes we'll do a three-way with me in the middle. I feel a little guilty playing Danny this way, but maybe a good hard come is just what I need to get me through till morning. At least it will stop Danny from asking any more questions.

We make love slowly, almost like it's a first date. When we're naked, I can see Danny's totally ready, but he can tell I'm not, so he lays me on my back and strokes my nipples, my belly and my pussy until the fire ignites. I push his face between my legs and let him do me until I come, then tell him to lie on his back so I can return the favor. After sucking and stroking him for a while, I climb up on his chest and slide him inside, moving as slowly as I can to make it last. Finally, he grabs a shoulder and my butt and moves my whole body back and forth, comes with a shudder, and I do too. After he's done, I crawl up into the crook of his arm and bury my face in his chest. He strokes my hair and my face, then his head falls to the side and he begins snoring. Men are so predictable.

It takes me a lot longer to fall asleep, but every time the scene in Bader's office pops into my head, I push my face a little harder into Danny's chest, inhaling his scent deeply. Eventually, that works.

SNIPER!

Chapter 14.

The first thing I do after I get downstairs is turn on the TV to see who's dead today. The anchors are up to their usual political bullshit, but there's no mention of another sniper attack. Yet.

Danny is sitting at the pass-thru, drinking *café de olla*, and Lupe is in the kitchen, rolling a breakfast burrito for him.

"Good mornin', y'all," I say.

Danny wishes me good morning back, but Lupe gives me a dirty look. When did I pee in your cornflakes, Bae? She throws another flour *tortilla* on a hot *comal* on the stove, turning it with a pair of tongs to soften and toast it.

"Did you talk to anyone about getting Eduardo back yesterday?" she asks without looking at me.

I don't answer immediately—I have no intention of discussing what happened with Bader with the fam. But I have to give her an answer.

"I had lunch with Congressman Bader," I tell her. Danny starts and gives me a that's-news-to-me look. "He said that he doesn't have any direct influence with CPS, but that he'll make some calls and see if he can get some other people on our side."

"What people?" asks Lupe.

"Conservative groups. Gun people."

She throws up her hands. "What good is that gonna do? It was guns that started this trouble in the first place."

I know the signs; she wants a fight. Well, I'm not gonna give her one.

"Hey, something's burning!" says Danny. Black smoke pours from underneath the *tortilla* on the *comal*. Lupe shrieks, snatches it off the hot cast iron surface with the tongs and throws it in the sink. Then she turns and glares at me again.

I tole you, you got till Monday," she snarls. "Then I'm outta here!"

That's it! "Why wait, Lupe? If that's how you feel, you can just get your ungrateful ass gone today!"

"Nattie!" Danny shouts. "Lupe, she doesn't mean it..."

"The hell I don't!" I holler. To Lupe: "I've totally saved your ass a bunch of times, from the strip clubs, from ICE, from the Albanians..."

Lupe picks up a plate from the counter and acts like she's going to throw it at me. Danny damn near tumbles off the stool getting out of the way, and I shield my face with my arm. She finally smashes it into a zillion pieces on the kitchen floor, then bolts from the kitchen to her room.

"Go on, run!" I holler after her. "That's how you handle everything!"

As her bedroom door slams with a crash that makes me jump, I dissolve into tears. Why the fuck can't she just give me some space? I just lap-danced a perv to get her fucking kid back!

Danny's looking at me with a sad face. "You'd better go apologize to her. She didn't deserve that, and you know it."

I snap a glare at him, ready to take his head off too, then my anger melts and I run into his arms. He holds me close and kisses the top of my head. "Go on," he says.

I look up into his blue eyes. "Not now," I tell him. "She's way big mad. I'll talk to her later, after she calms down."

"If she's still even here..." He lets me go. "I gotta go. Leon's been on duty all night and is waiting for me to relieve him." A beat. "How 'bout we have a family meeting tonight after we're done with vets' group, NA, Tai-Chi—get this mess aired out."

"OK," I say meekly. I totally don't think its gonna help, but whatever.

He kisses me again, on the forehead this time, then grabs his backpack and leaves.

OMG, I need to talk to Leland so bad!

***

It's 9 a.m. I'm crossing the New Commons, heading for the Counseling Center. I'm early, but I just couldn't stay home anymore. I'm hoping that Leland doesn't have another appointment before me, and can get me in early.

I spot a newspaper holder ahead, which makes me remember the photo op yesterday. Did she do it? Dammit! She fucking did! There I am, in all my glory on the front page, spread-eagled on a wall!

I begin reading the article. It's a gun-control rant that makes little sense, blaming law-abiding gun owners for somehow being responsible for the shootings. As I feared, it labels me the face of the pro-gun movement on campus, even though I never carried a sign for that shit in my life, or for any other cause, for that matter. The article has a disturbing undercurrent that violence against me is perhaps justified, since the writer considers people who hold views like mine responsible for the deaths of innocents. That's just great. My pistol is locked in the Jeep, so now I'm a sitting duck for any whack job who wants to take her up on it. The article does contain one legitimate piece of news—the governor has told the legislature to continue its deliberations of the assault weapons ban. He's unabashedly anti-gun, and he said that he would implement the ban immediately if it passes, even in the face of the sniper's threats.

As I fold the paper before walking off, a voice from behind me says, "I told you! It is her!"

I turn to see four students facing me; two guys, two women. They're dressed in typical campus chic—jeans, ratty t-shirts and flip-flops, except for one of the girls who's in combat boots.

"How the fuck can you live with yourself after what you've done?" says a blonde girl who looks a lot like me.

"Get off our campus, bitch," a guy in a surfer t-shirt adds.

I start to answer them in kind, but I think for a sec, then turn and walk away without responding. The other guy, who's wearing a *Come Over When You're Sober* shirt, moves to block me. "No way, bitch," he says. "You just don't get to dis us and walk off. What do have to say for yourself? You gonna shoot us, bitch?"

My hand reflexively goes to my front pocket, but of course, there's nothing there.

The four of them have moved to encircle me, all still rashing me. "Cunt!" "Fuckin' whorebitch!" "Why don't you just kill yourself?"

Enough! I zero in on the girl who looks like me. "Get the fuck out of my way, asshole!" I walk straight toward her.

Suddenly, I'm pushed way hard from the rear. I stagger forward, and the blonde girl raises her arms to thrust me away from her. I twist as I stumble towards one of the guys, who pushes me again. I'm being passed around in a circle like a ball! Panic grows in my belly and spreads through me—I'm helpless! These thugs can do whatever they want to me!

101

SNIPER!

Another hard push, and I twist towards the blonde again, who's got an evil smile on her face as she waits with hands extended to pass me along. I don't know where it comes from, but I abruptly turn sideways a little and grab her extended hands as she pushes, falling away from her, rotating my hips, pulling her forward. She sails across the circle like a rocket, right into Surfer Boy, and they both go down in a heap. Unfortunately, so do I.

"You fucking cunt!" screams the girl in the combat boots. She steps up to kick me right in the diaphragm, and all of the air in my lungs escapes with a whoosh. I roll on my back, and she delivers another kick that sends a jolt of lightning through my hip. My god, it hurts! She rears back for another, but Sober Boy grabs her by the shoulders and pulls her back.

"Enough, Susie! Don't kill her!"

"Why the fuck not? This privileged bitch is everything that's wrong with this world!"

"She ain't worth it, dude."

I'm laying there gasping like a fish on a dock, my hands on my belly, trying vainly to get up before Susie starts breaking ribs.

Susie shakes free of the guy holding her, steps up, and I steel my self for the blow. It never comes. Instead, she stands over me, hocks up a mouthful, and spits a yellow glob right in my face.

"Good one!" the other girl cries.

The snot runs down my cheek over my nose, smelling of old cigarettes. It continues into my open mouth, and the four of them begin laughing. The other three spit on me in turn.

"If you stay on campus you can expect more of this," Surfer Boy says, before they leave me lying there.

I don't move for what seems like an hour, looking at the blue sky and white clouds above, trying not to throw up, spitting out their saliva and catching my breath, all at the same time. Finally, I roll on my side and get my arms underneath me. Abruptly, I notice a crowd surrounding me, staring in judgment, it seems. No one moves to help me up. With a groan, I make it to my feet. OMG, there must be a dozen people! I'm fuckin' dead if that mob starts in on me!

But no one does. They simply move aside as I lurch toward them. I try to run, but that ain't happening. I find a bench in front of the Octagon and sink down on it. People pass by, going about their business, paying me no attention.

What am I gonna do? I want to just go home and crawl into bed, but I need to see Leland. Can I even tell him about this? I didn't do anything wrong, but a deep sense of shame and humiliation consumes me just the same. I've got to see him!

I rise slowly and begin making my way to Counseling Center. I have a hard time climbing the stairs to the front door. Inside, the receptionist barely looks at me as I tell her I'm here for Leland Marks.

"He's probably still over in his office in Overton Hall," she says. She checks her monitor. "Your appointment's not till ten. Just have a seat until he comes in."

I slip off my backpack and totter toward one of the plastic chairs.

A few minutes later, Leland enters by the front door. He doesn't see me—I say his name. He turns, takes one look at me, says, "Nattie! Oh my God, what has happened?" He helps me out of my chair, grabs my pack, puts his other arm around me and ushers me to his office. Once inside, he asks again, "What's happened?"

I open my mouth to speak, but the tears well up and my throat closes. I can't even!

He leads me to the daybed and lays me down. "Wait here," he says and goes away. I close my eyes and inhale the comforting scents of leather and Old Spice.

I feel that he's back, and something cold touches my arm, followed by a sharp sting. Then he's bathing my face with a warm, damp cloth, wiping away the spit and the disgrace.

I open my eyes and see his face, a mask of concern, hovering over me.

"Close your eyes, Nattie," he says. "Focus on my voice and relax. I cannot help you if you do not relax. Relax your feet, your legs, your tummy, and your chest. Good, good... Relax your face, your forehead. Let it go, let it all go."

A warmth is spreading through me, making my muscles like jelly. I want to go to sleep, but I can't; his singsong voice is keeping me awake.

He says again, "Tell me what's wrong Nattie. What's happened to you?"

I slowly tell him about the attack. This isn't what I came here to talk about, but I have no choice. He's quietly insistent, drawing out all of the details.

When I've finished, he says, "Nattie, I want you to listen to me. You are not who you think you are."

"What do you mean?"

"You are not who you think you are. Did you have any part in what happened this morning?"

"No! I was just coming to see you..."

"But you do realize that your words on television could be considered inflammatory by some, especially in the wake of the shooting? Everyone is stretched very tightly by what is going on. Don't you see that the actions of those students were understandable in that light?"

My eyes snap open. There's pressure in my forehead and my tongue is heavy as I say, "No! I didn't do anything wrong!"

"I didn't say you did, Nattie. Don't think in terms of right and wrong. Put yourself in the place of those who hurt you—try to understand why they did what they did. Don't you see that they had a reason?"

"It was Betsy Kiefer! She wrote that horrible article with that terrible picture..."

His rebuke is sharp. "Stop blaming others, Nattie. You must own your part in this if you are to get past it. You do want to get past it, don't you?"

Crying again, I nod. The last time I spoke with her, Rebecca told me that my problems were of my own making. Now Leland's saying the same thing. Maybe they're right.

"Don't you agree that you did have a part in what happened today?" he asks. "Don't you see that you angered people with your comments to the media? Don't you see that you gave them an excuse to do what they did?" His face above me is cold, stern, accusing.

"I guess so," I answer.

"Guess so, isn't good enough, Natalie. If you'll work with me, I will help you. If you just want to shift blame onto others, I can't abide that."

"Okay," I say. "It was partly my fault."

"Partly? You're still equivocating."

"Okay, okay, I shouldn't have said what I did to that reporter. But I was hurt too…"

"No more excuses," he barks. "Say, 'I was wrong, Leland.'"

The words stick in my throat, but I cough them up. "I was wrong, Leland."

"Wrong about what, Natalie?"

I know what he wants to hear. "Wrong when I said what I did to that reporter."

That boyish smile of his blossoms on his face, and tingles run from my head down to my toes. "There! That didn't hurt so much, did it?" he says.

The fuck it didn't.

"Now we can start getting at root of some of your issues," he continues. "What's happening with Eduardo?"

I tell him about the fight I had with Lupe this morning.

"It seems that you had a lot of culpability in that too," he says. I don't give him any argument, but he pushes it. "Didn't you?"

I nod.

"So, what are you going to do going forward?"

"What Puryear wants. Lock up the guns. And apologize to Lupe."

"Are you sure that will be enough?"

"No, but it's a place to start."

"And what will you do if Lupe decides she doesn't want to wait for you to get it right and moves out?"

"Let her go, I guess. What else can I do?"

His frown is back. "Well, if you love her as you say, I would think you would do everything you can do to get Eduardo back so she doesn't have to go. If that means getting all the guns out of the house…"

"But Danny's job…"

"…is more important than getting your son back? If he loves you as he says, I would think he'd be willing to make some sacrifices too. Think about it." He looks at his watch. "I have somebody else coming in, in a few minutes. Are you well enough to go home?"

I sit up on the daybed and my head spins. "What did you give me?"

"Just a little diazepam to calm you down. After you leave here, go up to Lee Street and get something to eat, wait a couple hours before you try to drive, and you'll be fine."

I realize that we never talked about what I came here to discuss—the sexual assault. But I guess we don't have time to get into that now. Maybe I had a part in that, too?

Leland moves to his desk and consults his PC. "I want to see you daily for a while, until we get you stable. Is one o'clock tomorrow all right?"

"I guess so." He glares at me. "I mean, yes, that's fine." He smiles at me again, and I release my breath.

Later, on the Counseling Center porch, I think about what to do next. I totally should go see Rebecca, but just looking down the long brick staircase makes me feel wobbly. The damn drug is still in my system. Leland's right—I don't have any business driving right now. I know! I'll call the hospital and see if there's been any change in Rebecca's condition.

Nurse April's on the line. "No, she's the same. Doctor said it's too early to bring her out of the coma. It's the best thing for her to just let her heal."

So, there's really no point in visiting; Rebecca won't even know I'm there. I go down the stairs a step at a time, both hands on the railing like an old woman, then make my way to a breakfast place on Lee Street. I keep my head down, looking around for anyone who might recognize me. I wish to God I'd never talked to fucking Darren Murphy!

After a pot of coffee and some food, I feel like I can make it to the Jeep. It's a long walk, but I'm afraid to get on the bus. Somebody might recognize me.

It's nearly two in the afternoon when I finally get home. The place is dark and empty, like my heart. I'm too dragged out to go upstairs—I grab a couple of ibuprophen, a blanket, then curl up on the futon in the great room.

Chapter 15.

T
he hot sun beats down mercilessly on the black tarpaper rooftop—reminds me of the 'stan, that pisshole where I honed my skills. Now I hunt a different kind of terrorist; so-called non-combatants whose very existence supports a corrupt system. I selected this FFP because the roof is black, and crafted my ghillie suit accordingly. Another criterion was the low wall surrounding the roof edge, pierced by a line of rectangular openings large enough to accommodate the barrel of my weapon, permitting me to scan the streets with my target acquisition system. The fools thought they could deprive me of targets by closing campus. I've just moved to different locations—downtown, this time.

It's lunchtime, so MLK Plaza is teeming. I survey the crowd with my scope. Young and old, male and female, white, black, Hispanic and Asian, it makes no difference to me. They're all facilitators of a repressive order that must change. Let's make that happen.

There! A fat cat banker in a three-piece suit. Fucking unwitting pawn of heartless capitalists. My finger twitches. His head pops like a melon. That mofo'll never foreclose on a needy family again.

There! Young black guy on a skateboard, weaving between pedestrians on the mall. Damn near knocks an old lady down. Got him in the left ear. Take that, you entitled prick!

There! Fortysomething white bitch in a mumu and flip-flops, sashshaying down the block like she owns it. Aging hippie with fucking tits hanging like udders, falling out of her dress. Her eyes grow wide as saucers as I put a round right between her mammaries.

The herd is starting to notice something's off; individuals scurrying around like roaches when the kitchen light comes on. The oiled bolt works smooth as glass between shots; I take out three more targets—a well-dressed women getting out of an Uber, an old fart hawking tchotchkes on the sidewalk, an Hispanic construction guy eating lunch with his co-workers. Shoulda stayed in Mexico, asshole!

Blue lights flash and sirens blare as two cop cars close off an intersection. More pigs appear, cordoning off an area around my FFP. Fine, I expected this. I take out two of them several blocks apart, just so those mofos know they're not safe either, then I pull back from the roof's edge and begin dismantling my weapon system. I hear the staccato whirr of chopper blades above. After jamming the pieces of my weapons system in my pack, I belly crawl to my hideout—a pile of black plastic trashbags next to the elevator maintenance shed.

Bending my knees, I zip up the bottom of my ghillie suit, then lean against the wall of the maintenance shed. Right now it's sunny here, but that will change as the afternoon wears on and the shed provides a wedge of shade. Still gonna be hot AF, tho. I pull my Kimber compact 1911 out of its holster, take the nipple of the tube leading to my water bladder in my mouth, tuck my head down and zip up the top of the ghillie suit from the inside. Now anyone looking over here will see nothing but another black trash bag in the pile. In the unlikely event that the pigs do find me, the Kimber will ensure I go out in a blaze of glory. I might even get to exfil if there's not too many of them.

Chapter 16.

Charlie Evans shoves the two books he'll need to finish his article into his black backpack and swings it onto his shoulders, then crams his afro under a red ball cap. He's going home to read, because it's just too damn loud in the office. The *Capitol Communique* is a weekly free newspaper available at all kinds of businesses, detailing political and social news, events in the downtown area, and containing classifieds for hookups. Charlie suspects that most of its readers pick it up for the latter reason. He still considers himself lucky to be employed as a feature writer for the *Communique* even though the pay sucks, because it will provide the all-important clips he'll need to get a job on a real paper someday. WTF, he's only twenty-two; all the time in the world, right?

Officer Tessa Albertson has been on the job a total of three weeks. She was just settling into the routine of street patrol when this sniper shit hit the fan. One factor that contributed heavily to her joining the Capitol City Police was last year's appointment of Elaine N'Dour as chief. As a woman of color herself, Tessa really thought she could go places in a progressive department like that. The Chief's murder hit her hard, as it did most of the other officers. Cops, regardless of gender or race, close ranks when one of their own is taken down. And of course, the pressure from the top to find the shooter is epic.

Tessa and her partner get the call to close off this building because it has been identified as a possible location for the sniper, who just took down eight people, two of them cops. Tessa's nerves are on a razor's edge. A single mom with two young children, she's all they have. Their asshat baby daddy can't be counted on for anything. Approaching the front doors, Tessa sees a dude in a red ball cap and a BLM t-shirt coming outside.

Charlie knows something's very wrong just as soon as the doors close behind him. Sirens are wailing and people are running every whichaways. Two cops, a black woman and a white man, are fast approaching. The woman shouts, "You! In the red hat! Get back inside!"

Charlie's not stupid—he instantly figures that sniper is somewhere near. Holy shit! This is big news and he's right in the middle of it! His hand darts for his pocket to retrieve his press ID, in the hope that the cops will allow him to accompany them. He never hears the shots that tear into his heart.

Officer Rolf Arnold, Tessa's partner, is staring at her dumfounded, her smoking service pistol clutched in both hands. The guy she just took down is crumpled in a rapidly spreading pool of blood.

"Fuck me, Tessa, what did you do?"

Tessa slowly lowers her weapon. "He was going for his pocket, Rolf!" she says through her tears. "I thought he was going for a gun! I've got kids... I couldn't take the chance. I couldn't take the chance!"

Chapter 17.

My dreams are troubled. I'm running, running, running from an unseen enemy. My hips hurt, my back hurts, and I feel like I'm gonna go down any second, then they'll jump on me and tear me to pieces.

Something soft touches my cheek. I struggle into wakefulness. It touches me again, and my eyes pop open. Danny's smiling face is hovering over me, his hand stroking my hair.

"Wake up, sleepyhead," he says.

He moves back as I roll on my side and try to sit up. A groan escapes my lips as I put pressure on my injured hip.

He looks concerned. "What's wrong, Nattie."

"Nothing." I don't want to get into what happened on campus this morning with him. His expression says he doesn't believe me, but he doesn't push it. Instead, he gives me another gentle kiss, and I bury my face in his chest.

After a moment, he pushes me away. "I got us something," he says.

"What?"

He reaches for a shopping bag behind him, on the floor. He pulls out a brown corrugated box about the size of a shoebox and hands it to me.

"What's this?" I say as I flip back the little cardboard tab that holds the lid closed. Opening the box, I pull out an item wrapped in bubblewrap, which appears to be made of dark metal. Danny snaps open his knife and offers it to me—I use it to slit the tape holding the bubblewrap closed, then unwind the plastic from the object. I'm holding a metal box about a foot long. The cover is on the long side and has a keyhole with a key in it, with a small clear lens and a four-digit keypad above it. I turn the key and raise the lid, which causes a drawer to slide out. I look at him questioningly.

"It's a gun safe, with a biometric lock," he says.

I smile. That's my guy—he brings me a gun safe!

"They hold two guns," he goes on, "and I got one for each of us. You just put your finger on the lens and it scans your print, then it will open only for you. There's a backup combination lock in case the biometric lock malfunctions. And I got myself a big one to go under my bed for my AR-15.

We can lock up the guns today, and call Puryear and tell her we're ready for inspection ASAP."

I smile and thank him, even though I think having these is not gonna make any difference. That Puryear bitch has an agenda—she'll find another reason to keep Eduardo.

Suddenly, the front door opens and Lupe comes in. She looks way shook, her hair frazzled, her eyes red and her cheeks tear-streaked.

"Bae, what's wrong?"

"You did not hear? The sniper! He is killing people downtown! They send me home from work."

Danny grabs the remote and turns on the TV. The screen fills with a helicopter shot of MLK Plaza. It's eerily empty of civilians; only blue-clad figures and police vehicles with flashing blue lights fill the streets.

"... word of a shooting by police has just reached WTCD, but details are sketchy at this time. It's possible that the police have taken out the sniper. Regardless, a ten square-block area has been closed off by the authorities and all civilians are instructed to remain indoors until the curfew is lifted. We have reports that several people have been shot, but..."

Danny clicks the remote and the TV goes dark.

"Hey! Turn that back on!" I tell him.

"Why? We know it's happening. We don't have to immerse ourselves in it."

"Danny is right," says Lupe. "Listening to that will only upset us more."

"Maybe we need to be upset," I say.

"What purpose will that serve?" Danny asks. I don't have an answer for him. "Hey," he continues, "Let's show Lupe what we've got." He pulls one of the biometric safes out of the bag and explains to her how it works.

"I dunno," she says when he's finished. "Maybe it would be better just to get the guns out of the house all together."

"WTF, people!" I holler. "Don't you get that the guns are only an excuse? This Puryear bitch doesn't like the way we live. She's trying to break up our fam!"

"Maybe you're right, Nattie," Danny says in a reasonable tone. "Maybe we'll need to do something else—get a lawyer, go to family court. But right now, the guns are the issue. I don't want to be without a gun in the house,

112

and neither do you. So, let's set up the safes and call Puryear back for an inspection. If she refuses to give Eduardo back after that, we can do something else."

"If she won't give my son back, I will dig her fucking eyes out!" snarls Lupe.

"Oh yeah, that'll work." I say.

Lupe whirls on me. "Then maybe I should just get my own place," she spits. "You two can have your precious guns!"

"Sure, run away again," I say. "That's all you're good at!"

Lupe's eyes widen like two black sinkholes, then before I can react, she slaps me so hard she nearly knocks me down. I stand there stunned as her hands fly to her cheeks, her mouth agape.

"N–Nattie," she stammers. "I am so sorry! I did not mean..."

Anger burns in me like a raging fire. Nobody fucking hits me! Nobody! I cock my fist, but sanity strikes, and I resist the urge. Turning on my heel, I head for the door, grabbing my keys from the hook as I go by.

"Nattie, come back!" hollers Danny. "We have to talk about..."

"Bye Felica!" I holler as the door slamming behind me cuts him off.

I jump in the Jeep and start driving. To anywhere! My mind is awhirl. She fucking hit me! I don't believe she fucking hit me! I take her in off the fucking street, save her goddamned life, get her out of the strip clubs, get her a job, marry her so she can stay in the fucking U.S.A., and she fucking hits me! I glance down at the speedometer. OMG! I'm doing fifty on a residential street. I mash the brake before I get pulled over. The sane part of my mind tells me to stay the hell away from downtown and the freeway, so I head south, out into the country.

She won't have to move out. I won't ever be able to go back to that house again! But where will I go? I think about Uncle Amos. Would he even take me in after what I've done, living in sin, as he puts it, with a man and a woman? Do I even want him to?

My phone dings. It's probably a text from Danny or Lupe—I let it lie. After a moment, it dings again because I didn't check the message the first time. Driving one-handed, I dig the phone out of my pocket.

Dojo closed tonight because of shooting downtown. If you want lesson, come to house.

There's a Google Maps link beneath the message.

Fucking Tai-Chi is literally the last thing on my mind, but I totally have no place else to go. Fuck it! I tap the link, then tap again to activate the routing function.

Siri's mechanical voice says, "Turn left at the next stop sign..."

Eventually, she brings me onto a road that runs along the shore of Green Lake, about ten miles out of town. Half of the lake is in a state park and the other on private land. The only signs of human habitation are mailboxes marking dirt driveways that disappear into the thick woods. Siri turns me right onto one of them, and I throw the Jeep into four-wheel because it's so rough. The road winds through the trees for about a quarter of a mile, then an odor of fish and rotting vegetation announces my arrival at the lake shore.

A structure with a peaked, sheet metal roof supported by wooden pillars, enclosing a rectangular area about 20' by 40' rears up in front of me, with an unobstructed view of the lake on the other side. A banner sporting Chinese characters is anchored on the long side at either end of the roof. I pull into a dirt parking area in front, next to a familiar old pickup. It's got a square body with those big bug-eye headlights set on each side of the grille and skinny black tires on spoked wheels. It's painted a faded green that matches the color of the lake water.

I kill the Jeep, but click the key so the AC stays on; it's hot AF out there; must be nearly a hundred. I still don't feel so good—I think the drug Leland gave me is still in my system, and the cool air eases the nausea.

Ye-ye comes out of a bright green tiny house, about 20' square, set off in the trees. It's way smaller than the pavilion, but it does have two stories—the dormered upper one is probably a sleeping loft.

He looks like some oriental god, striding toward me in nothing but a pair of gym shorts and flippies, his sweaty bronzed torso gleaming in the afternoon sun. Dude is the hottest old geezer ever! I cut off the AC, pocket the key, and open the door; the air that rushes in feels like it's blowing out of a furnace. I'm wearing jeans and a t-shirt when I should be in shorts and a halter top. Beads of sweat spring from every pore, and I weave unsteadily as I jump out of the jeep.

"You're early," Ye-ye says. "Wassamattah?" His expression is one of concern.

Like I said, I really don't want to get into my personal life with him. "Heat's getting to me," I tell him. I point to the banner. "What's that say?"

"No say..."

I make him talk to the hand. "Don't!"

"OK. It says Green Lake Pavilion. Come inside out of the sun."

He leads me into the structure. Small, colorful square flags—red green, blue, orange—hang around the perimeter of the roof inside and streamers decorated with more calligraphy hang down from the rafters. Chinese statues and potted ferns are placed artfully around the outside of the gleaming wood floor.

Ye-ye grabs a broom from a corner and hands it to me. "Here. You sweep. I'm going inside for a minute."

What am I, the fucking maid? "Why?" I ask him. "Looks clean to me."

His eyes harden. "Show respect for the space. Besides, you don't want to step on a twig or a stone while you train. Sweep." He turns and heads for the house.

I look at his back, then at the broom. I could make a smartass remark, but I don't.

I'm sweeping when he comes back, carrying a white bundle of cloth. He offers it to me. "Here. You can't train in those jeans today—it's so hot you'll pass out. Put these on. I think they'll fit."

I take the clothes from him, and he faces the lake with his back to me, gazing over the water. He's given me a pair of baggy linen pants with a drawstring and a roomy top that wraps around my chest and secures with a strap on the side. I shed my sodden jeans and pull on the pants; they're a little long, but I roll up the cuffs and they're fine. I peel off my t-shirt and bra and slide into the top. The whole outfit is as light as a feather. I'm still hot, but it's more bearable now.

"Since you came early, we'll do the whole form today. Follow me, and watch my feet. Don't forget to breathe."

Ye-ye stands with his back to me, facing the water, then begins a series of slow, deliberate movements. His motion is mesmerizing; I gradually get that I'm fighting an imaginary opponent, countering his actions with my own. At first, it's difficult for me to move because of my injuries, but in time as I limber up, the pain lessens. We assume various postures in succession

115

for what seems like hours—standing with one arm thrust out in front, the other coiled behind like a striking snake; delivering two-handed pushes to our imaginary opponent's chest; extending the right arm over head with the left palm down towards the ground. Sweat pours from my skin, but a cooling breeze from the lake penetrates the linen. My breathing begins to conform to the rhythm of the movements; inhale when I retreat, exhale on a strike. The pain in my hip has subsided to a dull ache. My head clears as the last vestiges of the drug Leland gave me leaves my system. We extend one leg in front while lowering the body to almost sit on the floor; Ye-ye's butt actually touches the deck, but I fall over backwards trying to go as low as he does. My muscles are like jelly as I try to scramble to my feet to continue following.

"Almost finished," he says without turning around.

After a few more pushes and strikes, he straightens up, ends by standing with feet apart, looking left, bringing his arms to his sides. Thank God—it's over!

"How do you feel?" he asks.

"Like I'm going to fall down."

"Then sit. I'll go and get some refreshment."

He goes to the house as I try to sit without falling again. While we were doing the form, I didn't think about Lupe, Eduardo, Rebecca wasting away in the hospital, the shootings or anything. But now that I've stopped, all of those negative feelings emerge again. My anger at Lupe rises in my gorge, my muscles tense and a tight band wraps around my forehead.

Ye-ye returns carrying a tray with a teapot and two small handleless cups. He sits next to me and pours; steam rises from the cups.

"Seriously? Hot tea?"

"No electricity—no ice," he says. "But this is a cooling tea."

"How the fuck does somebody live without power?"

"Our ancestors did it for thousands of years."

The tea is herbaceous and citrusy; a cool spot forms on top of my head as I sip it and the heat seems to flow out of my body, taking the rest of my anger with it.

"I can feel the disturbance in your *chi* from here," he says. "What's eating you?"

116

"Nothing." His raised eyebrows indicate his disbelief. His blue eyes drill into mine, seeming to penetrate to the depths of my soul. I want to look away, but I can't. Damnit! I feel the tears welling up again.

Suddenly it all comes pouring out—Rebecca, Eduardo, Lupe, everything. I go on and on and he says nothing, just sits there listening—it's like he's drawing all of the poison out of me, letting his warm energy flow into me to fill the emptiness. A cold wind springs up and thunder rumbles; for a sec I think he's making that happen too—but that's ridiculous! The sky opens up and the rain pours down, rattling off the metal roof like BBs. We're safe from it here, but it still feels as if it's cleansing me inside and out.

I finally wind down and we sit quietly for a while.

"This storm is an omen," he says, "a signal for you to atone. Pardoning the faults of others and dealing softly with those who sin against you brings you peace. Look inside yourself and set your life in order. Feel the lightness in your soul that results from accepting others as they are, not as you want them to be. Concentrate not on what others may have done to you, but on your love for them."

"That's easy for you to say," I tell him.

"But difficult for anyone to do," he answers. "If you come to me each day, practice the form, drive the bad feelings out, it will become easier. Do you believe this?"

I hesitate, then, "I think so."

"That's good enough for right now," he says. "Stay and take a meal with me."

"OK."

The downpour has slackened to a steady rain. We trot over to the house, which has a small covered porch in front where it's dry.

He goes inside, returning with a hibachi-style grill, which he fills with charcoal and paper, then lights. "You want to come in?" he asks.

I shake my head. I'm relatively cool for the first time today, enjoying the patter of the rain and the sweet breeze off the water. He disappears again, then comes out with a wicker basket filled with vegetables—lettuce, tomatoes, cucumber, peppers—with a colorful porcelain bowl and a knife on top. "You make salad," he says. I'm not much of a cook, but salad I can handle.

117

When the grill is ready, he brings out two skewers of small bream, heads on, and lays them on the grill. They cook quickly, and the smoky, fishy odor suddenly has me ravenous. He produces a covered bowl that proves to contain rice, and a small pitcher of dressing for the salad. He has no forks, but after a quick lesson, I find that manipulating chopsticks wasn't as hard as I thought.

After dinner, we just sit watching the lake, listening to the music of the water, the cries of the birds and the gulps of the frogs. Soon the sky takes on an orange tinge. He gently takes my hand in both of his; a tingle runs up my arm and down into my belly.

"I give my *chi* to you," he says. "Go now, and share it with those you love. Remember to forgive."

***

It's fully dark when I pull into my space at the townhouse. The windows glow with yellow light; Danny's vets' group is probably still going. Once inside, I see it's only Danny, Kay and Andy tonight.

"Nattie!" Danny greets me, relief evident in his tone. Andy gives me the look.

I ignore him. "Where is everybody?" I ask.

"Mike couldn't make it," Kay answers. "He's got something else going on."

"Maybe he's out shootin' up the town," says Andy. "He's sure got himself a hard-on for that sniper."

"That's enough, Andy!" says Danny. "You wouldn't talk about Mike like that if he was here."

"The fuck I wouldn't," says Andy. "Y'all heard him. He thinks that fuckin' shooter's a hero."

"That's not what he said," Kay counters. "He said he thinks the guy's good because he's got military training. I do too."

"You oughta know," Andy retorts.

Kay's eyes narrow.

"Y'all know Mike got cut from the Navy for killin' another sailor," Andy persists. "They prolly let him skate on a chapter fourteen 'cuz he was a SEAL..."

118

Danny cuts him off. "That's enough, Andy!" He looks at me. "There's a civilian here. Mike told us that stuff in confidence."

"I'm sorry," says Andy. He doesn't look it. "But that shit with Mike was all over the news. A gazillion people know about it."

I change the subject before Danny totally goes off on Andy. "Where's Jay?"

"Quit again," Danny says, shaking his head. "She says her shrink doesn't want her getting conflicting messages. I guess that's understandable."

Her shrink is Leland, same as me. I wonder what he's got against the vets' group?

"She's got the hots for you, Sarge," Andy leers. "That's why she dumped Mike after they got here. Maybe she's finally figgered out that's going nowhere."

"Don't call me Sarge, Andy. And I think it's time we wrapped it up for the night." To me: "Lupe's not back from her meeting yet."

"Sure," says Andy to Danny, still ogling me. I'm still wearing Ye-ye's Tai-Chi outfit—my other clothes stank so bad they were not fit to put back on. I feel sorry for Andy as a disabled vet, but if he doesn't quit, I'm totally gonna go off on him.

Ye-ye's voice echoes in my head. *Feel the lightness in your soul that results from accepting others as they are.* OK, OK, already.

Andy picks up his backpack and heads for the door. "See you tomorrow, Sa..., uh... Dan," he says. The door closes behind him.

Kay looks at me, his face sad. "Andy can be a real a–hole," he says. "But he lost that leg saving a buddy. Cut him some slack, Nattie."

"Totally," I say.

Kay grabs his stuff and follows Andy out. Danny looks relieved when he's gone. He says to me, "We have to talk."

I go over and give him a peck on the cheek. "OK, but before we start, I want you to know that I'm gonna tell Lupe I forgive her for hitting me."

He seems a little taken aback. "Good. Because she feels terrible about it. She called her sponsor right after you stormed out of here."

"I didn't storm out, Danny. I left before I did something to make it worse."

119

He smiles. "Sorry. Bad choice of words. Anyhow, she helped me get the gun safes installed. There's one in your room. When you're ready, I'll show you how to set the combination and input your fingerprint. We can call Puryear about that inspection in the morning."

I'm about to thank him when the door opens and Lupe comes in. She freezes when she sees me, a look of pure dread on her face.

I turn to her and open my arms. "C'mere, Bae."

Dropping her pack, she runs to me, and I enfold her in a hug. "Nattie, I am so sorry, I am so sorry..."

I kiss her softly on the lips. "Shhh... It's OK, sweetie, it's OK. You didn't mean it. You were worried about Eduardo. Me too."

Danny embraces the two of us, pulling us close, into his broad chest. "We're gonna get through this, guys. We have to."

Chapter 18.

My world consists solely of dead black heat. My clothes are saturated, but little sips of precious water through the nipple stave off dehydration. I doze fitfully—a good thing; it helps the long hours pass.

Loud voices jolt me from sleep: "Clear!" Thudding footsteps and jingling equipment near; I grip the Kimber tightly, ready to unleash a fusillade if my camo is compromised. But it isn't—the sounds recede until it seems I am alone on the rooftop once more. But that belief does not justify my breaking concealment. Not yet.

It becomes cooler as the day wears on. I check my watch: 1740. Still daylight. I will not come out of my chrysalis until at least 2100. I close my eyes and try to go back to sleep.

Sometime later, I awaken again; chilled, my sodden clothes clinging to my damp skin. I check my watch again: 2037. Almost time! I take a long drink of precious water through the tube. No more conserving now.

Finally, the numerals on my watch face flip to 2100. I ease open the top of my ghillie suit, squinting against the glare of the city lights. A quarter moon hangs in an indigo sky. It's still warm and humid, but the punishing daytime torpor is gone. I'm alone—I can feel it. I slowly emerge like a butterfly from a cocoon, inhaling a deep breath of night air sweet with exhaust fumes and smoke. Smoke? I shiver again. I wish I had brought along a change of clothes; I'll have to file that for next time.

I slide the Kimber into a pocket and bundle up the ghillie suit, cramming it into a pouch on the outside of my backpack. Suddenly, an explosion rents the air, coming from the street below. I rush to the roof's edge to see what's going on.

The street teems with people, and an orange glow from several burning cars dances up and down the sides of the buildings. I hear a muffled crash—someone has broken a window! Several people invade a store, coming outside a few minutes later, arms full of stuff. Looters! Beautiful! Once I get downstairs, it will be easy to lose myself in the crowd.

SNIPER!

Chapter 19.

By unspoken agreement, the three of us end up in the big bed in Lupe's room. There's no sex—we just fall asleep cuddling with Danny in the middle. My slumber is restless, filled with jumbled dreams of endless frustration. I awaken hot and sweaty, Danny's broad arm thrown over me. The bedroom reeks with the sour stench of body odor, and an overwhelming desire to get out of there grips me. I slither out from under Danny's arm and escape to the great room. Goosebumps ripple across my skin as I pass in front of the AC vent in my underwear. With Eduardo gone, modesty doesn't seem to matter all that much anymore.

It's become a morbid habit to turn on the TV to see who's died today. This morning's toll is totally awful—the sniper's lunchtime spree yesterday killed seven and put a cop in the hospital in critical condition. Almost worse, a policewoman accidently shot and killed a black reporter, triggering protests that devolved into riots after sunset. The mob was screaming for the officer's head and eight more people were hospitalized during the resulting chaos, with scores arrested for looting and burning.

The legislature is steadfastly refusing to stop debating the assault weapons ban, but some members are refusing to participate, sparking fears that there won't even be a quorum when it comes time to vote. The city has been virtually shut down, with only essential businesses allowed to open, a list of which scrolls continually across the bottom of the screen. Gyms are not considered essential, so Lupe doesn't have to go work, but as a contractor, she doesn't get paid either.

I go into the kitch and get out the fixin's for *café de olla* (yes, Lupe taught me how to make it). When the warm coffee aroma fills the room, the bedroom door opens and Danny emerges. Lupe soon follows.

All of us are walking on eggshells this morning, stiffly formal with each other in a way we've never been. I want to talk about the killings yesterday just to come to terms with them myself, but I don't want to bring up anything that could lead to an argument, so I stay quiet. Lupe retreats into the kitchen to prepare *chilaquiles* for breakfast. Maybe I can discuss it with Leland this afternoon.

After breakfast, Danny calls Uncle Amos, who informs him that the agency is suspending all operations until the sniper is no longer a threat. Fucking A! Danny isn't gonna get paid, either. Then Danny calls CPS to request an inspection. After hanging up, Danny tells us, "Ms. Puryear says she'll be here at eleven."

An endless repetition of the same shit drones on TV. It's totally depressing, so I cut it off.

"Why don't we police the area before Ms. Puryear gets here?" Danny asks. "Won't hurt to make a good impression."

It probably won't help, either, but whatever. The downstairs is pretty clean, but I know that my room upstairs, where my new gun safe is, needs some love. I go up to get dressed and pick up my mess. I'm salty AF that I'm having to do this because that bitch has my kid hostage, but I take my time, doing a good job, mainly because I don't want to go back downstairs and sit with the fam with nothing to say.

The doorbell rings at eleven on the dot—I can just see the bitch standing on the doorstep, looking at her watch with her finger on the button, ready to ring when the second hand hits twelve. She slithers in, dressed in the same tired, grey business suit she had on the other day. I'll bet she has a closet full.

Danny takes the lead. "Good morning Ma'am. Thank you so much for coming so promptly." Gag me!

"No thanks are necessary, Mr. Merkel."

"If you'll just follow me upstairs, I'll show you our new firearms security systems..." Danny begins.

"That won't be necessary," she says, digging in her briefcase and producing a manila folder that she hands to Lupe, who looks at it obliviously for a moment before passing it to me. I flip it open and begin reading...

"What the fuck is this shit?" I blurt, looking at Puryear, who's wearing an evil smile.

"It's a petition to juvenile court, Ms. McMasters, which I am required by law to file within 48 hours after removing a child from the home. It says that I have determined that there is an unhealthy environment in this house and requests that court place the child in a foster home until such time as that situation is rectified."

"B-but we've locked up the guns..." Danny stammers.

"The guns are no longer the problem, Mr. Merkel. The unlawful cohabitation I found occurring in this house is now the issue."

"Unlawful cohabitation? You've got to be kidding me!" Danny shouts.

"I assure you that I am not kidding about so serious a matter. It is still a misdemeanor in this state for unmarried people to live together in a sexual relationship. It is my understanding that you are married neither to Ms. McMasters or Ms. Ibáñez; you can't be, since they are married to each other. We also have laws in this state that prohibit conduct that outrages the sense of public decency, as well as lewd and lascivious behavior. Those are all misdemeanors as well. Since such activities are ongoing here, my petition alleges that they cause an unhealthy environment for the minor child." She looks at me. "And your past indictment for breaking and entering and manslaughter isn't going to help either, Ms. McMasters."

WTF! "That was years ago, and it was rescinded!"

"We shall just have to see what the judge thinks," she sneers.

Lupe is paralyzed, staring at Puryear open-mouthed. I see the deer-in-the-headlights look in her eyes change to fire, so I move in front of her, gripping her wrists tightly before she can go off on Puryear. "Shush, Bae," I say. "Don't let her get to you." She glares at me, then big tears well up and she buries her face in my bosom.

"If Mr. Merkel were to move out, perhaps I might amend the petition at some later date," Puryear says.

Danny is standing ramrod straight, his face frozen, looking every inch a Marine. "Get out of our house, you fucking piece of garbage," he grates. "We'll see you in court."

"You can be sure of that, Mr. Merkel," she says smiling, and leaves.

After the door closes, I look at Danny in disbelief. "Where the fuck did that come from?"

"This is no longer a negotiation, ladies," says Danny. "That woman means to destroy our family. It's time to fight. Why don't you call Gary McDougall, Nattie? We don't have a lot of time to get ready for that hearing on Monday."

SNIPER!

I met Gary McDougall when I was working for Uncle at 3M, who used him for legal services. I call his downtown office. We're in luck—he can see us at one this afternoon. "You'll need to be careful, though," he says. "There's a crowd on MLK Plaza protesting the police shooting last night. It was getting bigger and uglier by the minute when I arrived this morning. It might be better to wait till next week..."

I cut him off. "We can't Gary; we've got a hearing Monday morning. I'll explain when we see you."

"OK, but be careful."

I've got an appointment with Leland at one today, so I call to cancel that.

"Please hold while I ring Dr. Marks," the receptionist says.

"I don't need to talk to him," I counter. "Can't you just reschedule me for Monday?"

"He's left standing orders that he must talk to all patients who want to cancel or reschedule," she says. "Hold, please."

He comes on the line. "Nattie? What's this about rescheduling?"

I briefly explain the situation.

"That's all well and good," he says, "But it seems that Lupe and Danny ought to be able to handle the appointment with the attorney without you. It's vital that I see you regularly during the early phases of your treatment, and I don't have any other openings today. I was even going to suggest that I see you at my home tomorrow and Sunday to avoid a break in our sessions."

I didn't expect this; my mind is racing. I make a decision. "I'm sorry, Leland, but this is a family crisis, and my place is with them. What time would you like to see me tomorrow?"

His voice is low and stern. "I need to see you today, Nat."

"Don't call me that," I snap. "A gnat's a bug—my name is Nattie. And I can't make it today."

"I'm not going to argue with you, Nat. Be here at one," he says. The phone goes dead.

I don't believe it! He killed the call? Shit! I totally have no choice—I have to be at the meeting with Lupe and Danny. I'll have to try to patch it up with him later.

A minute later, another call comes in. An unknown number. I let it go to voicemail, then access it, holding the phone to my ear.

A man's voice: "Hi Natalie. Ralph Bader here. Got a few things to talk over with you about getting your boy back. It's not safe to meet at my office downtown, so why don't you come to my place tonight." He gives the address. "And wear something sexy."

Shit. I look guiltily at Lupe and Danny. I never did get to talk to Leland about what Bader did. Do I really want to put out for this asshole on a promise to get some gun nuts to pester CPS? I shudder. I don't think so. I punch some buttons to delete the voicemail, then block his number. He should get the message.

Damn it! I was totally counting on the congressman to help us shake up CPS. A thought occurs. Ralph Bader is not the only representative we have. I bring up the Internet on my phone and do a quick search to find a phone number. There! I touch the number and it connects. It's ringing.

A receptionist answers. "This is the office of Senator Samantha López. How can we help you today?"

"Hi, this is Natalie McMasters. I have a problem and I was wondering if the senator could help me with it...". I go on to tell her about our situation.

"I'm sorry you're having these issues," is her canned response. "I'll certainly pass your name and number on to the senator. Please realize that it may be a few days before your call is returned."

Yeah, or never, I think. But I give him the info anyway, and hang up.

***

Danny's pickup has a bench seat that will accommodate the three of us, so we take it. It's usually about a twenty-minute drive to downtown, but today it's over an hour because we run into another roadblock. The cops demand ID from all three of us, not just Danny, and inform us that the governor has issued an order discouraging all non-essential travel. Danny assures him that this trip is essential.

"That's what everybody says," The cop replies, but he waves us on anyway.

SNIPER!

Gary McDougall's office is on MLK Plaza, a pedestrian mall in the heart of downtown that has two multi-story parking decks on either end. Many of the businesses here hate that arrangement, because their customers have to walk too far to get to them; the restaurant owners and shopkeepers have been agitating the Council to convert the mall back to a thoroughfare for several years. I'll bet they're gonna be saltier than ever after yesterday's shooting has shut things down.

Gary's building is in the middle of the mall, so it doesn't matter which parking deck we choose; we're closer to the south one, so we park there. The deck is almost empty—people are staying away from downtown for the obvious reason.

Or so I thought until we get outside. Two huge charter buses are parked at the head of the mall, and people are getting out. I hear chanting in the distance. As we approach, the words become clearer.

"Who do you protect? Who do you serve? Who do you protect ..."

A solid line of people, hands linked, stretches across the Mall, barring access to the buildings beyond. A line of cops in riot gear faces them.

I grab my cell and hit the speed dial for Gary. When he comes on the line, I tell him what's happening.

"I was afraid of that," he says. "I'd come to you, but there isn't any access to our building from the street behind MLK."

"Can we try for tonight or tomorrow?" I ask him. "Maybe you could come to our place?"

"I'll see what I can do," says Gary. "There's no guarantee that we'll even be able to get out of here tonight."

"Call me in the morning," I tell him, then kill the call. Turning to Lupe and Danny, I say, "We'll just have to reschedule."

"No!" hollers Lupe. "We have to do this now! Those *hijos de puta* cannot keep us away from our lawyer!"

I'm about to take Lupe in my arms to calm her down when a coarse voice speaks up from behind. "Wassamatter, *Chica*? Don't you care that a brother was gunned down here yesterday? Ain't nobody's bidness more important than that."

Four people have come up behind us from the direction of the parked busses; three guys, one white, one black, one Hispanic, and a white female.

All four look to be twentysomethings. They're wearing hoodies despite the heat of the day, and their lower faces are covered with bandanas. One guy carries a "No justice, no peace!" sign and the woman has one that says "Silence is compliance". Both look to be professionally printed.

I take Lupe's shoulder to pull her back, while Danny steps in front of us, his hands held up in a mollifying gesture. "Hey guys," he says, "we're not looking for trouble."

"Brutha that got shot yesterday wasn't lookin' for none, neither," the black guy says. "Didn't help him any." He steps right up to get in Danny's face. Bad choice, asshole.

Lupe snaps. *"Chinga tu madre, pendejos!"* she shouts. "Get the fuck out of our way!" The Hispanic obviously understood what Lupe said, because he drops his sign and lunges for her. That does it!

Danny drops the guy in front of him with a stiff hand to the solar plexus, while Lupe lunges for the guy coming for her, claws out. I'm behind both of them and in no position to do anything; worse, I see that some of the people who came out of the busses have noticed us. Lupe's opponent gets his arms around her and wishes he hadn't—she digs her fingernails into both of his cheeks and clamps her teeth on his nose! The other guy moves to help his comrade, but Danny blocks his way. Apparently, he noticed what happened to his friend, because he backs away from Danny. The woman has dropped her sign and is coming for me.

I know what to do—I've been practicing like Ye-ye said. Automatically stepping back and putting most of my weight on my left leg, I raise my hands chest high in a defensive position. The biotch reaches for me, completely ignoring my empty right foot. Wrong move, sweetie! I snap a kick into the side of her knee, and she goes down. I take another step away from her. She tries to struggle to her feet, but her knee no longer works.

Half-a-dozen dudes have broken from the crowd by the busses, and are stalking towards us in a disciplined manner, like they've done this kind of thing before. Danny is an awesome fighter, but he can't take on an army by himself, Marine or no. We are totally in trouble here, people!

Apparently, Danny sees that too. He yanks up his shirt, pulls his 1911, draws down on the charging crowd.

"Stop!" He hollers. "I don't want to shoot anybody!" I hope not! There's no way that would come out well for him, even if he's a victim.

Luckily, our attackers are not suicidal. One hollers, "Gun!" and all of them nearly fall over backwards trying to stop their charge. Lupe's assailant manages to get her off of him by pushing her to the ground, but he can't follow up with an attack; his torn nose is streaming crimson and he claps both hands to it, blubbering. The girl I kicked has made it to her knees, but still can't seem to get on her feet. I hope she fucking needs a knee replacement!

I notice several people behind the attackers have cell phones pointed our way. "Look," I say, "all we want to do is leave. Let us go, nobody gets hurt." I start moving in the direction of the parking deck, Lupe and Danny following. The thugs, fixated on Danny's gun, don't move. Once inside the structure, Danny holsters it and we make a beeline for the truck. We exit the deck onto the street and head for home.

Sitting between Danny and me in the truck, Lupe is beyond ratchet. "Why those *pinche puto pendejos baboso* can't leave us alone? Now we never get Eduardo back!"

I put my arm around her, drawing her face into my chest. She's got blood on her cheek, which stains my shirt—I totally hope she doesn't catch something from that guy she bit. "We'll get Gary to come over tomorrow, Sweetie. Don't worry." The words sound empty, even to me. How the fuck can we not worry?

Back home, the first thing I do is click on the TV. Regular programming has been suspended to cover the growing demonstrations on the mall downtown. Holy shit! It looks like the crowd has more than doubled in size since we left. The camera pans back to show a line of protestors stretched across the mall. They've gotten hold of benches, waste baskets, traffic barriers and other objects to erect a makeshift barricade, denying entrance to the cops and everybody else. Tents and canopies have sprung up behind the barrier. Talk about your sitting ducks! Last place I'd want to be with a crazy sniper on the loose.

"...protesters are calling for the arrest of Officer Tessa Albertson, who shot and killed reporter Charles Evans during the sniper incident yesterday afternoon. Acting Police Chief Porter said that the department is reviewing body cam footage of the shooting, and will have nothing further to say until that has been completed. Police Union president Hayward Jimson also commented: 'This is an unfortunate incident, but we are confident that Officer Albertson acted to protect her own life and that of her partner. We decry that this officer's personal information, including her address and cell phone number, have been disseminated on the Internet, forcing her and her family into seclusion at an undisclosed location. It is inimical to our democratic system to try this dedicated public servant in the media....'

The anchor's face reappears on the screen. "The demonstrators are occupying MLK Plaza and have vowed that they will not leave until Officer Albertson is arrested and charged. There have also been sporadic incidents of looting and other violence. The following cell phone video has been posted to a number of social media sites by a group calling itself the Capitol City Anti-racists and Anti-fascists, showing a man threatening some CCAA members with what appears to be a gun."

OMG! It's a vid of me, Danny and Lupe outside the parking deck a little while ago. It's jumpy and grainy, so our faces are not clear.

The anchor continues, "The gunman, along with two female accomplices, apparently fled the scene in this pickup truck." Cut to a vid of Danny's truck, exiting the parking deck and driving away. Shit! "Police are examining the videos in an attempt to identify these individuals."

I hit the button and the screen goes black. I turn to Danny. "This is way bad."

Danny pulls out his phone. "You're right. I need to call the department ASAP and turn myself in."

"WTF, Danny! You didn't do anything wrong!"

"Right again. But it will make it worse if I they have to track me down, and they will."

"Why don't you at least call Gary first and run it by him?"

"Hell, Nattie, Gary can't even get out of his fucking office," Danny replies. "Trust me on this. I used to be a cop. I know how this will go down."

A sudden pounding on the front door interrupts us. "Daniel Merkel. This is the Capital City Police. Open the door!"

"Too late," Danny says. "They must have got my plate number off the video."

He goes to the door and lets in the law. Four guys in full riot gear come in, levelling ARs at all of us. "Everyone down on your knees, now! Keep your hands in view."

"Do as they say, ladies," says Danny as he complies.

"Isn't SWAT just a little overkill?" I say as I kneel down. Rough hands push me down on my face, plucking the Ruger from my ankle holster.

"What have we here, now?" A cop smirks.

"I have a CCH for that."

My arms are jerked behind me and zip-tied. A cop grabs my wrists and pulls me to my feet, sending waves of pain through my shoulders.

"There's no need to take the ladies, officers," says Danny. "The video shows they didn't do anything."

"This one was carrying," says the cop that's got hold of me.

"I'm in my own home, asshole," I say. I'll never learn.

He twists the wrist tie, causing me to gasp in pain.

"Don't hurt her!" Danny hollers.

"I won't if she watches her mouth," the cop replies. He's a squirrely little white fucker named Abercrombie, with a toothbrush mustache and bad teeth. He probably gets a hard-on from stroking his AR.

"Let's take 'em all to the precinct and let the D.A. sort 'em out," a guy with sergeant's stripes says. They read us our rights before perp walking us out and loading us in a van, with two, armed SWAT dudes to guard us. A news crew from WTCD is outside, filming the whole sorry mess. What do you want to bet that the cops tipped them, to get some free publicity while arresting us dangerous criminals? I'm way big mad, but poor Lupe's face is as white as a fish's belly—poor girl is scared shitless. She gets that American cops are not like Mexican cops, but that doesn't make her any less afraid.

What will this do to our chances of getting our son back?

"Don't say anything, Bae," I say to her. "Just tell them that Gary McDougall is your lawyer and you want him now."

"Shut up," Abercrombie says.

I ignore him. "And you've got your green card," I continue. "They can't send you back..." The little shit twists my wrists again, the pain cutting me off. Oh, I will remember this asshole!

They carry us to the local precinct instead of downtown, probably to avoid the demonstrators, and put us in separate interrogation rooms after taking away our phones and wallets. I've been through all this shit before. They'll let us stew for an hour or two, then come in with a spiel about how they can help us sort everything out if we'll just explain what we did. There's fucking nothing they can charge me with. You don't even need a permit to carry a gun in your own home. But I'm scared to death about what they might get Lupe to say.

My thoughts drift to Rebecca while I wait. Things happened so fast today that I never had a chance to check on her. I make a mental note to call the hospital when I get home, no matter what time it is.

I'm not sure how long it's been when that little shit Abercrombie and a policewoman enter the room. Before they can even get a word out, I say, "I want my lawyer. Gary McDougall. I'm invoking my right to remain silent." They go into their act anyway, but I'm not having any, so they finally leave me alone.

Much later, Gary McDougall comes in with Abercrombie. Gary is a laid-back older dude in his forties with a handlebar moustache, wearing a tan linen suit with no tie. By now I'm totally ratchet, and Gary looks like he's had a day of it, too. My arms are still tied behind me, I've got a splitting headache and I have to pee in the worst way. "Cut her loose," Gary says, not kindly, and Abercrombie complies. "Bathroom," I croak, and Gary takes my elbow to lead me there.

When I come back outside, I find that Gary has sprung Lupe too, but not Danny. "They're holding him on brandishing and menacing," Gary says. "The D.A. really doesn't have a choice—the mob is threatening violence if they let him go."

"That's not right, Gary!" I say. "We were being attacked! Danny just defended us and got us out of there." A thought occurs. "What about bail?"

"They've remanded him for his own safety," Gary says. "Your address is now on the 'Net. Do you and Lupe have any place else to stay tonight?"

SNIPER!

I briefly think about calling Uncle Amos again, but then my anger rises. "Fuck that! I'm not letting those assholes run me out of my home!"

"It's your funeral," Gary says.

It's dark and rainy outside, and thunder rumbles in the distance. I'm grateful Gary is there to give us a ride home. At the townhouse complex, a couple of people with signs are braving the weather on the main road—management forbids anyone but residents and guests from the parking lots. "Duck down," Gary says. Hopefully they won't know it's us since it's dark, and we're in Gary's car.

Once we're safely inside and Gary's gone, with a promise to come by tomorrow to discuss the Monday's hearing, I pour Lupe a big shot of tequila and get a boilermaker for me. But before I drink it, I go up to Danny's room and get his AR out of the safe under the bed. The cops still have my Ruger, so the rifle is all we have for protection if the mob descends on us. I slap in a mag of thirty 5.56s and pull the charging handle, click on the safety and carry the weapon downstairs. I totally hope I don't need it.

Once back in the family room, I drain my shot of Turkey, and chug my beer, then go to the kitchen for another. Then I call the hospital.

Nurse April is not there, but the nurse on duty tells me Rebecca is the same. More great news.

Lupe and I sleep together in her room with the AR on the top of the bureau. I really don't sleep much; I just hold onto Lupe for dear life.

Chapter 20.

We're not up an hour Saturday morning before Lupe and me have our first fight.

It's the same old shit. She's totally ratchet that she'll never see Eduardo again, and somehow, it's all my fault. I try to take Ye-ye's advice to heart and take the high road; let her be where she is and forgive her when she's wrong. But Lupe has a way of picking at me, testing each nerve until she finds a sensitive one, then going in for the kill. I know if I don't get out of here soon, I'm going to say something I'll totally regret.

I totally need to talk to Leland. I can't believe he's cut me off just for missing one stupid appointment; I mean, it's not like I even stood him up—I called to tell him I couldn't make it. I totally don't want to wait until Monday to try and patch things up, so I decide to let Lupe bitch at the pots and pans, and go upstairs to my room. I call Gary to find out what's up with Danny, and when he can meet with us about the hearing on Monday.

"They've transferred Danny to County," he says.

WTF! "You mean the County Jail?"

"Yes. They're pressed for space downtown because of the riots."

"Can I visit him?"

"Yes, but you have to give them a day's notice—you can't just waltz in. Call them and see if you can get a spot for tomorrow."

"I'll do that. When can you come over so we can talk about the hearing?"

"Let's shoot for tomorrow afternoon."

"You can't do it today?"

"All of that brouhaha yesterday really screwed up our schedule, Nattie. I'll see you tomorrow afternoon. I promise."

I don't like it, but I don't have a choice.

After Gary hangs up, I google the county jail, go to their website and find out that you can make visitation appointments online. I set one up with Danny at 11:00 a.m. tomorrow. It feels strange AF to type his name in a form that says *Inmate's Name*. Then I call the hospital to check on Rebecca—still no change.

I don't want to go back downstairs and deal with Lupe, but I can't hole up in my room all day, either. The Counselling Center appointment line is closed on weekends; maybe I can call Leland at home, if I can find his number. I try Google again and don't find a number, but I do get an address in Northbrick, a section of town that's totally bougie. So now I've got that feeling when you know what you gotta do, but you're totally shook about actually doing it. WTF. All Leland can do is dis me if I go over there, and I'll be no worse off than I am now.

I put on my best pair of jeans (meaning no holes) and the XO After Hours t-shirt that Danny got me last month. The Weeknd is not really my bop, so I've worn it only once to let Danny know I appreciate. I automatically reach for my ankle holster, then realize that the Ruger is history.

Lupe will prolly be in her room when I go down, and I see no reason to bother her. I put the AR and an extra mag in a gun case, grab my keys and head outside. The heat seems to have broken; it's actually just pleasantly warm with a slight breeze. I open the Jeep, stow the gun case in back, then get in. I tell Siri Leland's addy and ask for directions, then take off.

It's not long before I'm driving down a broad, tree-lined street with red brick walls on either side, occasionally broken by a driveway. This is the oldest part of town, where the privileged hang out. Many of the lots are two, five or even ten acres, formerly the estates of the city's founders. No houses are visible from the road; the elite totally crave their privacy. Siri's mechanical voice informs me that my destination is on the left. I swerve into a driveway flanked by tall green hedges, which spirals around to open onto a broad green lawn—a white, Old South antebellum Plantation House like Tara in *Gone with the Wind* looms ahead. The place just reeks of money. Two stories, a wraparound lower porch and an upper balcony; the whole thing sitting in the center of a lawn so green it seems artificial. The overhanging roof is supported by massive round columns, with dormers on top and an octagonal cupola in the center. The driveway loops around in front; I park near the steps and get out. I walk up a red brick walkway that leads between a row of yew hedges on either side to the porch, which is furnished with white rocking chairs and wicker settees.

The front door is made of luxurious dark brown wood with beveled, recessed panels in the lower half and three blue and green stained-glass panes on top. A small, black plastic square thingee mounted above the top right-hand corner of the doorframe catches my eye. It's got a tiny round glass eye in the center. A webcam? Is he watching me right now? I press the golden doorbell and chimes echo throughout the house. After a minute, the door opens.

WTF? Jay?

SNIPER!

Chapter 21.

Jay's eyes widen. "Nattie?", she says.

"WTF are you doing here?" I say at the same time.

Jay frowns, and I get the vibe that she's way tight to see me here. She's sporting her usual military motif; a camo t-shirt, olive drab fatigue pants, combat boots. Her short hair is slicked back and damp, like she just got out of the shower.

Leland's voice comes from another room. "Who is it, Jay?" A moment later he comes into the foyer, clad in a polo shirt, shorts, and knee socks.

"It's me, Leland," I say unnecessarily—I'm shook. "I'm sorry for showing up here, but I totally need to talk to you."

"You didn't seem to need me yesterday," he sniffs. "You wanted to take care of things yourself. Don't let me stop you." He turns away from me, his nose in the air.

"Please, Leland, I need to talk to you," I repeat. Fuck, I'm pitiful!

Leland turns back to me, his face still stern. "I'll make an exception, just this once." Jay is looking at me like I'm something on her shoe. What have I walked into?

Leland answers my unspoken question. "Jay is a good example of a dutiful patient, here for an early morning session and a game of tennis." He addresses her. "Your time is almost up, Jay. I'll see you tomorrow morning, same time." Now she's openly glaring at me, totally mad mad. "Jay!" Leland barks. "I said I'll see you tomorrow."

She jerks her head in his direction. "Yessir," she says meekly. "I'll just get my things," then she slinks out of the room.

"Come on back to my study, Nat," says Leland. I follow him, gawking at his lavish home like a kid at the circus. We pass through a living room smelling of lemon wax, all white upholstery and dark wood, with a large brown-and-white Persian rug underfoot and gold-framed engravings of game birds on the walls. We pass into a large dining room, where morning sunlight streaming through a pair of multi-paned windows illuminates an oval dining table, covered with a starched white tablecloth set for eight with gilt-edged, blue-and-white service plates and silverware. Portraits depicting soldiers in gray Civil War uniforms adorn the walls. Jay comes in through a door across the room carrying her yellow backpack; now she won't even look at me as she passes. Me and Leland go into a hallway past a flight of stairs covered with a bright red carpet that gives access to the second floor, and I follow him through a doorway at the far end.

Leland's study at the rear of the house is redolent with leather, wood and pipe tobacco. Just inside the door sits a massive, dark wood desk, a high-backed black leather chair behind it. A formal garden outside is visible through floor-to-ceiling windows on either side of the room. Black drapes brushing yet another huge wall-to-wall Persian rug frame scads of red, pink, blue, and yellow flowers, with a red clay cliff soaring in the background. Tall bookshelves filled with musty leather volumes line the walls between the windows. A dark wood, coffered ceiling made of grooved, sunken wooden panels holds a central hanging chandelier containing half a dozen electric candles. A black marble fireplace on the rear wall faces a red crêpe sofa and two black leather chairs on either side with a low table between them. Two ten-foot orange trees with arched windows behind them spring from large blue and white ceramic pots beside the hearth.

Leland seems not to even notice the luxury surrounding him as he waves me to one of the leather chairs.

"Wait here, Nat." he says. "I'll be right back."

I'm generally way hard to impress, but this place is blowing me away. How the fuck does he afford a crib like this on a college professor's pay, even moonlighting as a shrink? True, his late wife Daisy was a dean, but this place still seems to be more in pop star land than a house for a couple of academics.

Leland returns, holding a syringe in one hand, flicking it with the other.

"What's that?" I ask him.

"Same as last time. Something to calm you down."

"I'm way calm," I tell him. "I really don't want any drugs."

He sighs, an exasperated look on his face. "Look Nat, I'm doing you a favor by seeing you at all. If you want to argue about my treatment decisions, you're free to leave."

I ask him again, "What is it?"

"Diazepam. The common name is Valium. If you're going to stay, pull up your sleeve."

I know what Valium is. Mom used to pop it when her and Daddy were having issues. Calmed her way down. Sometimes too much.

He's beside me now—I can smell the sweat and cigarettes on him. I pull up my sleeve and offer him my shoulder, wince at the slight pinch as the needle goes in.

He lays the syringe on the table.

"Now close your eyes, Nat," he says, stroking my hair. "Focus on my voice and relax. I cannot help you if you do not relax. Relax your feet, your legs, your tummy, and your chest. Good, good... Relax your face, your forehead. Let it go, let it all go."

A familiar warmth spreads through me again. I go with the flow, sinking deeper into myself, riding the waves of his rising and falling voice.

"Open your eyes," he says. He's in chair across from me. "Now what was so important yesterday that you failed to show up for your appointment?"

It's like I'm speaking from the inside of a tunnel, with him at the other end. "I told you when I called you. CPS still has my son. We had to meet with our attorney to prepare for a hearing on Monday."

"A meeting you never had, apparently. I saw your little television performance."

"We couldn't get there because of the riots."

"They're not riots, Nat. They're demonstrations by concerned citizens to protest an out-of-control police force and government. And they should demonstrate to you that you're not nearly as important as you think you are."

My mouth goes dry at his words. I have to lick my lips so I can open them to speak. "What do you mean?"

"You are not who you think you are," he says deliberately, and it feels suddenly cold, like the blood is draining out of me. The very fact that you missed the appointment with your lawyer should tell you that it wasn't essential in the first place."

Now I'm feeling dizzy and it's hard to breathe. WTF did he give me? "But it wasn't my fault..." I begin

"There you go again! Blaming others for your own failings. If that appointment was as important as you say, you should have found a way to get there. Your life is never going to improve if you keep on making excuses for your bad behavior."

No, that's not right. I try to tell him why he's wrong, but my thoughts whirl around like balls bouncing off walls in a lotto machine. I lick my lips again and say thickly. "No! I didn't do anything wrong!"

"You are not who you think you are!" he barks. The words slap me in the face. "You must rid yourself of this self-centeredness! You say you have come to me for help, so listen to me when I try to help you. Stop shifting the blame for your own mess onto others."

I stare at him in the chair across from me. He seems to grow, filling my field of vision, then begins spinning like a top. I have to shut my eyes.

"You are not who you think you are. Take me through your day yesterday. Tell me everything you did."

Eyes still shut, I tentatively begin, "W...'we cleaned the townhouse because Danny had called CPS for an inspection..."

"Stop. Before that. Start from when you woke up."

It's way hard to think with that shit he gave me coursing through my veins. "Well, the three of us slept together that night..."

Later, I'm struggling to free myself from a clear, thick mass; it's like I'm drowning in Jell-O, swimming toward the light, pulling myself upward with flailing arms. Suddenly I'm aware again of the smell of the study. I'm lying on my left side, my cheek pressed into a soft cloth: it's wet, soaked with drool. My eyes open and I raise my head a little. My face is on a folded white towel, surrounded by red—I'm on the sofa. I push myself into a sitting position. My t-shirt has ridden up under my tits and my bra is pinching them. I straighten it, then stand unsteadily to pull my shirt down over my belly. Leland's no longer in the black leather chair.

His voice comes from behind me. "Finally."

I turn. He's at his desk, consulting papers spread out beside him as he types into a laptop.

"You must have been really stressed to sleep as long as you have."

"What time is it?"

"Nearly five."

OMG! I slept all afternoon! "What the fuck did you give me? Why did you let me sleep so long?"

He glares at me from across the room. "I'll thank you to watch your language and change your tone. Why must you always blame others? I didn't give you anything different than before. And I probably couldn't have woken you if I wanted to. This incident should demonstrate to you how desperately you need my help—such somnolence could be an early sign of clinical depression, you know." A chill passes through me.

He does something at the computer, then says, "I want to see you again, here at the house, tomorrow at 10." A beat. "As a matter of fact, all future meetings will be here, because of the danger currently stalking the city."

Ten? What's wrong with ten? I know. "I have an appointment to see my husband at eleven. He's in jail. Can I come afterwards?"

"He's not your husband, Nat. Bigamy is illegal. And you really must get your priorities straight."

I look at him the way I used to look at Daddy when he said no to something I totally wanted. "Please, Leland," I beg.

He crosses his arms in front of him and looks at the ceiling. OMG, he's gonna make me choose between him and Danny! He fixes his gaze on me again—he must see my choice in my eyes. "Okay, this time, you can come at one. But from now on, you check with me first before making any more appointments."

The rush of gratitude nearly takes my breath away. "I will! Thank you so much for understanding."

I look around for my backpack and see it on the floor next to my chair. I nearly fall over as I reach down to pick it up.

"Whoa!" Leland says. "You're still out of it—you can't drive in that condition. Come with me to the kitchen and I'll get you some coffee."

Leland's kitch is just like the rest of the house; gleaming white and silver, *tres* ostentatious. He fusses with a tabletop espresso machine that probably cost a grand or more, finally placing a large mug in front of me, full of insanely strong coffee with brown foam on top, along with a pitcher of cream and a bowl of sugar.

I reach for the mug to drink it black, but he says, "No. Use the cream and sugar. It will give you extra energy."

I do as he says.

Later, in the Jeep, I pull out my phone, intending to call Lupe to tell her I'm on my way. I see I've got some new recents and texts. Shit, she's called twice this afternoon—she must be totally shook by now. I switch to my texts; yep, she texted me a couple times too. And there's another text from a number I don't recognize. *Tai-Chi tonight at 7?* Shit! No, I can't make it. I put him off till Monday.

I bring up my voicemail. One from Lupe, an hour ago, wondering where I am.

I fire up the car and head out. I'm still a little wobbly, but I should make it home if I don't do anything stupid.

Chapter 22.

My heart jumps into my throat as I rocket straight up in bed. Wailing electric guitars and pulsating drums swirl through the air—maybe Ulcerate was a poor choice of wake-up music. Got the job done, though. I'm still a little wooly headed. I slept lousy AF last night, probably because of all the sleep I had at Leland's. I glance at the clock: 9:10. Shit! You mean I slept through that noise for ten minutes?

Lupe's in the kitch when I get downstairs. The house reeks of cinnamon, coffee, eggs and *chorizo*. My gorge rises at the smell.

"Good morning, Nattie," Lupe says in a cheerful voice. "I made breakfast—can I get you some?"

Fuck no!, I think, but I say, "No thanks, Bae. Just some coffee."

The look she gives me says disappointment, but I totally just can't. I pour me a big mug of *café de olla* and retreat back to my room.

After I've got the coffee down, I dress to conform with the jail's dress code—no revealing clothing, tube tops, see-through mesh materials, short shorts, micro-mini skirts, tank tops with thin straps, backless or sleeveless tops, midriff or cutout shirts or bathing tops, clothing with logos that inherently promote violence, hate, drug use, profanity, sex acts or gangs (whew!). I slip on my good shoes because the website was ambivalent about flippies.

I say goodbye to Lupe as I go out the door but she doesn't answer—yep, now she's ratchet about breakfast. She prolly fixed it as a peace offering, and I dissed her. I just can't do anything right!

The county lockup is on the outskirts of the city, about twenty minutes away. I stick to the back roads to avoid roadblocks. I click on the radio and punch buttons; all I get is music and preachers, so maybe the sniper hasn't struck again. Maybe he rests on Sunday like the Lord does.

The trip to the jail goes quickly, but that changes when I arrive. A long line of cars extends down the road. I join it and inch ever closer to the parking lot entrance. When I get close enough, I see that a guard is talking to the driver of every car. I remember the AR in the back. It's in a case and the back windows are tinted, so it should be all right. I look at my phone on its stand between the seats. It's 10:05 and my appointment's at eleven. Should still be plenty of time.

When it's my turn, the guard asks for my license and who I'm here to see. He checks his tablet, then waves me into the lot. I let out a relieved breath, as I drive around the parking lot for about five minutes before I spot someone pulling out, and I take the space.

It's another five-minute walk to the jail building—a modern sandy brick and glass structure that looks more like it should house patients than inmates. Inside, there's yet another line. A hanging sign says that only your identification, keys and a small wallet will be allowed in the visitation room. All other items, including purses, jewelry, cell phones and backpacks must be secured prior to visiting. Shit! I trot back out to the car to lock up my phone and my wedding ring, then go get back in line.

A microcosm of humanity is in line with me: a dignified African-American man in a charcoal pinstriped suit, dark purple paisley tie, and bright white wingtips, who looks like he just came from church; a white grandma in a bright green, crinkly dress with a long-sleeved jacket, gold glasses hanging from a chain and a pinned-on fur hat. A brown woman in her thirties with a round face, well-washed jeans and an *I love Manila* t-shirt looks as if she's holding back tears. And there's a Japanese guy in cut-offs and a paint-stained tee right in front of me, who prolly isn't gonna get in because of the dress code.

Sure enough, when we get to the metal detector, the guard tells the Oriental man that's he's dressed inappropriately; he argues for a couple more minutes before stalking off. Of course, the effing detector beeps when I walk through, so I have to waste even more time getting wanded.

As I follow the arrows on the wall down the hall, a bell skirls shrilly and a loudspeaker pops. "Attention all visitors. All visitation appointments have been delayed by 1 hour. We apologize for the inconvenience." Shit! Since my phone's now in the car, I have no idea what time it is. Well, my appointment's for eleven, so it will be at least noon before I get in. I hope that gives me enough time to see Danny and make it to Leland's on time.

The big clock on the wall says 12:20 when I'm finally seated at a cramped little table in the visiting room; the kind with a bench attached on two sides. It's gonna take at least twenty minutes to get to Leland's from here. I look at a door on the other side of the room where the inmates will likely come in. Come on, come on...

Fuck me! A guy in a uniform walking to the front of the room, reading from a clipboard: no physical contact with an inmate except a brief hug and a close-mouthed kiss at end of visit with a guard watching; keep your hands in sight at all times, don't give anything to an inmate, yadda, yadda, yadda.

It's now 12:30 and still no Danny! I can't wait much longer—I just know if I'm late for Leland he's gonna cut me off for good. I've got to be pulling out of that parking lot at 12:40 at the latest. I finally give it up at 12:35. At the exit door, the fucking guard doesn't want to let me out!

"Please! I've got a very important appointment I just have to make!"

"Well, Miss, maybe if you just managed your time a little better..." I'm gonna fucking rip his nuts off!

He eventually relents and opens the door. As I'm going out, I look over my shoulder and see the other door open and the inmates start coming in. There's Danny! I stand on my tiptoes and wave before the guard shoves me out into the hall and slams the door. The shocked expression on poor Danny's face will haunt me for the rest of the day.

At parking lot, I jerk open the door to the Jeep and grab my phone. 12:50! Oh shit...

I drive like a bat out of hell, but it's 1:10 as I'm pulling into Leland's driveway.

Standing in front of his front door, I ring the bell; the indoor chimes fill the air. Nothing. I look up at the webcam. "Leland, I'm sorry I'm late. Please let me in."

Still nothing.

Shit. Looks like the man means what he says. I look up at the webcam again, trying to hold back the tears. I tried, Leland. I totally tried.

I turn away to head back to the Jeep. If the man won't see me, he won't see me. I'll have to figure something else out.

Reaching the end of the walkway, I hear his voice behind me. "Nat." My heart leaps, and I turn to face him. He's standing on the porch, hands on his hips, looking supremely pissed. I open my mouth to apologize again, but he cuts me off. "Don't even. Don't even say it. I'm done with your bullshit excuses. The next time you're late for an appointment with me, don't bother coming. Now get in here." He turns and goes inside.

When I come in the door, the living room is empty. I follow the same path as yesterday, finding him in the study in front of the fireplace, his back to me. I can feel the chill coming from him across the room. I meekly go over and sit in a leather chair, waiting for him to acknowledge me.

Finally, he takes a filled syringe from the mantle, and turns to me, anger still evident on his boyish features. I meekly offer him my shoulder. A shark prick, and it's done. He takes the other chair and begins his singsong chant.

"Natalie McMasters, you are not who you think you are." The room swirls and bends. "Tell me all you did yesterday."

When I awaken on the sofa sometime later, he's sitting on the end at my feet, staring at me, a soft, almost loving expression on his face. It vaguely creeps me out. I struggle to sit up, pulling down my shirt to cover my bare belly.

"Why do I always fall asleep in these sessions?" I say.

"I'm asking myself the same question," he responds. The dose of diazepam that I'm using should not induce somnolence. It makes me worry that something else is going on." He cocks an eyebrow. "You're not doing drugs, are you? Or partaking of a little liquid courage before you get here?"

"No!" I answer, somewhat insulted.

"Well, something's causing it," he says. "How do you feel?"

I try to swing my feet to the floor and my head spins. "Not great," I answer.

"You'd better come to the kitchen for coffee. I don't want you running off the road on the way home." Me neither.

Later, my hands wrapped around a mug of his hellishly strong brew, I'm feeling some better. He's right about the cream and sugar—it totally jacks you up.

"I want to see you tomorrow morning," he says.

"I can't," I say. His features harden. "Don't get mad. The custody hearing for Eduardo is at nine o'clock. I have to be there."

"The child's mother can't handle it without you?" He responds in a sarcastic tone.

I force myself to look him in his cold blue eyes. "No, she can't. Lupe is scared to death of courtrooms, for good reason."

"You really need to get past this savior complex of yours. You are not..."

"...who I think I am." I shudder even when I say it. "Yeah, you told me. But I just can't miss the hearing, Leland. I won't. If that means we don't see each other anymore, then that's how it is." A chill runs into my belly at that last sentence, but I totally mean it. I hope he can see that.

Apparently, he does get it. "Okay," he says, shaking his head, "but you'd better be here at one on the dot."

"I will if I can. I'll call you if the hearing goes after lunch."

I can tell he doesn't like it, but he doesn't say anything.

When I get back home, I find out that my troubles aren't over. Lupe opens the front door before I even have a chance to touch the knob. She must've been peering though the peephole, waiting for me.

"Where have you been?" She spits, her eyes full of fire.

"I had an appointment with Leland..." I begin.

"We had an appointment with Gary!" She returns.

Holy shit! "Did he come?"

"Yes!" She replies. "And I had to deal with him by myself!"

I open my mouth to apologize, then the thought occurs; maybe Leland's right. She was able to deal with Gary herself. Maybe I do have a savior complex, and it's undermining Lupe's confidence in herself.

I follow her into the great room, where she plops down on the beanbag and I take a seat on the sofa. "So how did it go with Gary?" I ask.

She picks up a legal pad from the cocktail table. "I tried to write everything down. Gary said that this will be a pre..., pre...,"

"Preliminary."

"Si... a preliminary hearing where the CPS lady will tell the judge why she took Eduardo, and the judge will ask us questions about what the CPS lady said about us. Gary said that we should take pictures of all the gun safes, to prove that the guns are locked up now."

"Did you tell him that Puryear has a problem with Danny being here?"

"Si. He said not to say anything about Danny being our husband. We should just say he lives with us. And nothing about sex unless the judge asks."

149

"He prolly will, 'cause it's prolly in Puryear's petition," I say.

"Whatever. I'm just telling you what Gary said."

The anger has faded from Lupe's face; now she just looks scared to death. Fuck it! I get up and join her on the beanbag. She tries to push me away, but I'm not having it. I put my arms around her neck and pull her head to my breast. "Bae, I'm so sorry you had to do this all by yourself. I'll be there with you tomorrow. We're going to get Eduardo back." She cries softly for a bit, then pulls away. She's still shook, but I don't think she's mad at me anymore. "What else did Gary say?"

She consults her paper again. "He said the judge will decide if the CPS lady is telling the truth or not. If he thinks she's not, the judge will let Eduardo come home. If he thinks she is, he probably won't let Eduardo come back." She hesitates.

"What?"

"Gary say that the judge can also order Danny to find another place to live if we want Eduardo back."

Shit. And the judge will probably know that Danny's in jail—it was all over the news. It totally sucks that the government has this kind of power over us. We're not doing anything wrong! We just want to be a family, and they've taken our boy away from us.

"So that's it, then?" I ask. "Whatever the judge says goes?"

"Gary said we can ask for a trial. But he doesn't think it would help much if what the CPS lady says is true."

And it is pretty much true. So I guess we're screwed.

Chapter 23.

Since the only people that have to be at the hearing are me, Lupe, Gary and Puryear, it's held in the judge's chambers, a spacious room with floor-to-ceiling bookcases on three sides and a large window overlooking MLK Plaza. The courthouse has its own parking deck, so thankfully, we don't have to run the gauntlet of protestors outside.

Judge Ohno is a petite sixtysomething Asian woman, her black hair pulled up in a tight bun on top of her head, wearing a severe grey American business suit. Four short-backed, brown leather armchairs have been arranged in a line in front of her desk. Puryear arrived early and is sitting on one end. By unspoken agreement, Gary takes the chair beside her, with Lupe next to him and me on the far end.

"I want to keep this fairly informal," the judge begins. "I've read Ms. Puryear's petition and I trust all of you have as well." Gary nods. "Ms. Puryear. Is there anything you wish to elaborate on?"

"No, your honor. I think the petition speaks for itself."

The judge surveys us. "Is there anything that the three of you would like to respond to?"

Before we came in here, Gary told me and Lupe not to say anything unless the judge asked us a direct question, so we let him do the talking. "I would just like to say that while Ms. Puryear's petition is substantially accurate in its description of the living situation in the household, it's invoking outdated laws which are almost never prosecuted in this day and age. Ms. McMasters and Ms. Ibáñez are lawfully married, and their roommate Mr. Merkel is a former United States Marine and a former police officer whose reputation is above reproach..."

"Then why is he currently incarcerated in the county jail?" Puryear asks.

"Those charges have not been adjudicated yet," Gary says. "Technically, he's not guilty of anything."

"That may well be," the judge says, "but the petition alleges that there is ongoing, unlawful cohabitation in the household. Is that true?"

"As I said, your honor, those laws are outdated," Gary says.

"Then why has the legislature not seen fit to repeal them?"

I just can't help myself. "That's obvious," I say. "What Southern politician is going to say in public that any law about sex should be repealed?" Gary glares at me for speaking up.

"Be that as it may, Ms. McMasters, but the law is the law," the judge says. "Are the three of you engaging in sex with each other with a child in that home?"

So, there's the direct question. I'm not under oath, but I can't lie. "Yes, if that's anybody's business but ours."

"Regardless of what you may think, Ms. McMasters, it is the State's business." The judge looks at Puryear, who has a smug grin on her face. "Ms. Puryear's petition is upheld. The child will be placed in foster care."

Lupe rockets to her feet. "No!" she hollers.

"Mr. McDougall, please control your client before I find her in contempt."

I have nothing but contempt for this judge, but I swallow before I clap her back. Going to jail will accomplish nothing. I get up and embrace Lupe, pushing her back into her chair, shushing her as she weeps bitterly. After I've sat down again, Gary says, "Your honor, will you entertain an alternative to your ruling?"

The judge, who is gathering up papers to put away, looks up at him. "Let's hear it, Mr. McDougall."

"Prior to entering the household with his mother, Ms. McMasters and Mr. Merkel earlier this year, Eduardo Ibáñez lived with Mrs. Ruth McMasters, his step-grandmother, in Fayetteville for nearly a year. During that time, he attended public school and established other ties to the community there. Since it is CPS's established policy to place children with family members in lieu of strangers whenever possible, we ask that Eduardo be placed with Mrs. McMasters instead of in a foster family."

Now Puryear looks way salty. "Your honor, I fail to see how that would remove the child from the pernicious influence of his mother, Ms. McMasters and Mr. Merkel, unless visitation were strictly controlled."

"While it's not arguable that the relationship between Ibáñez, McMasters and Merkel is currently illegal," Gary says, stressing the word *currently*, "it is frankly outrageous to characterize their influence as pernicious. All three of them love that little boy and have acted in his best interests, as they have seen fit. You will note that CPS's petition makes no mention of the ostensible original reason that they became involved—unsecured guns in the household. We can demonstrate that those guns have since been secured as CPS requested, which indicates that Ibáñez, McMasters and Merkel are willing to provide a safe and healthy environment for the child."

"The guns are no longer the issue..." Puryear begins.

Gary talks right over her. "Ruth McMasters has proved an able guardian previously, and wherever Eduardo may be ultimately placed, I think it is draconian to deny him visitation by his loved ones."

"Mrs. McMasters is willing to take on the child?" the judge asks.

Gary responds, "Your honor, I talked to her last evening and she said she's even willing to formally adopt him if she has to." Love you, Mom!

"Then, provided a background check of Mrs. McMasters and an evaluation of her home by CPS is acceptable, I will direct that the child be placed with her."

Again, I have to speak up. "Your honor, it's hardly fair to have Ms. Puryear do that evaluation. It's obvious she has an agenda."

"Your honor, I protest..."

"She makes a point, Ms. Puryear. Let's not even have an appearance of prejudice. The CPS office in Fayetteville will conduct the evaluation. Until that time, the child will remain where he is."

"Can't I even see him?" Lupe cries.

"Ms. Puryear, you will make arrangements for Ms. Ibáñez to visit her son."

Puryear's expression says she doesn't like it, but she doesn't have a choice.

***

As we're driving away from the courthouse, the Jeep's windows are open because the weather is a lot cooler than it has been lately. A raucous cheering erupts from the crowd a block over on MLK. That can't be good. I turn on the car radio.

"...a crowd had assembled at the location where Officer Tessa Albertson, who was accused yesterday of killing Charles Evans, a writer for the *Capitol Communique*, had gone into seclusion. Capitol City police officers had surrounded the location to protect their colleague from the angry mob on their own time. A shot was heard from inside the house, and when officers entered, they found Officer Albertson deceased, apparently from a self-inflicted gunshot wound. A spokesman for the police department said…"

I feel sick to my stomach and I cut it off. I just don't need anymore of this shit today.

***

Standing on Leland's porch, I'm staring at the screen on my phone. 12:59. Wait for it…

1:00.

I press the doorbell, and chimes sound inside.

A pop, and a tinny voice from above. "Nat, I'm in the garden. Come around to the back of the house."

I follow the wraparound porch to the back stairs and descend into the greenery. It's early fall, so the flowers are sparse compared to summer, but there's still a riot of pansies, chrysanthemums, lavender and flowering shrubs. I don't see Leland, so I follow a flagstone path, calling his name. I pass a swimming pool on my left, sitting in a corner formed by a board fence, still calling. I'm about to run out of yard.

"Here, Nat."

I find him in a little nook surrounded by dark green bushes sporting huge clusters of white flowers. He's sitting in a folding chair, wearing a checked sport shirt and white pants; no doctor's smock today. There's an icy pitcher of lemonade on a little table beside him, and two glasses. I also notice a little silver tray holding a filled syringe and an alcohol pad in a little square package. For me, I guess. He rises as I approach, waving me to a chaise on the other side of the table.

"Sit, Nat, sit. It's so lovely out today after all of that heat that I couldn't bear it in that stuffy office." I do as he says. He picks up his chair and carries it with him, placing it near the head of my chaise, then takes the syringe and the pad to give me my shot. I don't say anything about the medicine this time.

154

"There," he says as he pulls the needle out. "I've lowered the dose to see if we can keep you awake longer today." He puts the syringe and the used pad and its packaging back on the tray. "Lemonade?"

I don't really, but I say, "Sure," just to avoid an argument. He smiles and fills my glass, pushing it over where I can reach it, then takes his and sits in his chair with a look of expectation. I sigh inwardly, then pick up the glass and take a sip. It's cloyingly sweet. I can't stand his satisfied smile, so I turn my head. The bushes block my view of the garden; all I can see is the cliff in the distance, with a forest on top.

He puts his hands on my face, his fingers splayed across my brow. "Lie back Nat, relax, close your eyes. Relax your feet, let your muscles go limp in your ankles, your legs, your thighs..." He drops his hands from my forehead to my shoulders, gently kneading as he talks his way up my body with that mesmerizing voice of his. "Natalie McMasters, you are not who you think you are." The heat drains out of me, replaced by an emptiness in my belly. "Tell me about your day," he orders.

I talk about the hearing in some detail; when I've finished, he says, "Good. I'm glad that the judge put Eduardo with your mom. Given your domestic situation, it's probably better that you don't have a child in the mix."

"What do you mean?" I say with an edge in my voice.

"Non-traditional families are non-traditional for a reason, Nat. They're inherently unstable. For example, will Lupe decide to move out because her son lives in Fayetteville? What will you do if she does?"

"Go with her, I guess."

"And what about Mr. Merkel?"

That's a good question. "I don't know. I'd like to think he'd come too."

"And give up his job here?"

Maybe he will, because he's been on the outs with Uncle Amos. But I answer Leland, "I don't know. I'd have to ask him."

"What about your aspirations for law school? Are you going to betray your ambitions for what you call love?"

I totally don't like where this is going. Rather than argue with him, I change the subject. "There's something else I've been meaning to tell you about." I tell him what happened with Bader. Well, almost all of it. I leave out the part about the lap dance.

"Hmmm. That's reprehensible, to be sure, but what was your part in it, Nat? Did you lead him on?"

I remember what I said to Bader. *"Please, Congressman. If you could help me, I'd be ever so grateful..."* But I answer Leland, "Fuck, no!"

He must see it in my eyes. "I don't believe you. You have told me that you worked as a stripper at one point in your life. I assume that you learned how to entice men in that context. Perhaps you do it without even being aware of it?"

I'm struggling to stay awake now. He may have given me less of that stuff, but something's still wrong. "No!" I croak. "I don't do that!"

"Yes, you do, Nat. You do it to me, all the time. You don't even realize it, do you?"

"I don't!" I say. "I don't think of you that way."

"How do you think of me? As your Daddy?"

"No!" He frowns. "I mean, I don't know..." He's stroking my hair, then he begins massaging my temples. I can feel myself slipping away.

"Relax, Nat. Close your eyes." I do it. Everything fades to black.

My dreams are dark. A man, it must be Bader, is on top of me, humping away. I try to push him off, but I can't; he's too heavy. His fingers dig into my hips, pulling me to him; my struggles serve only to make him fuck me faster, more violently. Despite my wishes, I feel an orgasm rising. He groans, and I come too. OMG, I have no protection! I don't want to get pregnant! CPS will take that baby away too..."

I awaken, for a moment unsure of where I am. A cool breeze chills me— I'm still outdoors. In Leland's garden. The sky is tinged with orange—WTF time is it, anyway? I swing my legs off the chaise to the ground, pull down my shirt, fumble in my pants pocket for my phone. 6:43! OMG, Lupe will be worried.

I make my way into the house and find Leland at his desk in his study, dressed in a white shirt and jeans, working. "Oh good," he says, "you're awake. I was going to come and wake you in few minutes. Would you like some coffee before you go? I could even fix you some eggs and toast?"

I still feel ratchet from the Valium. "Maybe something to eat would be a good idea."

"OK. Come on."

I follow him into the kitchen, take a seat at the island and watch him while he loads the coffee maker. A disturbing thought enters my mind. In the sex dream, I thought I was with Bader. But was it Leland? Is that why he's been dosing me with drugs? So he can fuck me?

"I've got to go to the rest room. I'll be right back." I jump off the stool, trying not to rush, at least when he can see me. I let out a breath as I close the bathroom door, fumble with the snap on my jeans, lower them, then my underpants. I feel between my legs for any evidence that I've been violated. There's no blood, no excess moisture. I stick a finger inside me, withdraw it, look at it. Nothing. But he could have used a condom. I don't feel any pain or irritation. I slide my jeans down further, stand sideways to the mirror. Is that a slight bruising around my hips? Maybe. I can't tell. This has got to be all in my head! Leland's never given me any indication that he's interested in me that way. For God's sake Nattie, the poor dude just lost his wife! This has got to be blowback from what Bader did!

"*You do it to me, all the time. You don't even realize it...*"

Stop it, Nattie!

I get dressed, wash my hands and go back to the kitchen. Leland's busy at the stove. "The coffee's ready," he says. "Get the cream from the fridge."

I force myself to eat the scrambled eggs he made, but I hardly taste them. I suck down three cups of his strong coffee, and finally feel ready to drive home.

"I've got some errands to run tomorrow morning," he says. "How about you come at three?"

"Yeah, sure..."

The sun has nearly set when I get to the Jeep. As I reach for the doorhandle, my phone chirps. I look at the text.

Where are you? Still want to do Tai-Chi Chuan?

Shit.

No, not tonight. I hesitate. *I'll call you when I want to start again.*

I've been going to therapy every day. Why do I still feel like my life is coming apart?

SNIPER!

Chapter 24.

I sleep shitty AF that night. Up at one, again at two. At three, I want a smoke, but I threw them all out. Back to bed at four, up at five. Fuck it! I drive to the all-night convenience store, buy me a pack of Lucky filters. As soon as I'm back in the Jeep, I tear the filter off one and light up. The acrid smoke burns my throat and lungs, but the nicotine rush feels like Leland's needle. By the time I get back home I want another one; I smoke it in the Jeep too, because Lupe doesn't like me smoking in the house. I leave the rest of the pack in the console.

I'm sitting at the pass-thru swilling down *café de olla* when Lupe comes out of her room. She sniffs as she passes me—she can smell the cigarettes, I'm sure, but she doesn't say anything.

I have no plan for today except to see Leland at three. I can't visit Danny because you have to make an appointment a day ahead. Lupe's not working—the gyms are still closed down because of the shooter. I know if we start talking, we'll get into a fight, so I wish her good morning and leave it at that.

My phone lights up and starts playing *Anybody*—my ringtone for an unknown caller. I pick up.

"Hello?"

"Is this Natalie McMasters?"

"Yes. Who's..."

"Please hold for Senator López."

Holy shit!

"Natalie. Sam López. How are you doing this morning?"

I open my mouth and the words don't come. I swallow and try again. "I-I'm fine, Senator. How are you?"

"Fine also. You called my office the other day concerning a problem you're having with Child Protection Services? Tell me about it."

"Well, it started when my son got into a fight at school..." I spend about five minutes telling her the whole sad story. "...We had a custody hearing yesterday morning, and the judge decided to place Eduardo with my mom in Fayetteville. That's better than putting him in a foster home, but we'd still like him to be back with his mom and his fam," I finish.

"Of course, you would," the senator says. "Who was the judge?"

"Judge Ohno."

"I know her. You know that I don't have any power over local agencies, but I can talk to Suki to see if she'll reconsider her ruling."

"Could you? That would be awesome!"

"There's just one thing I need from you first..."

Uh, oh! "What's that?"

"You remember the interview you had with Darren Murphy the day of the shooting?"

"What about it?"

"Now, I know you were very stressed and upset at the time. You had just seen a good friend and mentor shot down in front of you. By the way, how is Dr. Feiner doing?"

Yeet! I'm immediately overcome by guilt. I haven't checked on Rebecca in a couple of days. "I guess she's about the same—in a medically-induced coma. I haven't heard anything else."

"What's her prognosis?"

"Iffy." I'm trying not to cry, now.

"I'm sorry to hear that. Anyway, I know that interview came at a bad time for you, and you probably said some things you didn't mean. I wonder if you could approach Mr. Murphy and ask him for an opportunity to correct the record?"

Now I'm totally not liking what I'm hearing. "What do you mean?"

"You took a very strong position on guns during that interview. Next year is an election year for me, and commonsense gun control is one of the key planks in my platform. So, if we're going to be associated, I'll need you to publicly repudiate the position you expressed in that interview."

"I don't understand. What do you mean, if we're going to be associated? I'm just asking you to do me a favor. How do my personal beliefs affect whether you'll help me or not?"

There's silence on the line. Has she hung up? Then, "It's not your personal beliefs that are the problem, Natalie. It's your right to believe as you please. It's your public position that concerns me. There are people out there who watch everything that I say and do. If the media finds out I helped you, and there's a perception that my public position and my private thoughts are out of line, Fox News and the alt-right would be only too happy to rake me over the coals. People in my own party are lurking in the wings for a sign of weakness, ready to primary me. So, I'll need you to change your public position before I can intervene on your behalf."

Wow. "I don't know, Senator. I'll need some time to think about this."

More silence. Finally, "I get it, Natalie. You're young. You haven't learned to compartmentalize yet. Sure, take some time to think it over. Just realize that the more your son becomes entangled in the system, the harder it's going to be to get him out of it. Give me a call when you're ready, and we can set something up with Mr. Murphy." The line goes dead.

Lupe is sitting on the sofa, staring at me. "What was that about?" she asks. I tell her what the senator said. When I'm finished, she says, "That's great! You will do it, right? That judge will have to let Eduardo come home if the senator tells her to."

"It doesn't work like that in America, Bae. The senator can't order the judge to do anything."

"But she still might let Eduardo come home if the Senator asks her to. You must do as she tells you!"

"Lupe, it's not that simple..."

"Sure it is! Just say whatever the fuck she wants, so we can get Eduardo back!"

I don't know how to answer her. Integrity is way hard to explain. But I have to try. "If I do what she wants, I'll be lying in public."

"So what?"

Now I'm getting salty. "What do you mean, so what? That's so totally not who I am."

Lupe is staring at me open-mouthed. "Nobody gives a shit who you are!" she yells. "That is not important. And nobody loves Eduardo but me! I thought you did. If you care about him like I do, you would do anything to get him back.!" She angrily turns her back on me, grabs the remote and turns on the TV to stop any more argument.

Shit. How can I make her understand...wait! What's that on TV?

Scrolling across the bottom of the screen: *Legislature quashes assault weapons ban.*

161

Governor Janes in on the screen. "...legislature decided this morning to call a vote on the assault weapons ban, and by an overwhelming majority, the bill failed to pass."

Anchor: "Governor, doesn't today's vote reflect the fact that a terrorist is in control of the very processes of democracy?"

Governor: "Not at all, Jill. The legislature simply voted on the bill and rendered a result. That's how democracy works."

Anchor: "Then how do you explain all the no votes from legislators with a solid history of backing commonsense gun control propositions?"

Governor: "Jill, I don't have to explain it. Ask them."

A loud pounding on the front door erupts, followed by repeated ringing of the doorbell. I run over to the door, peer through the peephole. It's China Mike, from Danny's vets' group! He raises his fist to pound on the door again.

Mike nearly falls into the room as I open the door before his fist can make contact with it. He's dressed in camo pants and combat boots, an O.D. t-shirt, and wearing a black backpack.

"Mike! Whassup?"

He looks at me like a hunted animal. "I need to see the Sarge! Right now!"

"He's not here."

"Then where the fuck is he? I need him now, goddamnit!"

He sounds scared to death. I need to clam him down. "Come in and sit down. Tell me what's wrong."

"I don't want to sit down! I want the Sarge! Where is he?"

I've got to tell him. "He's in jail, Mike. You can't see him."

"In jail?" His mouth drops open and his eyes go wide, like he just got gut-punched.

I take him by the arm, guide him toward the sofa. "Come in and settle down, and I'll tell you about it."

He lets me steer him across the room, dropping his backpack or the floor with a thud as he reaches the sofa. Buddha, lying on the couch, takes one look at him and vanishes underneath it. Mike picks up the backpack and places it on the cocktail table. Lupe sidles over to give him room, and he sits, looking nervously at the front door.

"Can I get you something? Coffee?" He shakes his head. He still got that terrified look. "What's wrong?"

He undoes the backpack straps, flips up the flap and removes the contents. He lays the pieces of the rifle inside it on the table!

SNIPER!

Chapter 25.

"What's this?" I ask him.

"What's it look like? It's a Nemesis ANSR."

"A what?"

"A Nemesis Arms Advanced Sniper Rifle weapon system. I found it in my house this morning. Under my rack."

"How did it get there?"

"Damifino. I think somebody is tryin' to frame me..."

Our front door bursts open with a loud CRASH! knocking out a chunk of plaster as the doorknob slams into the wall. A small cylindrical object flies into the room, hits the floor, bounces, rolls.

Mike's hand flies to cover his ears and he squeezes his eyes shut. I try to do the same. Too late!

BANG! A flash of intensely white light.

When I can see again, I'm on the floor, looking up at a horde of guys in black coveralls, helmets and goggles covering us with AR-15s. Mike's got Lupe hugged up against him on the sofa, an ugly black semi-auto pistol pressed to her temple. His mouth is open like he's screaming, but all I hear is the ringing in my ears. The cops freeze—half a dozen rifles pointed our way.

Words emerge from the whining in my ears. "...fucking blow her brains out if you don't back the fuck off!"

The cops don't move. Then one of them twitches his gun muzzle a little, like he's gonna take a shot.

I jump up and thrust myself between the cops, Mike and Lupe.

"Please! Do as he says!" I can barely hear myself speak.

"Get out of the way, you," a cop barks, moving toward me. Oh no! It's fucking Abercrombie again!

"No! Get the fuck out of my house! Now!" I spread my arms wide in a futile gesture to protect Lupe and Mike more fully."

"I'll kill her!" Mike shouts. "I will! "One, two..."

A cop wearing sergeant's stripes makes a circular motion in the air with one hand. The blacksuits pile out of the room. I go over and push the ruined door shut; the top hinge comes loose so it hangs askew.

Mike's still digging his gun into Lupe's temple—she's scared shitless. "Does this place have a back door?" he asks.

"Yes," I answer. "Upstairs." About that time, I hear running footsteps on the second floor.

Mike rises from the sofa, bringing Lupe with him, backing toward her bedroom door. He shoves his gun in his pocket, opens the door with his now free hand, drags her inside, closes it. Another small cylinder bounds down the spiral staircase. This time I'm able to cover my ears and shut my eyes, but pain lances through my forehead as the flash-bang goes off, and I see red behind my eyelids.

SWAT invades the room again. A young, blonde SWAT dude steps in front of Abercrombie to roughly grab my shoulder, and she pulls me outside. Her name, Lester, is in white on her vest.

The first thing I notice in the parking lot is a black Winnebago RV parked in the center, surrounded by a ring of yellow crime scene tape. Lester steers me that way. She opens the rear door of the Winnie and pushes me inside where the sharp smell of ozone, coffee and unwashed bodies greets me. The interior has been gutted to accommodate the instruments necessary for a mobile command center—a counter runs along the length of one side, filled with monitors, computer towers and other electronic gadgets. Three TVs are tuned to different news broadcasts. A man and a woman wearing blue Capitol City Police uniforms and headphones occupy seats in front of the array.

A tall black man in a black SWAT uni, also wearing a headset with a mike, rises from a swivel chair in the center of the vehicle and extends his hand to me. I take it reflexively.

"Natalie McMasters? Captain Trevelyan, CCP SWAT. What can you tell me about the situation inside your house? Did Chiang say what he wants?"

"Chiang?"

"The perp. Michael Chiang."

"Oh." Danny was so protective of his peeps that I didn't even know Mike's last name. "I know him as China Mike. He said he wants to talk to my husband, Danny Merkel."

He drops my hand and consults clipboard hanging from his chair by a cable. "Husband? It says here you're married to a Maria de Guadalupe Ibáñez."

WTF are the cops doing with all that info on me? "It's a long story," I tell him.

"What about Chiang? Where is he? What kind of weapons has he got?"

"He's in the downstairs bedroom with Lupe. He's got a 1911." I don't mention the sniper rifle.

"Where is this Merkel?"

"Your squad has got him locked up." He raises an eyebrow. I briefly tell him how Danny came to be in jail.

"Well, that's it then," he says when I'm done. "Chiang will either talk to me, or we'll go in and get him."

My heart jumps into my throat. "He's an ex-Navy SEAL. He said he'll kill Lupe if you try to take him. He wants Danny. He trusts him."

"That may be," says Trevelyan, "but we ain't got time to get Merkel's ass outta the clink. We'll take it from here." He looks at Lester. "Take her out."

"No! Wait..." I might as well be talking to the wall. Lester escorts me outside to the crime scene tape, which she lifts for me to step under. I don't want to go.

"Please let me talk to the captain again. He really needs to get Danny..."

"Don't worry, Miss McMasters," she says. "We do this for a living."

Shit. I totally know that Lupe's fucking dead if they go busting in there. I look around in a panic, wondering what to do. It seems like the crowd is getting bigger by the minute, coming to get a glimpse of the infamous sniper who's been terrorizing the city. There! A bright blue WTCD news truck, it's antenna extending thirty feet into the air, is parked a little ways away. And there's a familiar face. Darren Murphy! I run over there.

A couple of guys move to block me as I approach, but Murphy spots me and says, "Natalie McMasters! Let her through, guys!" He shoves a mike in my face. "Can you tell me what's going on in there?"

I give him a brief summary, ending with, "Mike says he wants to talk to my husband Danny, but the cops won't let him."

"Why not, Natalie?"

167

"Danny's in jail. The cops are going to go busting in there. They're gonna get my wife killed!"

Murphy takes the mike away from me and speaks into it. "There you have it, Tim. The police are apparently rejecting a chance to talk the hostage taker out, instead employing the strong-arm tactics we've seen so frequently during this sniper crisis."

A couple of SWAT dudes are hurrying toward us. One is Abercrombie. Murphy sees them, too. "Tim, there's a good chance they're gonna take me off the air in a few seconds…"

The cops suddenly stop running, and Abercrombie cocks his head as if listening to something. He approaches at a slower pace.

"Ms. McMasters. Cap'n wants to see you again." He sounds disgusted.

Arriving back in the Winnebago, I notice that everyone is glued to a TV. The volume is turned up.

"…police have shut down our reporter, Darren Murphy, in an effort to control the information coming from the scene," the male anchor says.

"Tim, isn't it interesting that Natalie McMasters, whom viewers will certainly remember for her impassioned speech supporting gun rights immediately after the campus massacre, has once again become embroiled in this situation. I wonder how she feels now, with a loved one squarely in the crosshairs?"

"You bring up a good point, Jill…"

Trevelyan notices me and hits a button on the remote, silencing the asshat anchors.

"Ms. McMasters, I wanted you to know that I have contacted County and that Mr. Merkel is on his way here."

The power of the media!

"Take her back outside," says Trevelyan to Abercrombie.

"I guess I'll just have to talk to Mr. Murphy some more if you do that, Captain."

Trevelyan thinks about it, and his face tells me he doesn't like it a bit. But then he turns to one of the techs. "Get Chiang on the phone."

The tech hits some buttons on the panel in front of him. There's a pop on the loudspeakers and the sound of a ringing phone fills the room.

China Mike comes on the line. "Is the Sarge there?"

"Not yet, Mr. Chiang," responds the captain. "But he's on his way."

"Call me when he's here." He kills the call.

About fifteen minutes later, the door opens and a cop brings in Danny. In shackles!

I don't care. Dodging police officers, I run over to him and throw my arms around his neck, kiss him like I'll never stop. He puts his arms around my waist the best he can.

I let my husband go and turn to the captain. "Are the chains really necessary?"

"It's policy when transporting a prisoner," he says. To Abercrombie: "You can take them off, now."

When the shackles are off, Trevelyan gives Danny a quick run down on the situation. "The perp says he won't negotiate with anyone but you," he finishes. "We want you to convince him it's in his best interest to come out of there."

"How did he come to be in there in the first place?" Danny asks.

I answer that. "He came looking for you. He says that somebody planted a sniper rifle at his place. He was afraid that someone was trying to fame him for the shootings."

Danny looks at Trevelyan. "And why are you guys here?"

"We got an anonymous tip that Chiang was the shooter."

"And that was enough for you to send out SWAT for him?"

"Because of the gravity of the situation, we're taking all leads seriously. When we didn't find Chiang at his place, we tracked his cell phone and located him here."

"Mike posed no threat to us until you dudes came busting in," I say.

"I don't have to justify my actions to you, McMasters," says Trevelyan. To Danny: "We'll call Chiang. You'll tell him that he needs to come out, now. He won't be harmed if he does."

Somehow, I don't believe China Mike will see it that way.

The drone of an open line fills the RV. Trevelyan nods to Danny.

"Mike, it's Danny. What's going on, man?"

"Sarge! You gotta help me! Somebody is tryin' to make me out to be the sniper, get me killed. They planted a rifle on me. Don't let 'em do it!"

"Hey Mike, you've got someone pretty important to me in there with you. You pointed a gun at her. That's not cool, man."

"I'm sorry, Sarge. The cops made it her or me. And it sure as shit ain't gonna be me."

Trevelyan signals to a tech, and the drone stops—he's muted the line. "Tell him he's got to come out of there," he says to Danny. He signals again, and the line goes live once more.

Danny ignores Trevelyan's instructions. "Who planted the rifle at your place, Mike? Who else has a key?"

"The Navy's got it in for me, Sarge. NCIS don't need no stinkin' key."

"Mike, you've got to come out with Lupe."

"No can do, Sarge. But I'll tell you what. You come in, I'll send her out."

The captain is shaking his head at Danny, but Danny says, "You got it, Mike."

The captain mutes the line again. "No way, Merkel! I'm not trading one hostage for another."

"Look, Cap'n, I think I can get him outta there if you'll give me some time. And I'm a former cop and a trained Marine. I can handle him if he snaps. Lupe can't."

"I said no..."

"Maybe I need to go talk to Murphy again," I say.

"By God! I will lock your ass up!" Trevelyan threatens.

I fix him with a glare. "That ain't it. If you get my wife killed, I'll sue the city and trash you and the cops all over TV, get you your own hashtag on Instagram. You guys got enough shit happening because of that cop who killed the reporter. Do you really need any more?"

He's fucked, and he knows it. He waves for the line to be opened again.

"Mike, I'm coming in," says Danny. "Don't do anything stupid."

The captain cuts off the call. "Give him a vest," he says. Danny opens his mouth to argue, but the captain cuts him off. "No vest, you don't go in."

Danny takes the black Kevlar vest offered to him by a tech and puts it on over his head. He goes outside.

"Take her out and get her behind the tape," says the captain to Lester, referring to me. I start to argue, but think better of it.

170

As Lester escorts me across the lawn again, I see that the crowd has greatly grown—looks to be several hundred people now. I hope that the sniper is nowhere around; it would be a shooting gallery. Lester puts me behind the yellow tape as instructed, and I rivet my gaze on our front door. Danny has already vanished inside. In a moment, the door opens and Lupe cones running out. I duck under the tape again, ignoring Lester's "Hey you!" and run to her. By the time Lester catches up with me, my wife is in my arms.

Lester puts a hand on my shoulder to take me away from Lupe, but I slap it away. "She's my wife, goddamn you!"

"We have to debrief her," Lester says.

"Then I'm gonna be with her," I reply.

She rolls her eyes and takes both of us back to the Winnebago again. When we get inside, the captain glares at me, saying, "What the hell? Can't I ever get rid of you?"

Lupe and I are clinging to each other like we're sewn together. "I'm not leaving her." I tell him.

"Fine," he says. He starts asking Lupe questions about the bedroom layout, Mike's weapons, etc., but she's so triggered he don't get jack. In disgust, he turns back to the TV screen, which is now showing a view of our front door. The buzz of the crowd comes from a speaker next to it.

For a long five minutes, we all just mutely stare at the TV. Finally, the captain says, "I'll give him another couple of minutes, then we're going in."

"Remember what I said I'd do if you get somebody in my fam hurt," I tell him. He ignores me.

Time creeps by. Finally, he says, "Okay, I've had enough of this shit. Call Lieutenant Blevins and tell him to prepare to assault."

"Wait!" I say, pointing at the screen. "Look!"

The front door to the townhouse opens and Danny comes out, his hands held high. He looks over his shoulder and says something, then China Mike exits behind him. Spontaneous applause arises from the crowd. I go to the door intending meet Danny, but the tone from the crowd abruptly changes to a more sinister rumbling.

SNIPER!

"It's him! It's the sniper!" Somebody yells, followed by an ominous growl from the throng.

"Get him! Let's get him!"

The cops guarding the yellow tape raise their batons, but it's like trying to hold back the ocean by waving a stick. A cop hits one dude with his baton, but goes down as half a dozen more run right over him.

I dare not go outside into that chaos. My eyes snap back to the TV screen. Danny is standing in front of Mike, his hands raised in a futile attempt to shield his friend. A thug runs up and Danny decks him, but two more jump in. Mike rabbits back into the townhouse, a crowd following him in. Danny's disappeared, buried in a crush of bodies.

Fuck it! I yank open the door, shaking off Lester, who tries to grab me as I jump down the stairs. But I meet an impenetrable wall of humanity—no way I can get to my husband. My blood turns cold as shots echo from inside the townhouse. OMG, Mike, WTF did you do?

Lester is behind me, her hands on my shoulders. This time I don't shake her off. The crowd in front of us is roiling like the sea, thinning a little as more people press toward the townhouse door. I can just imagine what's going on inside! Suddenly, the crowd parts and Danny appears, his vest gone, his shirt torn to hell, his nose bleeding and his face covered with rapidly expanding bruises.

"Danny!" I holler. He sees me and falls into my arms. Lester slashes her baton across the wrists of a thug who's reaching for him, eliciting a scream.

"Get him into the command center!" she yells.

I do as she says. She backs in behind us, flailing at the crowd with her baton, then slamming the door and throwing the bolt.

The TV screen shows a scene from hell. People are now brawling with each other as all of the fear, frustration and hatred built up during the past week boils over like a pot of milk that's been on a stove way too long. Angry faces right next to the Winnebago fill the screen, and furious thumps on the door resound inside, but it must be reinforced because it doesn't give way. But then the entire RV lurches, and I grab frantically for a handhold as the floor slides from beneath me. Oh no! The crowd is picking the whole damn Winnebago up, rocking it, trying to overturn it! I fall

172

forward as the Winne slams to the ground again, bouncing on its tires—they couldn't quite flip it over. Blue sky appears on the TV screen as the command center rises again; this time I can't find anything to grab, so I tumble into the computer consoles on the back wall, knives of pain stabbing my elbows and my spine. Up, up, up the floor rises, then the Winnie reaches the tipping point and over we go! A horrible metallic grinding fills the air and we're plunged into darkness as the RV crashes onto its side.

The acrid smell of gasoline suddenly fills the air and my eyes begin running like faucets. OMG, are they gonna burn us alive? Then bright daylight scorches my retinas—someone has gotten the back door open! I haul myself along the floor towards the light as do others in the RV. Lester has climbed into the doorway and extends a hand, pulling me up, then moving her hand to my ass to tumble me out onto the ground. I brace for an assault, but it looks as if the crowd lost interest in the Winnie once they tipped it.

I turn to help the others as they come out—one of the techs; Lupe; another tech; Abercrombie, who gives me a nasty look; then Danny. Last of all is the captain, like he's leaving a sinking ship, directing Officer Lester to go first.

We scatter away from the RV because there's gas all over the ground and electrical cables running to an outside generator could set off a conflagration any second. Lester runs to the generator and disconnects it—somebody better give that lady a medal tomorrow!

After a while the crowd has thinned considerably, and ambulances arrive to take us to University Hospital. I don't want to go—I'm worried about the state of our townhouse. And Buddha. Where the fuck is my cat?

"Nattie, we can't do anything about Buddha now," Danny says. "Please get checked out. We'll deal with it tomorrow."

"We just can't leave him!"

"Cats are great survivors. We'll find him tomorrow."

A couple of EMTs are rolling up a stretcher with shrouded form on top. Danny steps up to pull the cover from the body, exposing the face. "Sir, don't do that!" say an EMT. Danny does it anyway.

173

SNIPER!

China Mike is barely recognizable. His face is swollen, covered with blood and caved in in places. Little blobs of spit still cling to his features. He was literally beaten to a pulp. For what? For nothing!

Chapter 26.

The emergency room at University Hospital is a scene from Hell. Gurneys jam the corridor, and more and more patients are wheeled in every minute—some just knocked around a little like me, others with more serious injuries. A nurse gives me a quick exam and wraps a yellow band around my wrist. I see Lupe on a gurney down the hall and I slide off of mine on to the floor, but the nurse notices and says, "Please stay here until we can get you in to see a doctor." Shaking my head, I hop back up on the stretcher.

It seems like hours before I'm wheeled into a curtained nook where an intern clad in pink scrubs waits. She asks me the typical stupid questions and pokes and prods before she says, "You're fine." I could have told you that, dude! "Please wait here until someone can come to check you out." I sit and spin for another thirty minutes until an orderly with a wheelchair and a clipboard arrives. He hands it to me, saying, "Sign at the bottom, and hop in the chair. I'll take you to billing…"

…where I'll probably wait another hour or two. I've had enough, people. I sign, and hand the clipboard back to him saying, "You take it to billing. I'm outta here." I jump off the gurney."

"Wait! You can't…"

"Just watch me." He follows me out of the niche, but stops as I weave through the crowd of stretchers in the corridor.

Lupe and Danny are nowhere to be seen. I go outside through the emergency room doors. The heat smacks me in the face—it must be nearly a hundred out here! I try to get my wife on the phone, but it goes straight to voicemail. "Call me when you get this. I'll wait for you. We can Uber home together." I kill the call. I know I won't get Danny—he's still in custody.

I'd like to check on Rebecca while I'm here, but I can't get into ICU without my badge, which is in the Jeep back at the townhouse. Shit. I call Nurse April, and she picks up.

"It's Nattie, April. How is Rebecca doing?"

"Oh hi! You'll be happy to hear she's doing a lot better, Nattie. Doctor Hall is thinking about moving her downstairs in a day or two."

"That's great! Is she awake? Can I talk to her?"

"No, Doctor is still keeping her sedated. But I'm sure he'll bring her out when he moves her out of ICU. You can talk to her then..."

Something in her tone ain't right. "What's wrong?" I ask.

"It's just that you might have to prepare yourself. She might not be the same when she wakes up, is all."

"What do you mean?"

"Doctor says he's not completely sure that the hypovolemic shock she suffered because she lost so much blood hasn't caused some brain damage."

Brain damage? No! It's that wonderful brain of hers that makes her everything she is. I feel the tears welling up, but I stifle them. I don't want April to hear me crying on the phone. "Can you please call me if they move her?"

"I will if they do it on my shift. But you should call the main number and check every day."

Right. I thank her and hang up. What now? I can chill here and wait to hear from Lupe, or get my own Uber and go home. But do I even want to? The mob killed China Mike in the townhouse, so I can just imagine what I'll find inside.

Uncle Amos' voice rings in my head. *If'n you don't get that yallerjacket out of the outhouse, you're gonna have to shit in the woods.* And I need to find poor Buddha. So let's go get stung.

An hour later, I'm back at my front door, or rather, what's left of it. The door itself lies on the ground, torn off the hinges. The cops were nice enough to string some yellow crime scene tape across the open entryway. Yeah, that'll keep the vultures out! I duck under it, go in to check out the damage, calling for Buddha as I go. It's as bad as I feared. No cat—he probably escaped outside. All of the furniture in the great room is overturned and torn up. Our big screen TV and gaming console are gone. All of the kitchen cabinets are open and most of the contents strewn all over the floor. The fridge is open too, and is nearly empty. What kind of fucking asshole would steal somebody's food?

Across the room, Lupe's bedroom door is also open, and I can see more disarray inside. I look inside. The furniture is in much the same condition as in the great room, with the decorative addition of blood spatter on the walls, the ceiling and everywhere else. Chalk marks on the floor indicate the position of bodies. Mike must've put up a hell of a fight, but even a Navy SEAL can't beat a crazed mob.

I back out again. No fucking way Lupe and me can deal with this mess ourselves. I go up the spiral stairs and into my room. Yep, the fucking animals ran wild up here too, but just maybe...

I root around in the mess, and find my firebox in a corner. Yeet! It looks as if it's been thrown against the wall a few times—yep, I see the dents it made when it hit, but it's still locked. All of our important papers are in here, including my and Lupe's marriage certificate and our homeowner's policy. I open it and find the policy—there's a number on the front to call to submit a claim.

I punch in the number and spend a good ten minutes pushing 1, 2 or 3 in response to an endless list of stupid pre-recorded questions. Finally, a person comes on the line.

"This is Marta. How can the Old Reliable Insurance Company help you today?"

I give her my name and tell her what happened. When I'm finished, she says, "Wow! That's terrible. Please let me look up your policy and see how Old Reliable can help you today." She puts me on hold for a good ten minutes. Finally, she comes back on the line. "I'm sorry to tell you that Old Reliable can't help you today, Ms. McMasters. Your policy specifically states that damage arising from civil unrest or a riot is not covered."

Seriously? I argue with her for a few minutes, but all I hear is that "...I'm sorry that the Old Reliable Insurance Company can't help you today."

"Then why don't you just cancel the fucking policy, lady?" I say, exasperated.

"Again, I'm sorry, Ms. McMasters. Our company policy is that you must cancel in writing. Please confirm your address and I'll get that paperwork out to you today." She starts to read out the address, but I savagely mash the button on my phone to kill the call.

I go back downstairs and look at the mess, tears leaving a cold trail on my cheeks. I know! I'll call Leland. I hit the home button on my phone and the screen lights up. Holy shit! It's nearly four o'clock! I suddenly have to pee. I had an appointment with him at one—surely, he's heard about what happened, and realizes why I couldn't keep it.

I hit speed dial. It's ringing, ringing, ringing... "Hello, you've reached Dr. Leland Marks. Your call is very important to me. Please leave a message and I'll get back to you as soon as I can..." Shit! I kill it, hit speed dial again. "Hello, you've reached Dr. Leland Marks..." Fuck! I hang up again. I'm totally weeping now, and I have to run to the bathroom.

As I'm coming back into the great room, my phone begins playing Khalid's *Talk.* It's Leland! Thank Christ! I pick up.

"Leland, I'm so sorry..."

"Nat, I told you what would happen if you were late again, or if you missed another appointment, didn't I?"

"Leland, please! I totally couldn't..."

"Natalie McMasters! You are not who you think you are!"

My knees turn to jelly and I crumple down to the carpet like a puppet with its strings cut. I'm freezing and I'm shaking and I want to throw up— I haven't felt like this since I was jonesing for smack last year. Leland's voice grates harshly in my ear.

"You have continually refused to follow simple rules. It's obvious that you have no interest whatsoever in getting better. I'm done with you, Nat. Don't call me anymore." The line goes dead.

No! He can't mean it! I hit speed dial.

"Hello, you've reached Dr. Leland Marks. Your call is very important..."

"Hello, you've reached Dr. Leland Marks..."

"Hello..."

I curl up into a ball on the rug, in the midst of the wreckage of my life, and everything blurs to grey, then black.

Chapter 27.

The first thing I notice as I struggle to wakefulness is the sour smell of decaying trash mingled with the coppery odor of blood. Where am I... in my townhouse! A cool cloth sponges my forehead, a hand supporting my head from behind. I open my eyes.

A light blinds me, then moves to illuminate the white blur of a face hovering over me. Who? The blur coalesces, sharpens. A wrinkled brow over piercing blue eyes. Ye-ye!

"What are you doing here?" I ask him.

"You didn't come for training the last few days. I was worried. Then I heard about what happened today. So, I looked up your address on Internet and came to see if you were OK."

His hand drops to the middle of my shoulders, pushes to help me sit up. My head spins; I feel weak as a baby.

"You can't stay here," he says. "You got someplace else to go?"

I think about it. I could go to Uncle's, or to Fayetteville. But do I want to?

"No," I say.

He picks me up bodily and carries me toward the front door, nimbly stepping around the wreckage on the carpet. Once outside, he sets my feet on the walkway, keeping me supported with a hand on my shoulder. "You can walk?" he asks.

I nod. He removes his hand and leads me to his pickup truck, parked next to my Jeep.

"I can drive," I say, but he shakes his head,

"Maybeso tomorrow," he says. "Tonight, you come home with me."

I stop arguing.

We're silent on the ride out to Green Lake. I cast a sideways glance at Ye-ye, whose attention is firmly fixed on the road. In profile, he looks like a much younger man; his craggy features are ruggedly handsome. Given how I've been treated by men lately, I'm not totally sure of him—it would break my heart if he tried to get into my pants. But he does seem to have my best interests at heart.

179

Finally, we pull up in front of his minihouse, and get out of the truck. There's no moon; the night is as black as Bader's soul, and the shrill drone of the peepers in the lake lends a surreal atmosphere to the surroundings. It's still hot and humid AF, and wisps of mist swirl like smoke in the headlight beams.

Ye-ye points at the house. "You had a bad day today," he says. "You go inside, sleep upstairs."

"Where will you sleep?" I'm almost afraid to hear his answer.

He leads me to the back of the truck, drops the tailgate and raises the hatch cover. A light comes on inside, so I can see a snug little bed chamber.

"You'll roast in there," I say.

"Is not so bad. Where do you think I slept while I was building this house? I can open the windows and it's got a fan in the roof." He sits on the tailgate. "Bad *chi* is coming off you in waves," he says. "We must fix it. First step, you get some sleep. In the morning, I'll make you breakfast, then we'll do *qi gong*. When your *chi* is right, you can decide what to do about your house. Good night." He waves towards his front door again.

Inside, his tiny house smells like a Chinese restaurant. It's laid out like a ship's cabin, with a neat little galley on one side and wall hangings with birds, reptiles and Chinese characters framing a low wooden table surrounded by beige floor mats on the other side. A ladder on the wall at the rear leads to the loft. Climbing up, I find a soft mattress on the floor, with half-a-dozen ornate pillows scattered around and a silk coverlet in a pile on top. Push-out windows on both sides of the peaked roof let in a swampy breeze from the lake, so the temperature is bearable if not totally comfortable. I strip to my underwear and crawl in, gathering pillows around me like a shield. Thunder rumbles in the distance, then the light pitter-pat of rain starts on the metal roof. It doesn't take long before I'm out like a light.

Muted daylight coming through window wakes me. Shielding my eyes with the backs of my hands, I grimace as pain lances through my shoulders when I move my arms. Every joint in my body aches—OMG, I feel older than Ye-ye! Must be all that bad *chi* he's talking about. The odors of cooking fish and rice waft up from below. I pull on my shorts and shirt, and climb down the ladder.

Ye-ye's in the kitchen, tending a simmering pot on a hot plate. "Good," he says. "I was just going to come get you." He ladles the mixture from the pot into a bowl, then places a spoonful of something from a frying pan on top. He hands it to me.

The bowl contains a white porridge topped with flakes of fried fish. Ugh. "What's this?"

"Breakfast. You eat, then we go outside."

I'm totally not sure about this stuff, but I guess I'll try it. "Got a spoon?" I ask. He extends his right hand with his fore- and middle fingers pointing at me and makes a scooping motion toward his mouth. Oh, brother...

I go sit by the low table and try a little of his concoction with my fingers. The rice porridge is bland, but the fish is highly seasoned with salt and garlic. It's an unusual combo for breakfast, but not totally bad. Carrying a bamboo tray containing a teapot, two handless cups and a bowl of the porridge for him, Ye-ye joins me at the table. He sits cross-legged, then pours a cup of tea and places it in front of me. He says, "First, finish your *congee*. Then you tell me what you been doing to get your *chi* so messed up."

Starting with Puryear's visit, I relate the events of the last few days. I feel myself tearing up as I'm talking and I try to stifle it, but he says "No. Go ahead and cry if you need to. Tears cleanse the body and the *ling-hun*." I totally don't want to get weepy in front of him, but I'm not going to be able to tell him what he wants me to if I don't, so I let the tears flow. As I'm telling him about the riot at the townhouse, I'm surprised to see tears on his cheeks, too.

I try to talk about my sessions with Leland, but my throat totally closes up when I do, making it difficult to breathe. Ye-ye's eyes narrow, and he reaches over to me, putting both hands on my shoulders. "Stop," he says. "Go and sweep the pavilion. Meditate on the lake while you do it and try to forget your troubles. I'll take care of the dishes and come in a little while."

Once outside, I see that the heat and humidity are already building. The pavilion is pretty clean, but I get that the sweeping isn't necessarily about cleanliness, so I grab the broom and have at it. The lake is a mirror reflecting the morning sunlight, a blanket of mist hovering a few feet above its shining surface; circles occasionally disrupt the stillness as a fish grabs a meal. I try to do as Ye-ye has asked, concentrate on the water, clear my mind of troubling thoughts. But I can't even—worries about Lupe (I don't even know where she is!), Danny (is he back in jail?), Eduardo (who's taking care of him today?) and even about poor Buddha keep pushing their way in. Leland's mantra keeps echoing in my head—*you are not who you think you are*—sending icy waves through me. Who the fuck am I then?

I hear a noise behind me and turn. Holy shit! Ye-ye is dressed only in a white cloth wrapped around his waist and passed between his legs. I'm again struck by how his body seems so much more youthful than his face—his muscles are even better developed than Danny's, and that's saying something.

Without speaking, I put the broom up and move to stand straddle-legged, facing him in the middle of the pavilion. He places both hands on his *dantian* and says, "Breathe." I inhale through my nose as I watch his stomach contract until it's nearly concave, then breathe out through my mouth as it expands again, mimicking his motions with my own diaphragm. As I breathe in again, I feel a familiar energy flowing into me through the soles of my feet, up my legs then into my torso as I exhale. We stand there breathing for a long time, then he clasps both hands in front of him at his loins, rotates his arms up and out towards me until they're over his head, then separates his hands and brings his arms back to his sides. I swear I can feel the bad *chi* flowing out through my fingertips as I imitate him, replaced by nurturing energy from the earth.

He goes through more exercises with his arms and waist, for what seems like an hour or more. Sweat pours off me taking the poison in my body and soul with it, until my shirt is clinging to my chest, saturated from sweat streaming through every pore. I'm suddenly aware that my nipples are no longer concealed, but then I remember stumbling into the dojo half-naked after the thugs attacked me, and my self-consciousness vanishes.

Ye-ye assumes a resting position with his arms at his sides, waits a moment, then fetches a two-handled ceramic jug decorated with Chinese characters from a corner. He raises it above his head and pours a stream of water into his open mouth, then hands it to me. "Drink."

The water is not ice-cold, but it's gotten so hot outside that it's refreshing nevertheless. I hand the jug back to him, and as he returns it to its place, I realize my sodden shirt is way uncomfortable, so I take it off and toss it to the side. It wasn't hiding anything anyway. Ye-ye doesn't even raise an eyebrow as he returns.

"You feel up to doing the form?" he asks.

"I think so."

For the next hour or so, we repeat the exercises that we did the other day. When we're finished, I sink slowly to the floor, every muscle quivering, as Ye-ye goes to fetch the water jug once more. The dull pain I experienced on awakening is totally gone, and a warm sun now smolders in my belly, radiating outward to my fingers and toes. After I get a drink, Ye-ye places his hands on my bare shoulders, and I feel some of that energy flow into him.

"Good," he says. "Bad *chi* almost all gone. Now it's your job to make sure it don't come back."

"How do I do that?"

Hands still on my shoulders, he gives wry grin. "You keep on doing what you doing, you keep on getting what you getting." Good God! My Chinese Uncle Amos. "Maybeso now, you can talk about what you couldn't before?"

He means my sessions with Leland. I try to begin, but my throat constricts again. Dammit! I try harder. 'I..., I've been seeing a therapist," I finally spit out. "He's been giving me drugs. I missed an appointment with him the other day, and now he says he won't help me anymore." A cold chill washes over me as I say it, and Ye-ye's face tells me he feels it too.

"Good," he says. "I think this guy is messing you up bigtime. Better you should come here every day, do Tai-Chi Chuan."

You know, I think he's right. The warm glow slowly returns, driving out the icy tendrils. "I will," I tell him. "But I'm done for the day." A pause. "I don't suppose you have a shower?"

He smiles. "What do you think I am, a barbarian?" He leads me around to the back of the house, where he's set up a porcelain shower stall, connected to a pump, a hose running into the lake. And no shower curtain!

"Errr... I think I'll go home and shower there."

I put my top back on, and we take his truck back to the townhouse. The sun is high and it's hot AF, but since his truck has no AC and we both smell like goats, we roll down the windows. The ride home is quick—no roadblocks. I wonder if the cops think the sniper is no more?

When we arrive at the townhouse, Ye-ye turns to me and says, "Okay. Come see me tomorrow, eight o'clock."

"I'll call you," I tell him. "I've got a home to fix up, you know. But I promise I'll come when I can."

"Okay," he says. Again, I'm struck by the difference between him and Leland. I think I know who I'm going to be relying on for help from now on.

When I get to my front door, I see that it's not hanging off the hinges anymore—it's been replaced! I try the knob—it's unlocked. I open the door and hear a vacuum cleaner humming. It's Danny! He's righted all the furniture in the great room, gotten rid of the pieces too broken to sit on, and is cleaning the carpet. I charge him with open arms, and our mouths lock together. After a minute, we come up for air.

"When did you get out of jail?" I ask him. "Why did they let you go?"

"This morning after breakfast. Apparently, I'm something of a hero," he says in a tone of disgust. "People seem to think I had a big hand in taking down the sniper. I guess the D.A. no longer wants to keep the golden boy locked up." He looks as close to crying as I've ever seen him.

"Have you seen Lupe?" I ask.

"She called. She's staying with her sponsor for a few days."

"Hey, sweetie, I'm real sorry about China Mike," I say. I know he's not the sniper."

"You're right, and I hope the cops don't find that out the hard way."

I feel like there's something he's not telling me. "What's wrong?" I ask.

"The sheriff has revoked my CCH," he says. "I can't legally carry concealed anymore."

OMG! That's a huge deal for a P.I.! "Is there any way you can fight it?"

"I don't know," Danny answers. "This is a shall-issue state, meaning that, if I meet the requirements, they have to give me the permit. But while the D.A. got me released on my own recognizance, she hasn't dropped the charges. I still have to go to court next month. If I'm convicted of a gun offence, the sheriff can legally refuse to issue. So, I'll have to get Gary involved."

"That totally sucks."

A welcome sound comes from the spiral staircase, "Meow."

"Buddha!" I rush to scoop him up. "Where have you been, boy?" I nuzzle his neck as he purrs loudly.

"He was here when I got here," says Danny.

"I'm so glad he's not hurt," I say. "He must've run off when the crazies trashed the place. I guess it was lucky that the door was broken, so he could get back in."

"I talked to management this morning," Danny tells me, "and they said it would be a few days before they could fix our door, so I got one and did it myself." He points to a giant box against the wall. "I also got us another TV. Why don't you help me hang it?"

Thankfully, the thieves didn't tear the mounting bracket off of the wall when they stole our big screen, so all we have to do is hang the new one. Danny does the bulk of the lifting, while I help him guide it on to the bracket. Once it's secure, I plug it in.

"Want some news?" I ask him.

Before he can answer, I hear the front door open, and Lupe walks in. We both run over to gather her up in a hug. She's somewhat aloof about returning it.

"How are you?" I ask her.

"Okay. I stay with Julieta last night. I just come to get a few things to take back with me."

"You can stay here tonight, Bae. Danny's fixed the door." She looks sad. "What?"

"I talked to your mom this morning. She's gonna take Eduardo to Fayetteville on Friday." A pause. "I'm thinking of getting a place down there to be close to him."

Goddamn it! I worked way hard to get this fam together—I don't want to see us broken up over shit like this. "Why don't you let me talk to Mom before you do that. Maybe I can convince her to move up here."

"Why would she wanna do that when she's got a paid-for place in Fayetteville?"

A good question. "I don't know," I admit. "Just please let me talk to her before you do anything drastic."

Danny says, "You know, I've been talking about leaving 3M. Maybe I could get a job in Fayetteville."

"But I still have to finish school..."

"It's obvious that we're not going to get this squared away right now," Danny says. "Lupe, why don't you stay with us until Nattie can talk to her mom?"

"Okay. But I don't want no two-hour drive between me and my son."

Neither do I, Bae. Neither do I.

Chapter 28.

*L*eaves crunch beneath my boots as I hike through the woods in the early morning darkness. There's hardly any wind here at the forest floor—the trees block it effectively, but when I got out of my pickup on the roadside, I could barely feel a humid ESE breeze, making it no more than 5 mph. That's still enough to require a significant correction at 1,000 meters. The world through my nightvision goggles is a vivid emerald green, but I still must tread lightly, so my foot doesn't catch on a root or a rock. I occasionally cut off the infrared and check my GPS to ensure that I maintain a bee-line to the FFP. It's sloppy opsec to use a GPS with an illuminated screen, but I'm not worried—there's no enemy in these woods at this hour to notice the light.

Sporadic traffic noise tells me that the FFP is near. After turning off and pocketing the GPS, I scan the forest for the stunted tree I previously designated as a landmark. There it is! Moving slowly six paces to the right, I reach down and pick up a platform I made out of pine boughs last week, to reveal a painstakingly excavated shallow trench. With this set-up, a ghillie suit is unnecessary. I take off my nightvision goggles, then shrug off my backpack, kneeling next to the depression that will be home for the next few hours.

It only requires a minute to unlimber my rifle. This AR is not as good as the Valkyrie, but it'll do. I put the weapon in the trench, then crawl inside, pulling the platform over the top so I vanish into the forest floor. There's a cut-out in the front of the trench for the suppressor.

In a couple of hours, the rising sun illuminates the area. The FFP is on a ridge looking over a four-lane highway. It's early, so traffic is still pretty light. I chose a position above a curve so a target directly in front of the FFP need not be engaged, making it more difficult to ascertain where the shot came from. Peering through the scope, I locate a large pine in the highway median and use a laser range-finder from my pocket to verify that the range is approximately 1,000 meters. The traffic is coming towards me, so it's a cinch to hit a driver. In this case, a one-shot kill is unnecessary—a wreck at 70 mph should be sufficient to take out the target.

I set the elevation knob on the scope to 10, then wait as traffic builds. Since the mission objective is to cause maximum chaos, the traffic should be heavy, but still moving at highway speed so damage is maximized.

SNIPER!

Finally, it's time. Even with the precision scope, I can make out few details about individual drivers, but the specific target really doesn't matter. Ah! A perfect situation. A tanker truck approaching in the left lane. A warm wind is blowing from six o'clock, which will make the bullet rise, but the truck is coming straight at the FFP and I'm shooting downwards, which should compensate. The shot will have to be just a tad early though, to account for the forward speed of the truck. I establish a proper stock weld and peer through the scope with both eyes open, exhale to the natural respiratory pause while bringing the rifle to the desired point of aim at the grille of the truck, and squeeze the trigger gently until it breaks. The subsonic rounds have little recoil and the sound of the shot is all but drowned out by the road noise. I can't see whether the windshield has been hit because I maintained my sight picture for a proper follow-through, so the rear of the truck is now in the scope. I then survey the entire scene.

The truck shimmies, then abruptly fish-tails before lurching hard right. A SUV plows into the cab, providing enough impetus to cause the sixteen-wheeler to flip, taking the trailer with it, and begin sliding down the highway. I can read the logo on the side of tank—Smithson LOX. The tank wasn't constructed to take this kind of punishment-it splits open and an evil white cloud boils out, instantly engulfing the truck and nearby cars.

Holy fuck! The tanker carries liquid oxygen. It immediately vaporizes on contact with the warm air, but remains cold enough to speedily freeze to death the occupants of the Honda Civic next to the wreck, as well as anyone else swallowed up by that terrible cloud. They are the lucky ones.

Sparks generated by the crashing cars ignite the cloud, and my face burns as if from a sunburn as a ball of orange light invades the FFP up to nearly a kilometer away from the explosion. The massive fireball consumes vehicles on both sides of the highway, setting the forest and the underbrush in the median ablaze, and even the asphalt of the roadway itself catches fire. Many will be killed, but many others will take days to die in the burn ward. Days filled with pain and suffering. I know. I saw many like them in the 'stan.

An unwanted thought comes into my mind. What did these poor people do to deserve this?

They're targets, not people.

Through my scope, I see a tiny figure emerge from the flames, stagger, fall down. It's a kid!

No, not a kid. A target. Just a target.
OMG! What have I done?

SNIPER!

Chapter 29.

Like the rest of America, Lupe, Danny and me sit with stunned faces, staring at the utter destruction on the TV screen. Blackened hulks that used to be cars, trucks and buses lie scattered across the blistered asphalt like in a scene from a war movie. Only this is no movie, it's totally real. The charred figures spread out between the vehicles used to be living, breathing people, with hopes, dreams and families. Why would somebody do this? What does it prove?

A voice on TV says, "...preliminary estimates put the death toll in the hundreds, with an equal number seriously injured. All of the burn wards in the city's hospitals are overwhelmed. The governor has declared a state of emergency, paving the way for the president to order the deployment of mobile combat hospitals and forward surgical teams to take up the shortfall. NTSB is sending investigators to establish the cause of the disaster, but an anonymous tip phoned into WTCD indicated that this is the work of the sniper who has been stalking our city over the past ten days. A mob of enraged citizens is surrounding police headquarters downtown, demanding answers."

Danny said yesterday that he hoped everybody didn't find out the hard way that Mike was not the sniper. Looks like they just did. But if it was not China Mike, then who? My mind snaps back to the argument among the vets' group members. Kay attacking Andy when he pointed out that Kay had sniper training. Is Kay the sniper? But why?

The female anchor's face fills the screen.

"While we're waiting for updates from our roving reporters, we'd like to put these events in perspective for our viewers. With me today is State University Professor Leland Marks, who tragically lost his wife Daisy, the dean of the University College, in the shooting on State campus that began this terrible series of events. Dr. Marks is a psychologist, and can perhaps offer us some tips about how to cope with the trauma arising from this horrific occurrence." The camera pulls out to reveal Leland sitting next to the anchor. "Thanks so much for agreeing to be with us today during your time of mourning, Dr. Marks."

"Please, Jill, call me Leland. And you don't have to thank me. I feel that it's my duty to put aside my personal feelings and to help everyone deal with the issues arising from this horrible tragedy."

Seeing Leland on the screen causes an utter sadness to overwhelm me. I don't understand. The man has literally kicked me to the curb, refusing to help me because I couldn't follow his stupid rules. Why am I so sad? I should be grateful that I no longer have to deal with him.

"That's very noble of you, Leland," the anchorwoman says. "As a psychologist, can you give us any insight about what's going on in this man's head? Do you think he's killing people just to advance a political agenda vis a vis the proposed assault weapons ban?"

"That's an excellent question, Jill. I think the sniper's anti-gun-control stance is only the ostensible reason for his killing spree; it has to go way deeper than that. I see it as primarily an act of outrage against the strictures of society, which he obviously feels are unfair and not applicable to him. He's killing people to show the rest of us that he cannot, will not allow himself to be controlled."

"So, he's a sociopath who cares only about himself?"

"That's the simplistic explanation. One thing is clear. The sniper is not who we think he is."

I go cold at those words. It's suddenly hard to breathe.

"What do you mean?" the anchorwoman asks.

"We need this man to be evil personified. We need to be the victims here, because it absolves us, individually and collectively, from any responsibility for these tragic events. But I think to really understand why this is happening, we must ask ourselves if we had any part in it."

The anchor's features darken. "Surely, you're not saying that we deserve this, that it's some kind of just retribution?"

"No, no, no, not at all, Jill. While the sniper himself may certainly feel that way, it's absolutely no justification for the mass murder that happened this morning. However, I think that we must acknowledge that there are certain facets of American culture that may have encouraged these killings, at least in the sniper's mind, or maybe even abetted them. The ready availability of guns in the U.S.A. is one such factor. Our puerile, cultural resistance to authority, rooted in our own revolutionary history, is another—

it validates people like the sniper acting out, gives them permission, if you will, so they can become heroes in their own eyes, and in the eyes of the deluded masses who make folk heroes out of them. It's also very likely that this sniper has a military background, so we're responsible for training him to do the very thing that he did. Do we just expect him to forget all that training when we no longer require his services? Additionally, a personality capable of such horrific actions doesn't just arise overnight. How many warning signals did this man give out that were simply overlooked or ignored? Don't you see how the actions of the sniper might be understandable, while not justifiable, in that light?"

The anchor still has an expression of disbelief on her face. "I agree with you about the availability of guns, but are you saying that American culture itself is to blame?"

"Don't think in terms of blame, Jill. As difficult as it may be, try to put yourself in the sniper's mind—try to understand why he's doing what he's doing. Don't you see that he must have a reason?"

She's still not buying it. "Couldn't that reason simply be mental illness?"

"Absolutely. But external stimuli were still likely responsible for triggering his killing spree." He picks up a pitcher of water on the desk and pours himself a glass; takes a drink before continuing. "This is a great tragedy on many levels—for those of us like myself who have lost loved ones, for our city, for our country, and lastly, for the individual who is carrying out these attacks. The best outcome he can look forward to is life imprisonment, and I think it's pretty likely that he won't let himself be taken at all, preferring to go down in a blaze of glory, at least in his own mind. I think our great challenge is to ask ourselves how we can prevent this kind of thing from happening again. We cannot do that unless we acknowledge our part in it."

Wow. An icy convulsion runs through me—this is so much like what Leland said to me during my therapy. Do we all have responsibility for everything that happens to us?

Danny grabs the remote and clicks off the TV. "That's the biggest load of fucking bullshit that I've heard in a long time," he says.

My skin burns, and anger rises in my throat. "I think he's got a point," I say. Why the fuck am I defending Leland?

Danny stares at me open-mouthed. "Seriously? You think that you and me had a part in encouraging this scumbag?"

"I know that I did not," says Lupe. "That man is evil. He is the devil."

"You mean the sniper?" I ask Lupe.

"Him too. But I mean that man on television. He is blaming us, blaming America for the actions of an evil man. He should go to Culiacán and live with the cartels for a while. Then he would understand how great America is."

I glare at the two of them. "Leland Marks is my doctor, now that Rebecca has been hurt. He's even lost his wife to the sniper. I won't sit here and let y'all dis him like that!"

Danny is unapologetic. "Then maybe you should find yourself another doctor."

"*Sí*," says Lupe.

I open my mouth to lash out again, but the truth of what they're saying penetrates. I want to agree with them that Leland's a shit, that he blamed me for things I had no part in, made me feel guilty and worthless. Why can't I? Just the thought of agreeing with my wife and my husband causes my throat to close up again, a frosty ball to grow in my belly and an overwhelming urge to pee. I spring to my feet and run to the spiral stairs, seeking the protection and solitude of my room.

I throw myself on the bed, face down. A cold certainty is emerging inside me. I don't know how, but Leland has done something to me, without my knowledge, something that has me totally fucked up. I roll over and get up, stand with my feet shoulder width apart, my fists clenched. I breathe in through my nose, one Mississippi, two Mississippi... At eight, I exhale slowly through my mouth, unclenching my hands, flexing my fingers. Another inhalation, relaxing my hands now, turning them palms up, seeking energy from the earth. I feel it creep into my feet, flowing up my legs into my belly, expelling the ball of ice that lies there. I do this for several minutes until I'm filled with a sense of calmness.

My phone dings, breaking my trance. I've got mail.

Subject: I saw what you did!

I open the app, touch the message. There's no text, but there's an attachment with a nonsense name and a .MOV file extension. I tap the file.

A movie starts. A woman on a chaise, surrounded by flowers and greenery. OMG, it's me, in Leland's garden! A man comes into view. It's him! He stands beside me, facing the camera, takes off my flippies. His hands fumble at my waist. WTF! He's undoing my jeans, sliding them down and off! My panties follow. Now he's unbuckling his pants, lowering them and his boxers, kicking them away. He spreads my legs, strokes me between, then kneels beside me, lowering his face into my crotch. The camera zooms in so you can see his tongue working. After violating me with his mouth for a while, he turns me on the chaise and raises my hips. His dick juts out like a knife blade. He thrusts himself inside me— he's raping me! My anger begins to boil as I watch him pound away. He doesn't last long, giving one final push before collapsing on top of me. After a minute he gets off, stands staring at my nakedness with a smirk on his face, his cock a shriveled little bump. He disappears from the screen, then returns carrying something—a basin with a cloth and a bulb with a long nipple on it. He raises my hips and slides a white towel under my butt, then uses the equipment to clean between my legs, filling the bulb from the basin and squirting the water inside me. Finally, he dries me with the towel. No wonder I didn't find any signs of what he did when I checked later! He redresses me, then leaves the field of view again. The screen goes black.

I can't believe what I've just seen. Anger doesn't even begin to describe what I'm feeling toward Leland right now. I've never experienced this emotion before, but suddenly, I realize what it is. Hatred! I totally hate that motherfucker. I want to claw his eyes out with my fingernails and shove them down his throat!

I know what I have to do.

SNIPER!

Chapter 30.

Leaves crunch beneath my boots as I hike through the sweltering woods, sweat streaming down my face, my soaked shirt plastered to my chest. As I'm trudging up a hillside, the slope effectively blocks any whiff of a breeze. I pull on the strap of the rifle hanging on my shoulder with the vee between the thumb and forefinger of my right hand, as if I'm using that force to literally drag myself up that hill. Finally, I crest the top and move to the far edge of the cliff where I can look down to the valley, fifty feet below. Leland's mansion lies spread out before me.

I unlimber my AR, pull the lens caps from the scope and find a tree with a limb at the right height so I can steady the suppressor in the crook between the branch and the trunk. I peer through the scope, surveying the back yard. Unsurprisingly, nobody is out there—waves of heat rise from the stone pathways as the pavement broils in the late afternoon sun. I dial up the magnification all the way so I can see through the windows into the house. I check the study first—it's his fave room. There's the motherfucker! Sitting at his desk, all kicked back, waving his fingers in the air. Looks like he's listening to music, conducting an orchestra. Not a care in the world. Asshole!

After leaning the AR against the tree, I rummage in my belly pack for a pmag. Picking up the rifle again, I click the pmag into the receiver, then, holding it by the pistol grip pointing at the ground, I use my fore- and middle fingers to pull the charging handle. I check the safety and make sure it is off. Ready to rock and roll!

I place the barrel back into the fork in the tree and aim at Leland's office window. Prick is still there, making like Leonard Bernstein. I place the crosshairs right in the middle of his fucking face. His musical endeavors are causing him to weave in and out of my field of view—best to wait until the symphony is over to get a clean shot. My throat begins to close up, but I picture that video in my mind, see him on top of me, his scrawny ass bouncing up and down, and my throat muscles relax.

A little voice in my mind: *Are you sure this really what you really want to do, Nattie?*

Fuckin' A! The bastard raped me. I've got a right.

But rape isn't a capital crime.

Well, maybe it fucking should be.

What if they catch you? Do you really want to risk life in jail for this prick? That video is damning evidence; show it in court and there's no way he'll get off.

That may be, but there's still a chance. It's my word against his that I was really unconscious when he was fucking me. A smart lawyer could paint it as some kinky consensual sex game. And I know first-hand just how damned convincing Leland can be with that velvety voice of his.

A bullet in the brain is nothing but justice for what he did to me. And if I'm lucky, they'll blame it on the sniper. Won't even matter that the ballistics won't match the earlier shootings. China Mike brought the sniper's rifle that someone planted on him to the townhouse. It disappeared after the riot. Makes sense that this shooting would be from a different gun. After I'm done, I'll drive on out to Green Lake and deep six the AR. I'll buy Danny a new one for his birthday.

Leland's stopped with his musical antics—now he's just sitting back in his chair, eyes closed. I put the crosshairs on his nose. I've killed people before, but always in hot blood, in self-defense. So far, I haven't crossed the line to cold-blooded murder. But is this really murder? Retribution, I call it. Payback for something no woman should have to endure. Doesn't even make a difference that I wasn't conscious to experience it. I can't even begin to describe the shame and humiliation that overcame me when I saw that vid; the bastard having his way with me like I was his fucking sex doll. How dare he? I shift the crosshairs to his right shoulder. Maybe that's the way to do it. Imagine the shock on his face when the bullet shatters his clavicle into a zillion pieces that pierce his innards like so much shrapnel. Then another shot to his torso. Let him bleed out slowly, knowing what's coming. Or maybe one in the throat. Dying, unable to breathe, the coppery taste of warm blood filling his mouth, trickling into his throat. I smile at the thought.

I look away from the scope at a blue sky painted with a late afternoon yellow haze. I can't kid myself. It's murder I'm contemplating, no matter how much I try to rationalize it. I'm going to take another person's life because I totally fucking want to—makes me no better than the fucking sniper. No, that's not right either. The sniper killed innocents. That last attack on the beltline killed hundreds. He didn't even care who died, as long as somebody did. This is different. This is an execution.

198

Only the state has the right to take a life, and only after due process.

But I know if I turn Leland in, and if he even gets convicted, he'll be out again someday. Out again to do to other women what he did to me. My heart hardens. Not gonna happen, motherfucker.

Rebecca's face suddenly pops into my head. That day in her office. *"Mark my words, Natalie McMasters. One day you're going find you enjoy being judge, jury and executioner. And on that day, you're going to kill someone just because you think they deserve it."*

Looks like she was damn right after all.

I put my eye back to the scope, center the crosshairs on his forehead. Better to take him out with one clean shot. Shithead will never know what hit him, but that's OK. If I shoot him anywhere else, there's a chance he'll survive. That ain't happening.

I drop my finger to the trigger, take a deep breath like Danny taught me, find myself counting to eight. Fine. A little *chi* will speed the bullet along. I look away again.

What will Ye-ye think if he finds out what I've done?

Who cares? He wasn't the one who got raped.

Back to the scope again, realign the reticle. Finger hovering a millimeter above the trigger. Inhale, let it out slow, watch the crosshairs swing back and forth across the target. It will take only a touch on that hair trigger to send the bullet on its way. The arc gets shorter, shorter, the reticle centers on his forehead. My finger shudders as I prepare to tap the trigger...

Cold metal presses against my neck. A woman's voice says, "Pull that trigger, and you're dead."

I take my eye from the scope, turn my head slightly. I can't see who she is, but I know that voice.

"Careful," she says, removing the gun barrel from my flesh. "Put your weapon down slowly. My rifle is full auto. If that barrel moves an inch in my direction, I'll splatter your brains all over the trees."

I do as she says.

"Turn around."

SNIPER!

Chapter 31.

Ten feet away, Jay has an AR levelled at my chest. No way she'll miss at that range. I should be scared, but I'm not. I'm totally pissed. Pissed that I didn't have the gumption to pull the trigger and die with the knowledge that I paid that motherfucker Leland back for what he did to me. Now he's gonna fucking skate for raping me. Because I was weak.

Jay is wearing green forest camo head-to-toe, her face smeared with green and black paint, her short, blonde hair crammed under a military pillbox cap, a black backpack on her back. Her face is a blank mask, her grey eyes boring straight through me. I have not a doubt in the world that she'll kill me with hardly a thought.

"Put your rifle on the ground, Nattie."

I do it, and my last hope goes down with it.

I flash back to Leland's office the day the sniper first attacked. I remember Leland helping Jay put on a black backpack, not the yellow one she's wearing now. That pack was way heavy. Too heavy...

Later, when she came to vets' group, her backpack was yellow. Not black. But when China Mike brought the Nemesis sniper rifle to the townhouse, it was in a black backpack. Suddenly I get it!

"It's you," I say. "You're the sniper! You had the rifle in that backpack that day at Leland's office. You planted it at Mike's place. You had a key because you used to go together."

She jerks the gun barrel to the right. "Sit with your back against that big tree."

Never turning my back to her, I sidestep toward the huge pine behind her. She backs away to let me pass, keeping her AR on me the whole way. I put my back against the bole, slide downward. The sharp bark catches in my shirt and scratches my flesh.

My butt hits the ground, and I stare up at her, a goddess of death hovering over me.

"How did you find me?" I ask her.

"I saw your Jeep parked on the side of the road," she answers. "I had a pretty good idea of what you were going to do, and this is the spot I'd have chosen."

"How could you know what I was going to do?" I know! "You took that vid. You sent it to me! Did Leland even know you were there?"

She shakes her head.

I ask her the question I really want to know the answer to. "Why, Jay? Why did you kill all those people?"

Her face twitches, then hardens again. "Leland said it was for the greater good. Everyone would see how bad guns are. We would get them out of people's hands."

That doesn't make any sense! "Y'all tried to stop the assault weapons ban!"

"That was just so the cops would blame the right-wing nutjobs for the shootings."

I replay my sessions with Leland in my mind. My growing dependence on him. The hopelessness I felt when he scolded me, threatened to cut me off. "Leland did this," I say. "He made you kill those people. And I'll bet he was fucking you too!"

She jerks her weapon savagely and I brace for the impact of a bullet. "Don't say it like that! We were making love..."

Another realization. "And his wife found out, didn't she? That's why you killed her that first day."

"Leland had nothing without her." Jay replies. "Daisy came from old money; the house, all the stuff, it was all hers. He signed a prenup when they got married. She said she was going to cut him off after she walked in on us making love in his office. Tell everyone he was screwing his female patients—that would have finished him at State."

"But you shot him, too!"

"He asked me to. He said it would deflect any suspicion from him. The husband is always the first one that the cops think of when a wife is killed." A smile lights up her face. "He trusted me to wound him without killing him. He honored my craft."

"Your craft?"

She turns to show me the patch on her shoulder—a snake coiled around an arrow. "I was the first woman to graduate from the army sniper school!" she says proudly. But an undercurrent in her tone implies something else going on.

"So if you were such hot shit, why did you quit the military? Why did you join Danny's group?"

Her eyes flash fire. "Because the army is full of good ol' boys who just couldn't stand to see a woman show them up! They washed me out after my first mission."

I see her eyes harden as she lines up the gun barrel on my forehead. Wetness dribbles from between my legs. I've got to keep her talking so she doesn't shoot.

"Why did they wash you out, Jay?"

"I was providing cover fire for an assault group in a village outside of Kandahar. They were advancing on a mud house with a wall around it, so you couldn't see who was in the courtyard. My mission was to cover their six so they could concentrate on what was in front of them. All of a sudden, this Ali Baba pops out of an alley, goes running towards the guys. I blew the top of his head off. Later I found out it was just a kid. Nine years old. I did what I hadda do, you know, but a thing like that still shakes you. I had trouble sleeping. Bad dreams. Eventually, I told my captain. I guess it was just what he was waiting for, because he said it showed I didn't have what it takes to be a sniper. He washed me out of the sniper unit and sent me to a shrink, who suggested I put in my papers. Told me I wouldn't go anywhere if I stayed in."

"It was you that planted that rifle on China Mike. What did he ever do to you?"

"Leland was worried that the cops might be getting close and wanted to misdirect them. When Mike and me were going together, he gave me a key to his place. So, it was easy for me to do. Leland said it would be funny if there was another attack after everybody thought they'd arrested the sniper." Sadness comes over her face. "I didn't mean for Mike to get killed like that."

I don't believe it! "What the fuck did you think was gonna happen, Jay?"

"I thought they'd let him go after there was another shooting."

This woman is obviously totally cray-cray, but she still disgusts me. "Well, you showed 'em you have what it takes to be a sniper, all right. How many people did you kill on the highway again? A hundred? Two hundred?

How many did you put in the burn ward? Even little kids. WTF did they ever do to you?"

Her face is full of pain. "I didn't know what was in that truck," she says. "I didn't mean for that to happen."

"So congrats. You're the greatest fuck up in mass shooter history. I hope Leland was worth it."

For a second, I think she's gonna pull that trigger, but she sniffs and frowns. She says, "Leland shouldn't have done what he did. I was afraid he was going to eighty-six me for you. He did the same thing to me. The first few times we made love, I was drugged, so I didn't know. But then he told me. He said he knew it was wrong, but I was so beautiful he couldn't help himself. He said he wanted me as a willing partner. Everything was going great until his wife found out."

I can't believe what I hearing. I don't know which one of them is more fucked up, Jay or Leland. "So what are you gonna do?" I ask her. "kill me and sail off into the sunset with Leland?"

"He shouldn't have done what he did with you," she says again. "He said I was the one. He said he and I would change the world, then we'd retire and go away somewhere, be together for the rest of our lives."

I'm past caring, past fear. This cray-cray bitch is gonna do what she's gonna do. "Yeah, and how did that work out for ya? Go ahead and kill me and run off with your Prince Charming. And please, don't think about all those whose lives you took, or their families." I take a deep breath, maybe my last. "Leland played both of us for fools, Jay. The difference between you and me is that I know it."

Now she looks like she's totally going to lose it. Time to double down, Nattie! "You know what? You kill me, and he'll prolly turn you in as the sniper. Say you're cray AF. I saw him on TV the other day, basking in the limelight. He loved it! He'll tell them how he was horrified when he found out you killed all those people. He'll come out the hero, the media darling, and your ass will rot in jail until somebody shanks you."

"He won't do that!"

"Didn't take him long to dump you for me, did it?"

Now I've done it! Her eyes harden and she drops her finger from the side of the receiver to the trigger. I turn my head away and mutter a prayer to a God I don't believe in...

SNIPER!

Chapter 32.

You fucking bitch! He loves me! Not you!

Then why did he fuck you?

Rage fills me as my finger drops to the trigger. The little coward's just sitting there, shivering, looking at the ground. Waiting for me to end her miserable life.

It hits me. She's right! Fucking Leland did use me. He used me to kill his wife and all those other people.

I go to the tree Natalie used to steady her aim and slide the suppressor of my rifle into the vee, dial the scope up to high. There's the bastard! At his desk in the study, writing. He leans back in his chair, the point of his pen touching his tongue, empty eyes looking straight at me. He looks like a little boy doing his homework. Of course, he has no idea I'm there.

Bastard! You shouldn't have fucked her. You said you loved me! Me! I killed hundreds for you...

My finger caresses the trigger, sending a three-round burst on its way. His face dissolves into a bloody pulp.

SNIPER!

Chapter 33.

I'm no longer looking at Jay—I don't want to see it coming. The strident hiss of her suppressed rifle splits the air, and I reflexively clench my teeth. Sharp pain lances through me as I bite my tongue. I'm still alive!

My eyes snap back to Jay. She's at the cliff edge, her rifle still propped in the fork of the tree, surveying Leland's mansion below. OMG! Did she do what I think she did?

I have one chance. I get quietly to my feet. Remembering Ye-ye's lessons, I stalk towards her, moving one foot at a time, silent as death. If she senses me, I'm done for.

When I'm five feet away, her head snaps around. She jerks her rifle, but the sling snags on the branch, pulling it out of her hands. It tumbles onto the ground next to the tree. Stepping in, I feint at her face, letting my *chi* fill my front foot, flow to my empty back foot, rotating my hips as my rear foot drives forward in a snap kick to her knee. Her hand reflexively moves to cover her face, then my kick hits her knee and the joint collapses. Arms flailing, she gives a shrill cry as she tips backwards. Her hand flashes out, grabbing the tree limb. She wobbles back and forth, scrambling to get her feet underneath her.

Jay is an Army Ranger. If she gets her footing, I'm fucking toast. I dive to the ground and snatch up her AR, roll on my back, aiming center of mass. She regains her balance, ready to dive at me. I pull the trigger. The rifle spits, the three shots coming so fast they sound like one—a gaping hole appears in her belly. Her hands flash to cover the hurt and she staggers. Her scream pierces my ears as she tumbles backwards over the cliff.

Peering over the edge, I see her splayed on her back fifty feet below, her broken body contorted into a swastika. I take up her rifle and look through the scope at Leland's office window. I can no longer recognize the face of the person at the desk.

I pull off my sweaty shirt and thoroughly wipe down her AR, then toss it down with her. The scope pops off as it hits and goes tumbling across the stony ground. I put on my shirt again, collect Danny's rifle, and head off towards my car. I'm not going to report this—the cops will find the bodies soon enough.

Chapter 34.

A week later. It took three days for someone to notice Leland's absence and send the cops to find his and Jay's bodies at the estate. Initial reports attributed the killings to the copycat sniper that the cops were blaming for the highway massacre (they're still claiming that China Mike was the actual sniper). Since there have been no more attacks for a week, things have calmed down considerably. State is opening again on Monday for an abbreviated fall semester. With any luck, I'll have my B.A. in December next year.

Lupe, Danny and I are still together in the townhouse. Since our insurance wouldn't cover damage resulting from civil unrest, we had to take out a second on the place to fix it up. It's a lot more minimalist than it used to be, but we have everything we need to live comfortably, if not luxuriously. My inheritance from my late BFF is nearly gone, so I'll have to find a job for the spring semester. I'm hoping that Uncle Amos will take me on at the agency again. Danny has decided to stay on with Uncle for now, so we'd be working together if Uncle agrees.

Mom came to visit with Eduardo last weekend. He looked none the worse for his adventures, although everybody (even Danny!) cried when we were all together again. Lupe told Mom that she was going to move to Fayetteville to be close to Eduardo, but Mom said Lupe didn't have to. She said that our fam was way too special to break up, so she is going to sell the house in Fayetteville and move up here. That Puryear bitch fought it, but Gary was able to secure unlimited visitation rights for the three of us as long as Mom agreed. Eduardo still isn't allowed to live under the same roof with Lupe, Danny and me, but this is the next best thing.

I've been spending two hours a day working out with Ye-ye at the pavilion. While I'm no Bruce Lee, Ye-ye says he's very pleased with my progress, and that I'm now more than capable of defending myself against a much larger, nonskilled attacker. He's troubled by what he calls "a blot on my *you jing*", which is interfering with the free flow of the *chi* throughout my body. He said he suspects it is arising from "unresolved issues".

Is my "unresolved issue" that I basically decided to murder the man who raped me? That fact that I didn't actually kill him has no bearing on the issue—the only reason I didn't was that Jay stopped me. I've thought about that a lot this week and I'm a little worried that I can't seem to dredge up any guilt. Maybe Rebecca was right—maybe it is getting easier for me to kill. I'm way glad Leland's dead and totally sorry that it wasn't me who made him that way. But I suppose Jay had a claim too—he fucked her up way more than he did me.

I haven't been able to work out exactly what it was that Leland did to me. It must have been some form of mind control facilitated by drugs and hypnosis. I feel much better now that he's dead, but every once in a while, the phrase "you are not who you think you are" arises in my head and I get short of breath and week in the knees. When that happens, I just stand in *wuji bu* and do my *qi gong* until it passes. Problem is, I'm pretty sure he was right, because before last week, I would have told you that I could never murder anyone in cold blood. Now I know different.

I'd love to be able to talk with Rebecca about all of this, but I don't think that's ever going to happen. As of yesterday, she was still in ICU, but Nurse April is sure that she'll be transferred out to a private room any day now. Even if the ugly specter of brain damage does not appear, I can't really forget that Rebecca tried to have me arrested for carrying on campus. Maybe I shouldn't have done that, but a true friend would not try to ruin my career and my life over so trivial a thing. One of the last things Rebecca said to me was that my troubles were of my own making. Maybe she's right. Maybe she was telling me that I'm not who I think I am too, and I just wouldn't listen. Ye-ye's been saying that the secret to a happy life is to simply discover who you are, and to be that person. Maybe that's where I should direct my energy from now on.

My phone is playing Taylor Swift's *Cruel Summer*. Nurse April! I snatch it up, hit the button.

"April! Wassup?"

"Hey, Nattie! Just wanted you to know they moved Rebecca a little while ago. Doctor stopped her meds last night after my shift, so I didn't know they were sending her downstairs till I got here."

"Holy shit, that's totally great! Is she awake? Is she...," *brain-damaged*, is what I'm thinking, but what comes out is "...OK?"

"Not sure," April says.

212

Shit! "Will there be somebody there when she wakes up, in case she's confused?"

"No worries!" April says brightly. "Her fiancé showed up this morning and has been with her the whole time.

Who? OMG, no! Oh holy fuck, no!

"April, listen to me. Call security and get them to her room right now. Tell them that Rebecca is in is great danger."

"What? Oh no, Natalie, I met him. He's a great guy! A hunk!"

"April, do as I say. He's a killer!" I shout the next word. "Now!" A pause. "I'm coming over there."

I kill the call, shove the phone in my pocket and dash to the door, grabbing my keys from the hook on the wall, then tear it open and run outside. "Danny's "Hey, Nattie!" echoes behind me, but I do not stop. I see him come out the door as I fire up the Jeep, but I do not wait. I slam it into gear and back out, tires squealing, then pop it into first and lay rubber out of the parking lot.

Rebecca's fiancé is Leonard Ashworth, who she met in college when he called himself Barrett Tybee. As the serial killer, the Marquis, he's raped and tortured two dozen victims over two decades, strangling them before removing their eyes. Of course, Rebecca knew nothing of this when they became engaged. Barrett sent me a letter last spring, blaming me for ruining their engagement among other things, telling me that he would come for me in time. Well now, he's here.

Heedless of law enforcement, I drive as fast as I can without wrecking the Jeep—the road blocks are gone, but it still takes the best part of twenty minutes before I make it to University Hospital. There are a couple of cop cars out front—not good sign. I pull up behind one and exit the Jeep, caring not whether it's still there when I get back. The guards are gone from the front door, the metal detector no longer in the lobby. I run to a console and type in Rebecca's last name, hit Enter. Room 302C. I've been in this hospital enough to know just where that is.

When the elevator opens on the third floor of C wing, I exit into chaos. Blue lights flash in tandem with electronic alarms, as security personnel attempt to keep the hallway clear. My eyes flash to the room number sign on the wall and I head for 302, dodging an overweight rent-a-cop who tries to stop me. I'm too late! The doorway to 302 is blocked with yellow crime scene tape; two University cops stand nearby. One sees me as I run up and moves to stop me, but I duck and sidestep, sliding under the tape. Rebecca's in a hospital bed, a crash team frantically working on her. A doctor steps aside and I see she's not moving.

OMG! Her eyes!

————The End————

Thomas A. Burns, Jr.

About the Author

As a kid, I started reading mysteries with the Hardy Boys, Ken Holt and Rick Brant, then graduated to the classics by authors such as A. Conan Doyle, Erle Stanley Gardner, John Dickson Carr, and Rex Stout, to name a few. I have written fiction as a hobby all of my life, starting in marble-backed copybooks in grade school. I built a career as a technical and science writer and as an editor for nearly thirty years in academia, industry and government. Now that I'm truly on my own as a freelance science writer and editor, I'm excited to publish my own mystery series as well.

Follow me on Facebook at
https://www.facebook.com/3MDetectiveAgency/
Twitter @3Mdetective
Instagram at 3mdetective
Tumblr at nataliemcmasters
BookBub at https://www.bookbub.com/profile/thomas-a-burns-jr
or email me at tom@3mdetectiveagency.com.
Be sure to visit the 3M Detective Agency website at
https://www.3mdetectiveagency.com/contact/
and subscribe to my newsletter to get all the news about Nattie and the 3M gang.
Don't miss the next book in the critically acclaimed Natalie McMasters series by Thomas A. Burns, Jr., coming in 2021.